Rave Reviews for This Explosive New Thriller

"POWERFUL AND CONVINCING!"
—*Montreal Gazette*

"GRIPPING . . . The first mystery to deal primarily and intelligently with the AIDS issue."
—*San Francisco Examiner*

"PROVOCATIVE . . . Topical and entertaining, a good read!"
—*TWT* (This Week in Texas)

"FASCINATING . . . UNSETTLING."
—*Toronto Star*

"AN IMAGINATIVE STORY . . . Warmbold has obviously done her homework!"
—*Philadelphia Inquirer*

"GRIPPING . . . Insightful . . . A promising debut!"
—*The Missourian*

JUNE MAIL
Jean Warmbold

JUNE MAIL

JEAN WARMBOLD

JOVE BOOKS, NEW YORK

JUNE MAIL

A Jove Book / published by arrangement with
The Permanent Press

PRINTING HISTORY
The Permanent Press edition published 1986
Jove edition / February 1988

ISBN: 0-515-09440-4

Jove Books are published by The Berkley Publishing Group,
200 Madison Avenue, New York, New York 10016.
The name "JOVE" and the "J" logo
are trademarks belonging to Jove Publications, Inc.

In memory of my Father

JUNE 11

A clear head at all costs, sweetheart. There has to be an explanation here. Some reasonable enough rationale for his disappearance which eludes me at the moment. Maybe a slip-up in information? A last minute change in plans? A wire that got by me, enroute between New York and this god-forsaken hellhole.

I make a pit stop at May's Diner, apparently the only restaurant in town, in order to take stock of the situation. Unfortunately, the coffee here is lukewarm dishwater and my mind's an exhausted blank. More to the point is the disquieting air of this stripped down hash house, reeking of a grease and loneliness which transports me onto some third-rate Edward Hopper canvas. Though even Hopper would have had the sense to skirt such obviousness as that bare yellow light bulb. And all these ~~dam~~

I light up what is to be my last cigarette of the day and take Frank's telegram back out of my purse:

> Great to hear from you stranger.
> Anticipate your visit with open arms.
> Call before arrival.
> Love and kisses—
>
> Frank

But when I tried getting in touch out of San Francisco, the number came up disconnected. And his address traced down to that deserted bungalow west of Colston this

1

afternoon. How to add anything up? Especially when considering that Frank's wire arrived two short days ago with no hints whatever of an impending move.

There is always the possibility that he is giving me the intentional slip. But then, why the telegram? That had never been Frank's style, to say one thing and mean another. Leastways, not the Frank I once knew. The man who had prided himself on being such an honest bastard. Blood-curdlingly so.

I order a refill on the dishwater and flash back to our last awkward encounter, some four years ago. It was Oscar's front bar, if I remember it right. With the usual Friday night rabble clogging up the place on stale cigarette smoke and beer. And it was I who first caught sight of him, engrossed in cozy conversation with a most striking latino woman nestled into his side. Considering the circumstances, which were somewhat less than propitious, I promptly buried myself in the pages of the letter I was in the process of reading—from my mother no doubt—in hopes that the Beautiful Couple would humor me by vanishing into the sultry summer night.

But when I finally risked a peek about, it was only to find Frank and Miss Costa Rica of 1981 right there at my elbow. She was a disgracefully slender creature, with the kind of liquid brown eyes one could kill for. And her name was Angelica. The Angelica? I darkly speculated, a smile freezing halfway across my face. *The* Angelica of crumpled napkin, tossed oh-so-casually onto my dresser that fatal evening, some three or four months before?

My suspicions were immediately confirmed by way of a certain nervous gesture of Frank's right hand to left ear lobe. A gesture which I had become all too familiar with over the ten or so months of our stormy and see-saw affair. My smile took on a distinctly bitter edge as the prerequisite banalities were exchanged. Soon enough I was making my excuses, gathering together the scattered pages of my letter and walking self-consciously out the door—bent on leaving all memories of Frank and the fifteen pounds I had gained since our final break-up, far far behind.

By and large, I succeeded in doing exactly that. Until last month, that is. While passing time on a flight down to

Boston, I chanced upon that *Time* write-up on Frank. What an erotic jolt that had been. Coming face to face with those familiar grey-blue eyes in the pages of a national magazine. "Why I know that man!" I had murmured incredulously to the lumpish businessman sitting to my left.

"You don't say," he had mumbled, head bobbing precariously low in my lap for a closer look before he lurched back up to toast my glory with another swig of scotch.

The article itself had been an extended wrap-up of recent strides in recombinant DNA, with particular emphasis given to its applicability in AIDS research. There were the usual hints of impending breakthroughs, the general drift being that Dr. Frank Winslow out of Genco Laboratories in Northern California was well on his way to developing a viable AIDS vaccine.

By the time we landed in Boston, I had made up my mind to locate the man and reconnect. I was in desperate need of a story, and his certainly looked like it could aptly fill the bill. Current, hot, and juicy. With yours truly on an unsuspecting inside track. Presuming of course, that our past relationship, in all its clichéd absurdity, could be said to represent an inside track. Or any kind of track, at all.

If I am to be brutally honest with myself, it was more than the prospect of a respectable scoop which was egging me on. For I suddenly found myself craving the man like honey. Something in his lean, sensual presence which had jumped off that glossy black and white and into the pit of my stomach, wreaking havoc with nerve endings that had been lying complacently dormant for months.

And so it was that I wangled his present address out of my connection at Time Inc. and dispatched a short note. It took two days for his return telegram to arrive. And two more for me to decide to withdraw what little remained of my dwindling checking account in order to cover the trip west. All that financial outlay, only to get out here and run up against this frustrating blank.

I stare glumly into the coffee grounds settling at the bottom of my cup and contemplate the options now before me. I must make contact with Genco's central offices and labs in Monterey, of course. But seven o'clock on a Friday

evening is hardly the ideal time to try extorting what is no
doubt classified information out of some private lab. I dimly
consider the possibility of flying on back to New York
tonight, as if a man named Frank Winslow did not exist.
But what would that get me but an empty bank roll and
enough unanswered questions to nag me for months to
come.

In due course, I decide to stick around Colston one more
day, in hopes of digging something up. Paying for my
coffee, I question the waitress apropos cheap lodgings for
the night. She recommends a Motel 6 some eight miles
north of town. I slip another quarter under the saucer and
head out into the hot desert night.

Enroute to the motel, I stop off at a 7 11 for the usual
stockpile of reserves for solitary evenings in far away
places. One Simenon mystery. One package of Parliaments.
And a cold bottle of cheap white wine.

Simenon works his usual magic. Plucking me out of that
tacky motel room and into the dusky streets of some canal
town in northern France. A provincial backwater where
Maigret and his pipe relentlessly track down their man.
Three hours and three quarters of a wine bottle later, I put
the finished mystery aside, annoyed at myself for not having
had the forethought to pick up a second book.

Pouring out the last of the wine, I settle back against the
pillows for a mental recap of the day gone by. A nightly
habit picked up reading Gurdjieff: memory equals experience and experience equals life.

First there had been the croissants and coffee back at
Amy's in San Francisco, the two of us catching up on past
lives while we waited on her teenage admirer to recharge his
motorcycle for their overnight in Carmel. Then the two
hours wasted at Rent-A-Wreck, and the four and a half hour
drive down Highway 5. Out from under San Francisco's
foggy mantle into the blazing badlands of California's
central plains.

Once here in Colston, my first stop had been the
antiquated Shell station across from May's, where I made a
sad attempt at freshening up in their cramped and filthy
restroom before heading out to Paradise and Frank's. Or
what had once been Frank's but apparently was no more.

Paradise Valley. One of the thousand and one arid little boom towns which have sprung up around this country over the last forty years. All of them with their vapid, treeless landscapes and split level claptrap homes. Row after depressing row of them hatched out of identical prefab molds.

Not Frank's style, that place. Down to the many blowsy dandelions dotting his front lawn. Frank would never have tolerated such obvious beacons of sloth and neglect. Which is precisely why my somewhat casual lifestyle—the peanut butter, the cigarettes, the white wine and hot baths and general state of disarray—used to exasperate the man so. All that benign neglect.

He hadn't always been so intolerant. Not in the beginning, at least. And putting aside my plastic cup, I close my eyes and will myself back. Some five years back. To that glorious and troubled first month. First week. First night of nights. When and where we first met.

The setting is Davies Hall, Columbia University, West side, New York. The very last place I want to be on that particular rainy Friday evening. But there I am, none the less. Covering a debate on the ethical and moral perspectives of recent advances in genetic engineering research. Should Man Play God? was the timeworn question. And I am too cold, tired, and hungry to give a damn about the answer, my mind racing ahead to the leftover pizza I will be polishing off in front of The Honeymooners sometime later tonight.

Then he begins to speak. There is something in his manner, not so much in what he says as in how he says it, that yanks me back into the here and now of that vast and poorly heated room. His words are so weighted. His tone so pensive and self-assured. And his looks, if one goes in for such things, quite first rate.

Members of the press are invited back to the usual post cocktail party-reception directly following the debate. As a rule, I eschew such events. Too many of the same faces, the same banal conversations, the same watered down punches and sweaty wheels of over-ripe brie cheese. But this evening I made an exception to the rule, heading home for a quick overhaul before taxiing over to a certain Esther Squire's East side flat.

The place is posh. Very posh indeed. And packed to the rafters with America's chic-intelligentsia elite. I make a beeline for the kitchen and a hefty glass of the nearest wine. A few gulps of an unusually sour cabernet sauvignon and I begin shouldering my way into the front parlour, ultimately staking claim on a foot square piece of territory to one side of an imposing marble hearth. From this particular vantage point, the man in question is nowhere in sight. Perhaps he will be making an appearance later in the evening? Or worse yet, has already arrived, paid his dues, and left? I drift in place, soaking up welcome heat from the fire blazing before me and sipping on a second glass of the red wine.

"Should get yourself a notebook, woman. All that paper shuffling can get on one's nerves."

The voice is startlingly familiar. I turn to lock eyes with the grey-blue, now grey, now blue eyes of my dapper geneticist, spilling what little is left of my wine in the process. A purple stain of Rorschach possibility materializes on the beige shag at my feet. "I was that bad?" I suggest with an ingratiating smile, beads of perspiration gathering instantaneously under both arms.

He nods, looking at me, or rather through me, and then back to the fire. Quite as if I have been found wanting in some essential virtue and tossed away.

"There was a lot to learn from you two tonight," I finally hazard. And after an excruciating pause, "Though it goes without saying that I'm on the other fellow's side."

"Without saying," he echoes drily, a finger tracing and retracing the delicate line of his finely chiseled nose.

"It's a matter of principle, don't you think? And safety. If you want to play the game, you better be willing for the others to make the rules. Especially when your game happens to involve experiments with the life process itself."

"On the contrary, my dear lady. Since we are the ones playing the game, we're the only ones who can possibly understand what the rules should be."

"Ha!" I exclaim with unintended emphasis, setting my empty wine glass down on the mantel and surreptitiously scanning the room for a loose cigarette. "I find it rather difficult to believe you geneticists—or any other scientists, for that matter—are capable of blowing your own whistles. Just not part of your programming. Not part of your game."

"Genetic engineering is hardly a game, as you insist on referring to it," he points out in the same dry, condescending manner.

"Isn't it? Well no, you're right. It isn't. But I imagine that is precisely how a lot of your people begin to approach it after awhile. Ensconced away in your pearly white laboratories, with all your test tubes and double helixes and the like. There's some truth to that, isn't there, Doctor?" I persist, in a soft insinuating tone, swooping a fresh glass of wine off a passing tray.

"You're sure you need that?" he asks, nodding in the direction of my glass.

"Why, yes," I stammer, giving the man a quizzical, sidelong glance. The savior type, is he? "Which is why I took it in the first place, thank you. So tell me, Doctor. In all seriousness. And off the record. How can you be as infallibly convinced as you sounded up there tonight that there will be no freak genetic mishap in our future? No unforseen calamities along the way to all of your miracle cures?"

"Such as?"

"The opposition brought up any number of possibilities tonight, didn't they?" I say, regretting that I had not taken time out to review my notes. "But let's take the obvious. Some new-fangled miracle bacteria which continues to mutate outside the lab. Becoming unexpectedly toxic and killing off half the human race before an effective antidote can be found."

He stares down at me a moment in pensive silence. "You don't really believe that crap, do you?" he finally allows.

"What crap? . . . Why shouldn't I?"

He rubs his eyes in weary disgust.

"Now *that*," I murmur, one finger dancing in the air, "is precisely what I find so exasperating about you people. This condescending, 'our work is above it all' attitude you always wear."

"Look, Miss . . ."

"Calloway."

"Miss Calloway. Recombinant DNA happens to be a very complex subject, about which I am fed up with having to discuss with every Tom, Dick, and—"

"Harriet," I interject.

"—reporter who happens to come along, and who invariably doesn't know a damn thing about what they're talking about. It's never the informed ones with whom I get mired down in these senseless debates."

"Is that so? Well! I guess I know when to beat a retreat," I demur, smiling crookedly up at the man, and surprised to find him smiling in return. "Nonetheless Doctor, as poorly informed as I may be concerning the particulars of your work inside the lab, I'm quite sure I know enough about the ways of the world *outside* the lab to rest assured that the wonders of genetic engineering, whatever they may or may not be, will inevitably be used for the worst possible purposes, and wind up mucking things up even more than they already are."

"That was some retreat," he murmurs wryly, and suddenly we both laugh. A slinky blonde strolls into the conversation at this point in time, linking arms proprietarily with my new friend.

"Aren't you going to introduce us?" she purrs, smiling oh-so-graciously in my direction.

"Afraid I didn't catch your name?" he says.

"Sarah Calloway," I enunciate crisply, pulling my purse up over my shoulder in preparation for a quick exit.

"Well Sarah, this is Esther Squire."

The hostess, of course. "How do you do," I murmur, deciding she isn't the type to shake hands. "I must say, you have a beautiful place here. I'm afraid I've forgotten your name, as well," I lie, turning back to Frank.

"But I thought everyone knew the great Doctor Winslow," Esther coos, twining a finger playfully around his ear. He jerks his head away. It is an infinitesimal movement, but one I take note of, all the same.

"Frank Winslow," he says, giving me one of those long searching looks which, unbeknownst to me, he had become famous for. "You're not driving home, I trust?"

"Why no. As a matter of fact, I was planning on catching a cab."

"Good. There are enough drunk drivers out there tonight without adding one more to the scenery."

Whether the man is playing with me or not, this last remark seems totally uncalled for. "Dr. Winslow," I begin hotly, the blood rushing to my cheeks, "whatever else I may be this evening, I am most certainly not drunk. I do thank you for a most enlightening conversation. And a pleasure to meet you," I add curtly, with a vague nod in Esther's direction before making an about-face and strutting indignantly out of the room.

I land in the adjacent dining area, where an opulent spread of goodies has been laid out on a huge buffet. Why not? I tell myself, picking a plate off the sideboard and proceeding to pile it high with a bit of everything in sight. Unfortunately my appetite has deserted me, and without bothering to take a single bite I set the laden plate back down on the buffet and return to the kitchen for my coat.

Romeo and Juliet are still going at it to one side of the refrigerator. All that insatiable puppy love depresses the hell out of me. I am in the motion of battling into my coat, wrong arm into wrong sleeve—okay so maybe I didn't need that last glass of wine—when an invisible hand helps me along.

"Running off so soon?"

I turn, staring incredulously up at the man. Unable to believe he has actually followed me out here. "I don't really dig these things, to tell the truth," I say, gesturing vaguely into the other room.

"And you were going to leave just like that? Without even saying goodbye? . . . Before we could even finish our conversation?"

"I thought you finished things off rather handily, now that you mention it."

He laughs, "So?" he murmurs, lightly touching the top button of my coat and sending chills all the way down my back.

"So?"

"When would you suggest we get together to wrap things up?"

Wrap things up? "Well, I don't know. Maybe sometime next week?"

"How about tonight?"

"Tonight? But don't you . . . ?"

"Don't I what?"

"Well, nothing. It's just that . . ."

"Just that what?" he asks, reaping obvious enjoyment from my obvious discomfort.

"Well what exactly do you mean?" I finally say. "Go some place and talk, or what?"

"I live right in the neighborhood," he replies, nodding in the general direction of the back door. "How does that sound? And I make a great pot of tea," he adds, drawing a finger along the collar of my coat.

"Yes. I bet you do."

He laughs again. "You do like tea, do you not?"

"Not particularly, as a matter of fact."

"Well, you'll learn to. It's an acquired taste."

When he returns to the living room to take care of some final farewells, I consider another quick swig of wine. But before I am able to translate thought into action, the man is back, a sport coat slung over one shoulder and a Carmen McRae album in hand. Whose album it is and how it happened to have found its way into this particular apartment, is not a question I care to go into at the moment.

We taxi over to his loft in the lower end of the Battery. Hardly in the neighborhood, as he put it to me earlier. But I am in no mood to quibble. And as promised, he really does make us up a pot of tea. And we really do talk. Or rather, he talks and I listen. Nodding along in my own sweet fashion as he expounds cryptically on cell fusions, vector molecules, incubated plasmids and the like. When all I can really think about is whether the two of us are going to be sleeping together tonight. Or not.

It is sometime around 3 a.m. that he hits me with the question. Should he call me a taxi home?

"Well yes. . . . I suppose you had better," I answer, making a hesitant attempt to rise.

"Or do you have a better idea?"

I laugh. What else to do under the circumstances?

"Good," he says, carrying the teapot off to the kitchen

and returning moments later with a bottle of Courvoisier, two glasses, and the Carmen McRae.

I never did acquire a taste for tea. But Carmen's smokey melodies have remained synonymous with love-making—the sweet, new, lingering kind—ever since.

It is not until morning, with the harsh light of a new day pouring through the bedroom window, that I am finally sober enough to take note of the slender band of gold adorning the fourth finger of his left hand.

"You're married?" I screech, pulling the bedclothes up around my neck.

"Of course," he answers, having the audacity to chuckle. "What self-respecting American male wouldn't be married off by thirty-five years of age?"

"Well then why in Jesus didn't you tell me?"

"I've never made a habit of announcing such things. Nor hiding them either, for that matter. The ring is here. Isn't that enough?"

"No, it isn't enough. And where is your wife?"

"With the kid, upstate. Any more questions?"

"Kids even," I mumble, too unnerved to bother hiding my total disgust.

"I was under the impression you had children squirreled away somewhere as well."

"What are you talking about?" I snap, yanking the sheet off the bed and whipping it around my waist.

"All that bleeding heart talk last night about having to put your children's destiny in the hands of a few mad scientists."

"I was speaking figuratively, for God's sake." Shrouded under the sheet, I march off to the bathroom, slamming the door behind me. And thinking how very much I despise that term 'bleeding heart.' The ultimate conservative-minded pigeon hole for people who just happen to be human enough to care.

When I re-emerge some fifteen minutes later, showered, dressed, and prepared to make a quick and cool exit, two glasses of fresh orange juice have already been set out on the breakfast room table, and some incredible smelling coffee is brewing on the stove. Ah well, I tell myself in

Machiavellian resignation, if I don't want him bugging into my drinking habits, what right do I have bugging into his bedroom habits. And what she doesn't know won't hurt her. An axiom which over time I have come to vehemently disbelieve.

But as matters were to unfold that week-end, I was to spend the rest of the day and the following evening holed away in that loft. Feeling terribly compromised and compromising. And madly in love.

JUNE 12

I wake up to migraine and terminal dehydration, shades of an overly active air conditioner and yesterday evening's Mountain Chablis. After a quick shower and change of clothes, I head back to May's Diner in the center of town; in the mood for something familiar, though it be so low and humble as their wretched coffee and that stolid waitress' implacable non-smile.

"Call me May," she says when I order my coffee. Which explains her dogged presence there behind that counter 16 hours out of every day. A quick cup and a run-through of the *Colston Times,* and I take a drive out to Paradise, intending to question a few of Frank's neighbors. Someone who may know of his present whereabouts or why the man skipped town.

My first stop is the pea-green bungalow just adjacent to Frank's. No one is home. I move on to the fading fuchsia with no better results. Wandering around to the backyard, I am confronted by an overgrown hinterland of rose bushes and crab grass, with a rusted out hand-mower beached in a stairwell by the garage. The sight of the mower inspires instant nostalgia for a time and place when such antiquated mchinery still prevailed. Those bucolic Saturday mornings of my childhood, long before my parents' separation and divorce.

The reverie having run its course, I walk back out onto the main road, heedful of a host of particulars which got by me in the dusk of yesterday's late afternoon visit. Frank's bungalow is far from the only place to have been shut down. On the contrary, every house in the general area seems to be locked up and deserted, a few parked cars and a passing motorcycle the only testimony to human habitation around.

I head back to the car, sliding listlessly behind the wheel and puzzling over a vague irregularity to Frank's front door. What is missing? His address, or course! The three brass numerals which led me to that sugar shack yesterday afternoon have disappeared. I walk back up for a closer look. The three beveled holes are there all right, so I'm not imagining things. I glance over at the neighboring units, my suspicions confirmed. No addresses on any bungalow within range.

Standing there on Frank's front porch, I am troubled by an eerie, unnatural stillness to this place. And without further ado, hop back into the car and hightail it out of that ghost town but quick. Once back in Colston, my trepidations appear foolishly ill-founded. All those missing numerals can be explained away by any number of innocuous possibilities. A scavenger perhaps. Or local junk man collecting his due. Sufficiently reassured, I follow through on stage two of today's agenda. The post office.

The old man slouched behind the iron-grated window looks to be asleep, his chin resting on a sunken chest.

"Hello?"

One eye cocks open, and then the other, as he slowly rights himself in the chair.

"What's happening out at Paradise Valley?" I ask, raising my voice in consideration for the hearing aids he wears on either ear. "Is Genco laboratories closing down?"

"Not so fast, young lady. Not so fast. Genco laboratories, you say?"

"Out at Paradise. I was just out there looking up an old friend. But apparently he's moved on. Apparently everyone's moved on."

"Only company out there's Chemix Pharmaceutical.

Been out there for the last twenty years. They cleared out though. Some three months back."

"Chemix Pharmaceutical. . . ? Would you happen to have the forwarding address for this gentleman here?" I ask, slipping him a piece of scrap paper with Frank's name and address jotted out on it. He takes the paper and shuffles over to a file cabinet in back.

"Seems this Winslow character didn't leave no forwarding address at all, Miss."

"Are you sure about that? I mean isn't the post office obliged to keep track of our addresses more or less?"

"Not if you people don't cooperate some by leaving behind a few clues," he says, easing himself back down in the chair.

"Would it be possible to tell me the last time Dr. Winslow received mail at his Paradise address? It's very important that I find out where the man's gone."

"He ran out on you, did he now?"

"Of course not," I reply with a laugh. "He's just an old friend I was hoping to talk to again."

"Because if he's run out on you, young lady, it won't do you no good hunting him down and dragging him home again. He'll only be slipping back out the minute you turn your back."

"He is just an old friend," I repeat hotly, "Now about that mail?"

"It's not me you'd be wanting to talk to about that. I don't sort the mail. And I don't deliver it. That'd all be in Lucy's department."

"Lucy?"

"Our postmistress. Been working the job for ten years now. Ever since Harry passed away."

"I see. And where might I be able to find this Lucy at the moment?"

"She'd be out making her rounds. Could be anywhere in a thirty mile radius, so I wouldn't try tracking her down if I were you. She's generally back by two, if you got some questions for her."

"Then I'll be back at two," I tell him, stuffing Frank's address back in my purse.

"Should let the poor sucker be," the old man mumbles under his breath as I walk out the screen door.

Things are getting more muddled by the minute. More questions. No answers. And this heat isn't helping any. Must be near ninety by now. A dry, blistering desert air that hurts going down. I drop back into May's, settling at one end of the counter and ordering a cold beer.

Two business men are conversing in low tones at a table in the rear. And a stooped, wizened character is huddled over a stack of pancakes at the other end of the counter. The blue uniform and leather mail bag at her feet tell me this must be none other than the postmistress herself.

This Miss Lucy may look old, but she sure doesn't eat old. And the pancakes aren't to be the end of it either. The first course finished off, she moves to a second. Hot apple pie buried in mounds of freshly whipped cream. Five or six masterly swipes and she shoves the empty bowl aside, calling out to May for her receipt.

"Would you have a minute?" I ask, slipping onto an adjacent stool.

"Depends what the minute's for," she drawls saucily, bringing a bar of Hershey's chocolate from her purse.

"I'm trying to track down a friend of mine. A Dr. Frank Winslow?" I say, refusing her offer of chocolate. "You must have delivered mail to him at one time or another over the past two years? He lives out at Paradise. That is, he did live out at Paradise, until a week or so ago."

"Child, there hasn't been a living soul out at Paradise for two three months now. Not since the Chemix plant closed down." She pops a square of chocolate into her mouth and slips off the stool. Shrinking to somewhere under five feet tall.

"But that's impossible! You see, I sent a letter to Dr. Winslow just a week ago, and I know that he received it. Because he wired me back," I explain, pressing Frank's telegram out on the counter top for her inspection. She slides it back in my direction without giving it a glance.

"All I can tell you dearie is what I already told you. I haven't been delivering to Paradise since early spring. For the very excellent reason that there's been nobody out there to deliver mail to."

"And you never saw this man on one of your trips there?" I persist, shoving the *Time* profile under her nose.

She frowns at the photograph, shaking her head. "Can't say that I did. He sure is a looker that boy, though, isn't he," she chuckles. "If I were any younger now . . ." And with a wink in my direction she heads on out the door.

One hell of a looker alright, I mumble under my breath, taking another long look at the photograph myself. Frank in his lab coat. That lab coat and Frank. An image which unleashes a chain of formaldehyde-laced memories. The countless evenings the two of us passed, holed away in that lab of his. Not the most romantic of love nests, that place, what with its black alabaster counters and bio-chemical paraphernalia scattered all around.

But I adjusted. As I adjusted to so many other 'inconveniences' of our affair. That was the underlying, if unarticulated, ground rule of our entire relationship. I must adjust.

I am eventually wrenched back into the present, and May's, by my pint-sized postmistress, who is waving an envelope under my nose. I grab for it. She jerks her hand out of reach. "When you first mentioned that gentleman friend of yours, it didn't ring any bells. Mind doesn't work like it used to, child. One of the trials of old age. But a few minutes to nibble on it, and I recollected having seen that Winslow name before. So I went back to the office and checked through our dead letter file. And sure enough! A letter addressed to your Dr. Winslow."

"That's wonderful," I say, hopping off the stool and reaching out for the letter one more time. She drops it into her mail bag, giving the weathered leather a salutary slap.

"Couldn't rightfully hand it over to you now, could I Miss. Against federal regulations, handing over personal mail like that."

"You can't be serious," I murmur, taking a step in her direction.

She grips the bag with both hands, pedaling back a couple of steps herself. "Lookie here, child. I been working for the United States Postal Service a good ten years now. And my husband, near thirty-five years before that. Which makes forty-five honest years of service between the two of us. And I don't plan on tainting that kind of record at this late date. You hear me now?"

"But you don't seem to understand, Ma'am. This could be a matter of life or death. If I could just find out who sent that letter? Any information at all would be of tremendous help."

She draws the envelope out of her bag for a furtive peek, then drops it back in. "Appears to have come from a J. M. Winslow. Out of San Francisco. If that will be of any assistance to you. Post-dated the 12th of May. And that, Miss Wisenheimer, is that."

J. M. Winslow? Obviously Jennifer, Frank's ex-wife. But what would she be doing in San Francisco, of all places? And after all these years, why still be in contact with Frank?

"Hold on a minute!" I yell after the postmistress, following her out the restaurant door and up to her jeep. "Something doesn't add up here. How can a letter sent to Dr. Winslow May 12 wind up in the dead letter file, while my own letter, sent the first week in June, get through?"

"Get through?"

"Why yes! Don't you see? Dr. Winslow received my letter sent around the 4th of June, while the earlier letter got derailed into your file."

She shakes her head in muted exasperation. "I'm just not coming across to you child, am I? Now you listen here, and you listen good. I haven't been delivering out to Paradise for almost two months. Not a single dad-burned letter to a solitary individual out there. And that includes your doctor friend there. You hear? And if I didn't deliver out to Paradise, well then nobody did."

"But Frank did receive my letter," I reiterated hopelessly.

"Lookie here," she says, resting a gnarled hand on my shoulder and blinking up at me through a noon-day sun. "It's never easy when a man chooses to step out on you. And it don't matter how he chooses to do it, neither. Whether it's by living, or by dying. Still all comes down to the same one-way ticket. And you got to live with it. You got to live with it because it's the only choice you got.

Understand me, now?" And with that last pearl of wisdom dropped, she gives my shoulder a reassuring pat and hoists herself into the jeep.

"But he didn't leave me!" I yell after the retreating vehicle. "I left him!" Obviously the lady has had words with the old geezer in the post office. Their morbid rendition of my interest in finding Frank is beginning to pall.

Minutes tick by and I remain rooted to the spot. Until the blue jeep is nothing more than a cloud of dust down the highway, and my shirt sticks to my back like bubble gum on hot cement. It is the heat which finally drives me back into the diner, where I finish off what little remains of a now lukewarm glass of beer.

What possible connection could this Chemix firm have with Genco? Or with Frank? It is becoming increasingly obvious that I must return to San Francisco. Any possible leads, including Chemix and Jennifer, head me back in that direction. The decision made, I opt for one last beer before hitting the road. May returns with my beer and a double decker club sandwich, as well.

"On the house," she mumbles, setting me up with cutlery and a bottle of Heinz.

"I don't understand," I say with a laugh.

"You got to eat, don't you? Doesn't matter how many problems you got. You still got to eat."

I am duly humbled by the woman's generous gesture. Especially considering the rash assessment I made about her the evening before.

"What makes you think I have problems?" I ask, daubing ketchup over the pile of greasy fries.

"Eat," she says, folding her arms under large breasts and leaning against a fifties Coca-Cola poster which adorns the back wall. Her solid frame makes an arresting contrast to the bikini-clad blond skiing into the sunset with a bottle of Coke. "Just eat."

And so I do. While May proceeds to serve up some new arrivals in the rear. "Couldn't help but overhear your conversation with Lucy," she says upon her return. "Something about life and death, was it?"

"I might have been exaggerating a bit," I concede. "It's

just that a friend I was supposed to be meeting out at Paradise Valley last night, disappeared without telling me where he's gone."

"They shut down and moved out last April."

"Everyone?"

"They may have a couple of watchmen around. They were a queer bunch out there," she adds, gesturing at the Time photo of Frank which is still on the counter. "Never mixed much with us folks in town. Fact is, they had no need to. The company built everything right into Paradise its employees could possibly ask for. A restaurant. Shopping center. They even had their own cinema out there, if you can imagine."

"This is Chemix Pharmaceutical you're talking about?"

She nods. "Brought their bulldozers in one February and were moving their people in by May."

"What year was this?"

"Must have been '65. Or '66. We were all pretty fired up about it here in Colston. Been led to believe it was going to mean money. You know—more business. And jobs. For our children. So as they wouldn't have to be always moving elsewhere in order to gain a decent livelihood. It's a sad thing when a town can't support its own flesh and blood. I got three daughters, and the closest one is down in L.A. Two hundred miles away. There's one of my grandchildren I haven't set eyes on yet. And she's near six months old. Now that's not right, is it? But it's the way it has to be."

"So Chemix didn't—"

"Didn't hire from Colston. Didn't buy from Colston. The only thing we ever got out of that company was funny tasting water."

"Contaminated?" Maybe that can explain their god-awful coffee?

"Who knows? But it sure don't taste the way it used to. Better dying through chemistry, as my daughter used to say."

I finish off the sandwich and wait up at the cash register to pay my bill. True to her word, May has only charged me for the two beers. "What was Chemix making out there?" I ask, after she hands over my change.

"Was all research and development. Or R & D, as those folks used to call it. Built themselves a couple of those high risk labs out there. The kind that can handle the tricky stuff."

"Like what?"

She shrugs. "Pesticides. Insecticides. Like I said. They were a pretty private bunch."

"So why did they suddenly close up shop like that?"

"Big business for you. It wasn't so sudden, though. Been rumors about them moving out for years. Guess they were hit by the last recession like a lot of other folk. Maybe there was something about better tax breaks down in Texas too, now that I think of it."

I head back to the motel, in dire need of an afternoon snooze before starting the four hour trek back north. Parking the car in front of my room, I am stopped cold by the sight of the motel room door hanging slightly ajar. I make a wary approach. Kick the door wide open. And let out a muted scream at the sight of my suitcase and all its contents strewn about the motel room floor.

I dash down to the motel's front office, only to be met with a sign tacked onto the door: "Back at two." Scrambling back into the rented Datsun, I lock both doors and gun it back to May's.

"Someone just broke into my motel room!" I whisper frantically, upon entering the diner and catching May's eye. She comes over directly and steers me to the nearest counter stool.

"Get ahold of yourself, sweetie," she says calmly, handing me a cigarette from the pack stashed in her apron pocket. "What did they take?"

"I don't know, actually. I wasn't about to waltz right in and find out. The creep could have still been in there for all I know."

May advises me to sit tight and heads into the kitchen. "Louie's going to cover for me," she says upon her return, removing her apron and stuffing it under the counter. "Why don't you and I just trot on over to the sheriff's office and see what he can do for us."

"But this is the post office," I say, stopping short of the familiar screen door.

"That too," she says, pushing me on through.

"Hold it," I whisper, stepping back out on the front stoop. "Who is Colston's sheriff?"

"John Kelly," she answers, shoving me back in.

I yank her back out. "You don't mean to tell me that old fart in there is actually your sheriff?"

"That's right," she says with a chuckle, taking a strong hold on my arm and dragging me back over the threshold. This time I am absolutely certain the man is asleep, his head jerking up spasmodically at our approach.

"Well now, May," he bellows familiarly, making what I consider to be an admirable recovery. "What can I be doing for you now?"

"It's the young lady here who will be needing your aid, John. Her room over at the Motel 6 was broke into this morning."

"Or afternoon," I interject.

"You don't say," he murmurs, pursing his lips in my direction. "Real sorry about that, Miss. But it wouldn't be the first time it's happened. That old motel's become a mighty popular target these days. Could be the same damn fella every time, too, as far as we can figure the whole thing out."

"But why wasn't I warned? Why didn't the manager inform me there had been so many burglaries in the place?"

"Wouldn't imagine it'd do a hell of a lot for business. Would you? Now why don't the two of us mosey on out there and see what can be done to fix things up."

"I'm coming along," May says, taking my arm once again. "I feel responsible for this mess. I was the one who recommended that motel to her in the first place."

I followed the two of them out to Sheriff Kelly's jeep and crawl into the back seat. What this Rip Van Winkle is going to be contributing to the situation out there is quite beyond me. He doesn't even seem to be wearing a gun. But I have little option at the moment than to sweat it out on the sticky plastic seat cover as we weave our way back to the scene of the crime.

JUNE 13

Sunday morning, San Francisco. Colston and the troubling events of yesterday appear no more substantial to me now than the fleeting impression of a distant dream. Vaguely disturbing perhaps, but so essentially unreal. Especially when juxtaposed against the resuscitating realness of the cup of black coffee now before me and the harmonies of Bach drifting in from Amy's stereo in the adjacent room. I'm in the mood to be grateful for the little things. For the fact that Amy's landlord was so kind as to let me in to the apartment last night at 2 a.m. And that a pair of cut-rate jade earrings were the only items of interest to my cat burglar yesterday afternoon.

After a brief perusal of Amy's morning *S. F. Chronicle* I pour myself a second cup of that excellent Java and look up Jennifer Winslow's number in the city directory. She's still listed as a Winslow, alright. Even after four or five years of divorce. I start to dial her number. Then think better of it. What's the sense in ruining her Sunday with a call from me. She didn't much take to me back in New York. And she certainly isn't going to be feeling any better about me out here. Time does not heal all wounds. Anyway, what point is there in setting up a rendezvous with the woman, or with anyone else for that matter, until Amy and her keys have returned. Which should be sometime this afternoon.

I pass the remainder of the morning leafing through a pile of *Ms.* magazines stuffed under the bed. Sometime after two p.m. there is a knock at the door. It is Amy's landlord, passing along a message from Amy for me to water her plants and feed her cat while she's away.

"Away?" What cat?

"She and her companion have decided to bike on down to Mexico for a week or two. She," and he stops to clear his throat. "She apparently wasn't expecting you back in town so soon."

"Yes, well you see I. . . . Things didn't quite work out the way I had hoped. It's okay if. . . . ?"

"Make yourself at home," he assures me, proceeding to unhook a bulky ring of keys from his belt and pairing up three keys with the corresponding locks on Amy's front door. Once the man has taken his leave, I turn the apartment inside out in an attempt to ferret out Amy's phantom cat. I look everywhere. Cupboards. Closets. Bookshelves. Bathtub. Laundry chute. Behind the refrigerator and stove. All I come up with is a bag of Purina cat chow and a couple of bowls. I fill one of them up and head outside in quest of a late lunch.

Walking east over Nob Hill, I find myself in San Francisco's Chinatown. Clumps of souvenir-hunting tourists, fresh fruit and vegetable stands, arcane little herb shops, sidewalk hawkers, and strings of pressed duck and chicken adorning butchershop windows along the way.

Once past a spat of tacky girlie joints off Columbus, the city moves into North Beach, a six block area of Italian restaurants, bakeries, and espresso sidewalk cafes. I duck into the first book store I see and emerge some thirty minutes later with two new Simenon Maigrets. Within minutes I'm nestled into a rear corner booth of a small Italian restaurant, with a bottle of beer and basket of fried calamari before me, as well as one of the Maigrets.

"Not one of his better ones, I'm afraid."

I look up to find a tall, thin, bespectacled gentleman standing before me, a drink in hand. It takes a moment to realize he is referring to my book.

"Not bad though," I say, diving instinctively for the pack of Parliaments lying at the bottom of my purse, wondering simultaneously how I'm going to manage to shake this guy without being obnoxiously rude.

"Ever read *Tidal Wave?* Or *The Man Who Watched Trains Go By?*" I shake my head. "Actually," he goes on, pulling a chair over from the adjoining table, "his best stuff comes out of his non-Maigrets."

"But I love Maigret!" I protest, getting drawn into the conversation in spite of myself. "The character's so unassuming. So . . . so undetectivey in his way."

"Undetectivey?" The man has a very pleasant laugh.

"You know. Fat. Middle-aged. Sexless." I lean into his lighted match, then stop myself, stuffing the unlit cigarette back into my purse. "Listen," I say, staring down into the pages of my open book. "I don't mean to be antisocial here. But I really wasn't in the mood for company this afternoon."

"Right," he says, jumping up so quickly that he turns over the chair he was sitting in. Then bending over to pick it up, scraps of paper and three or four pens drop out of his coat pocket. He stuffs everything back into his pocket and, smiling wryly, gives a vague salute and returns to the front bar.

Perversely enough, I find myself regretting his departure now that he has actually left. I've always been a sucker for klutzes. Besides, anyone who's a fan of Simenon can't be all bad. After a moment's deliberation, I scribble out a short note on a napkin and ask the waiter if he would be so kind as to deliver it up to my friend sitting at the bar.

And it works, just like I knew it would. My friend reading over the note, laughing, and returning to the table with drink in hand.

"Stanley," he says, offering his free hand.

"Sarah."

Stanley retakes his seat and gestures to the waiter for another round of drinks. I have a sneaking suspicion I'm going to be leaving this place a lot less sure-footed than when I came in.

"You look like a Stanley, interestingly enough," I say, pushing the basket of calamari his way.

He leans back in his chair, giving me a rather severe squint over his glass of scotch.

"Did I say something wrong?"

"Somehow I've never considered the idea of looking like a Stanley to be a particularly complimentary state of affairs."

"Oh?" He may have a point there.

"As a matter of fact, I prefer to blame all the existential angst of my adolescence on having to answer 'present' to *Stanley* every day of my young life."

"Is that so? Well things could have been worse, after all."

"You think so, do you?"

"Sure. You could have been a Sylvester. Or a Clarence, God forbid."

"My younger brother is named Clarence."

"You're kidding me, aren't you? Ha! And I suppose he's a bit on the short side, right? Plump? Wears glasses, no doubt. I'm close, am I? Well then, you can hardly blame your mother, can you? I mean, for having the insight to choose names which suited her children so well."

"Ah, but the real question here, sweetheart, is whether the name suited the child. Or the child grew up to suit the name."

The waiter approaches our table bearing our drinks and informing Stanley that he is wanted on the phone up at the front bar.

"Afraid I have to be heading out," Stanley tells me upon his return, slipping into the sport coat he had left hanging on the back of his chair.

"Oh?"

"A bit of an emergency here. Sorry to hang you up like this. It's been real nice." He glances around for our waiter, instructing him in sign language to put everything on his own bill. I should object, but don't. The man slips a cigarette out of my pack, lights up, and before I can collect myself enough to say some kind of goodbye, sets off for parts unknown.

Damn. Just when I was getting good and primed for an old fashioned afternoon of drinks and banter. And he was definitely the type one could banter with. Ad infinitum.

I return to my Simenon, but it doesn't work any longer. So I finish my drink and head back to the apartment, resolved to make contact with Frank's ex-wife.

The line rings three, four times. I am about to hang up when she answers, sounding somewhat out of breath.

"Hello Jennifer?"

"Yes?"

"I'm not sure you're going to remember me. I'm Sarah Calloway . . . An old friend of Frank's . . . ?"

"I remember you, Sarah." The coolness in her response turns my stomach.

"Yes. Well the reason I'm making contact is that I've been trying to get in touch with Frank. For professional reasons. Concerning a story I'm doing on the search for an AIDS vaccine." I pause. Silence reigns. "I lost contact with him years ago, you see. But hooked up again last month. That is, I was under the impression I had hooked up. But now I'm not so sure. You see, it appears that Frank has disappeared into thin air."

"He's no longer down in Paradise Valley?"

"Jennifer, nobody's down at Paradise! The whole company folded up its research labs and moved out over two months ago!"

"So that explains it," she murmurs, as if to herself.

"Explains what?" I get no response. "Jennifer, how would you feel about the two of us getting together for a drink or something? I realize I'm probably the last person on earth you care to see again. But I have the oddest feeling about Frank. That maybe he's in trouble or something. And you're the only one I can turn to about it. Maybe if we talked it over? . . . Say later on tonight?"

"If you could see your way to coming over here. I want to be home when Jaimie gets back from practice."

"Of course." We arrange to meet within the hour. I shower and slip into the one clean blouse left to my name, acutely aware of the psychic traces of yesterday's cat burglar, whose grimy paws have permanently desecrated every piece of clothing he touched.

Following the directions Jennifer gave me over the phone, I head straight up Larkin and then make a right at Vallejo, climbing to the top of the hill. It is a lovely summer evening. The heavy grey horizon having given way to the purple-orange splendours of a setting sun. But I'm in no mood to enjoy the scenery. Body and soul focused back on quite another Sunday evening, some four to five years ago.

It was the first and only time I ever met Jennifer. Unless one is to count the wedding picture on their dresser. Or the snapshots of Jennifer and son stuck into the wardrobe mirror. The pictures had prepared me for her beauty but not for that unworldly composure; that unnerving presence of hers which required no props or vitriolic displays of self-righteousness to let one know exactly where one stood both in her own eyes and in the eyes of the world.

How ironic really, that the particular Sunday evening in question was the only occasion, with the exception of our first week-end together, that Frank and I ever dared meeting in their Battery loft. The reason for the risk was simple enough. Jennifer was away on an unusual week long assignment, casting around down South for some situation comedy coming up on CBS. But the series head writer had a freak heart attack on the road. The junket was cut short. And Jennifer returned to New York four days ahead of schedule. Four nights too soon.

At least Frank and I hadn't been in bed when she arrived. Far from it, as the two of us shouted each other down in the middle of the living room. She entered the room with the unearthly calm of an avenging angel, sliding the satchel off her shoulder and settling into the rocking chair by the door, as the two of us stood gape-mouthed before her.

"You're quite right," she murmured, unsettling me with her assuring smile. "He is a bit of a chauvinistic bastard, at that. But then, what does that make you?"

I had no ready answer for that one. Still don't. And staring mutely over at Frank, then back to Jennifer, it was all I could do to grab my purse off the sofa and run shamefacedly out the door. The end! I murmured over and over, as I ran the thirty or so blocks to my west side apartment. Fatalistically relieved that Jennifer's untimely entrance had showed Frank and me up for the cheap and wasted twosome we had somehow become. The end.

But it hadn't been the end, after all. Not quite yet. For Frank walked out on Jennifer that very night, moving into my little apartment for a few weeks time. Until he could get around to digging up new lodgings of his own. And all he would ever tell me about their final split was that he was glad it was over. No more. No less.

By the time I reach Jennifer's residence, an attractive wood frame house at the top of Vallejo street, my lungs burn and sweat oozes down my neck. How San Franciscans can live with all these hills is beyond me. I ring. Wait. Then ring again. When Jennifer finally answers the door, my first thought is how much she has aged over the last few years. All that grey hair. And smile lines cutting into a once smooth and open face. How many of those lines am I personally responsible for, I wonder guiltily, as she leads me toward the back of the house.

"So? What will it be?" she asks, remaining standing by the hearth as I settle awkwardly into a rocking chair in one corner of the room. "A bit of wine? Some scotch?"

"Whatever you're having," I say, shrinking inside at her determinedly distant air.

She returns moments later with two frosty gin and tonics. We sip a moment in silence. "Great view you have here," I say.

"I trust you didn't come over here to discuss the view."

I smile wanly, then take another long sip on my drink before plunging in. "What started all this was that feature on Frank in one of the May issues of *Time*. You read it perhaps?" She nods. "Impressive, wasn't it?" She nods again, an inscrutable smile hovering on her lips. "Anyway, it was that story which induced me to get back in touch with Frank. I hadn't heard from him in over four years, you see. So I wrote him out at Paradise, suggesting an interview. He wired back his consent. And I flew on out, only to learn, once I got out here, that Frank and all the rest of them out at Paradise had moved on. Sometime in April I gather. Which doesn't add up at all, since I heard from Frank out of Paradise just a couple of days ago!"

"I had always imagined you were the one who accompanied Frankie out to Paradise in the first place."

"Good heavens no," I say with a nervous laugh. Frankie? "We split up long before that."

"So why do you come to me with all this?"

"Well because Colston's post office showed me one of

the last letters Frank received at his Paradise address. A
letter that wound up in their dead letter file. It was from
you, Jennifer. That's how I learned you live here in San
Francisco in the first place."

"That letter wasn't from me. It was from my son."

"I see. So they keep in touch?"

"At one time, yes. But Frankie hasn't answered one of
Jaimie's letters in months," she murmurs, head down as she
prods stray kindling back into the fire.

"The real puzzle here, Jennifer, is that Frank received my
own letter, which wasn't posted until the first week of June.
And never received yours, sent almost a month before."

"What makes you so sure Frank received your letter?"

"Like I said. He wired me a reply. Invited me on out."

"And you have no reason to doubt the authenticity of the
telegram?"

I stare at her a moment, more than a little non-plussed. In
all my wildest imaginings over the last few days, why had it
never occurred to me to question the validity of the telegram
itself? But who would go through the trouble of such a
forgery? And why? I bring the tired scrap of yellow paper
out of my wallet and hand it over to Jennifer without saying
a word. She reads it over and hands it back.

"*Love and kisses* were never Frankie's style," she
suggests. "Neither such endearing phrases as *open arms*."
Right. And right again.

"But I don't understand," I murmur, my head beginning
to spin. "Why would anyone . . . what would be the
point in someone other than Frank answering my letter? It
just doesn't make any sense."

She shrugs and rises. "Ready for another drink?"

While she retreats to the kitchen I stew awkwardly in
place, puzzled by her aloof posture vis-à-vis Frank's fate.
An uneasiness compounded by a vague sense of humilia-
tion. After all, how many countless times had I read and
reread that damn telegram, without getting the slightest bit
suspicious, while Jennifer had been able to pick it apart on a
single reading for the counterfeit piece of communication it
was likely to be.

"Franks still works for Genco?" I ask Jennifer upon her return.

"To the best of my knowledge."

"Then how does Chemix fit into the picture? Because that was the company down at Paradise. Not Genco labs."

"Chemix funds quite a bit of Genco's research. Some kind of arrangement where Chemix will distribute and market genetic engineering products developed by Genco labs. I gather it was the promise of huge bonuses from Chemix which lured Frank out here in the first place."

Jennifer rises from the sofa, walking over to the window and looking out over the bay. "So where do you go from here?" she asks.

"God only knows. I suppose over to Chemix. They're based right here in San Francisco, isn't that right?"

"Daly City."

"Right."

"How long did the two of you last?" she asks, turning around and fixing me with an intent stare.

"Frank and I?" I stammer, taken off guard by the personal turn to her questions. "Just under a year. We barely made that."

"What happened?"

"What happened was a certain sexy Chicano lady. That's what happened."

"Perhaps she should be the one for you to contact."

"Who?"

"This Chicano friend of Frank's. She might well know much more about Frank's present whereabouts than I."

"No doubt," I mumble, thinking that Angelica is about the last person on earth I care to contact about this thing. Besides, I never learned her last name.

The front door flies open, followed by the stamping of feet out in the hall. "Mom!" And into the room bursts the spitting image of Frank. A little shorter, perhaps. And ganglier, of course. But the spitting image, nonetheless. How could she have taken it all these years, I think. Living night and day with this constant and striking echo of the man who walked out on her one night, not so many years ago.

"Hello, Jaimie," Jennifer says, her voice turning remarkably warm, and her face breaking into a beatific smile. She is still a very lovely lady, I note. Very lovely indeed. "I'd like you to meet an old friend of mine, Jaimie. Sarah Calloway."

"Hello Jaimie," I say, grateful that Frank's name has not been dragged into the introductions.

"Hi," he mumbles, shuffling about in the middle of the room. And then turning to his mother. "I made the cut."

"Oh sweetie! Why that's marvelous!" she exclaims, jumping up from the sofa and giving her son an extended hug. A display of affection which Jaimie tolerates with a unique fusion of adolescent agony and ecstasy, his face turning the color of the red baseball cap on his head. "Jaimie's been trying out for the team three years straight," she says for my benefit. "Well now! I would say this calls for some kind of celebration. Wouldn't you? What shall it be?" she queries gaily, looking from me back to her son. "Big Macs? A pizza? Burritos? A little salsa and chips? I've just turned Jaimie on to Mexican," she adds, smiling in my direction.

"I could make up some of those submarine sandwiches like the other night," Jaimie suggests shyly.

"That's it! Jaimie makes the most incredible sandwiches, Sarah. Oozing of avocado and cheese. Here honey," she adds, digging into her purse and coming up with a five dollar bill. "Check out the refrigerator and then run over to Tony's for whatever you'll need."

He shoves the bill into his pocket and, nodding sweetly in my direction, trots out of the room.

"He's a doll," I say, and mean it.

"Isn't he?" she says with a laugh, her gaze following her son out the front door. "You can stay for supper, can't you?" she asks, her voice charged with nothing but friendly goodwill. Then, holding up her empty glass with a mischievous grin. "Do we dare have one more? We're celebrating, after all."

"Why not?" I say with a laugh, the woman's incredible flash of good spirits catching up with me. Watching her slender frame spring jauntily out of the room, I marvel at

the transformation which has taken place. Night and day
from the cool and ironic persona which greeted my arrival
only a half hour before. I find myself wishing there was
someone in my own life who could bring about such an
amazing transformation simply by walking in the front
door.

When Jennifer returns, her mood has sobered considerably. "Do you know how rarely the bastard ever writes
Jaimie?" she murmurs, sinking back into the love seat, her
drink in her lap. "The real victims of broken marriages. The
kids."

Tell me about it. We sip our drinks in silence. When I
finally hazard a look up, it is to find her studying me intently
once again. "Jennifer," I begin, then stop. Rendered
momentarily mute by a wave of guilt and remorse. "You
have to realize," I try again. "I had no intention of strong
arming my way into a family situation . . . I mean, I had
no idea that Frank was even married at the time . . . Not
until . . . well until . . ."

"Until it was too late?" she finished off for me, deep
irony back in her voice.

"It wasn't too late. It's never too late. I know that now.
But I pretended not to back then. I was such a damn fool in
those days. That's my only explanation for it. A God-
damned fool." I sit there, staring into my hands. Feeling
oddly relieved for having finally admitted to myself, as well
as to the one other person who seems to matter in this
instance, just exactly what I had been in those years. And
maybe still am.

"Really, I should thank you, Sarah. I was bound to leave
him sooner or later. You weren't the first, you know. And
you certainly wouldn't have been the last. It was best for
Jaimie and me that it ended when it did."

"So you left Frank," I repeat vaguely, the words sinking
in as I take another long sip on my drink. Wondering why
I'm still not feeling the slightest bit high. It is surely an act
of God which brings Jaimie into the house at this point in
time.

"I'd rather we not mention Frank's disappearance to
Jaimie," Jennifer murmurs before rising from the couch and
following her son into the kitchen.

I eventually join them there, settling at the kitchen table with Jennifer, where we sip our drinks and watch a true master at work. Jaimie labors over those sandwiches with the painstaking pride of a dedicated craftsman, meticulously spreading mustard and butter over the thick slices of sourdough. Then neatly layering on the tomatoes and cheese, followed up by avocado and ham. And then a final layer of cheese before the entire foot long concoction is placed under the broiler to re-emerge, moments later, browned, bubbly, and oozing, true to Jennifer's word.

With the submarines and pitcher of lemonade in tow, we move into the library and settle before the TV to watch the San Francisco Giants eke out a 3–2 victory over the Chicago Cubs. To my amusement, Jennifer is a true-blue aficionado of the game, well informed of every player's batting average, home run record, and field performance, right down to the intimate particulars of their private lives, all of which she and Jaime thrash over in the greatest detail with each new player who comes to bat.

I remain an envious onlooker and take my leave at the game's end, promising to keep Jennifer informed of any new developments, should and when they come along.

JUNE 14

Sometime around 4 a.m. I awake to find a furry ball of calico curled at the foot of the bed. When I go to touch the creature, he scampers off toward the kitchen. By the time I stumble in there after him, damn if he hasn't pulled the disappearing act on me again. God only knows where the little bugger manages to hide. I tear the kitchen apart end to end and still don't come across him. Which forces the obvious question upon me: if I am unable to track down one pea-brained kitty cat in a forty foot square apartment, how in hell do I plan on locating Frank?

The truth of the matter is, I'm not so sure I should be

looking for Frank anymore. The probability of that telegram being forged casts a different light on the picture, adding on murky highlights to what is a progressively murky affair.

Why, in spite of Frank's absence, was someone interested in me visiting Colston? To learn who I was? How much I knew? Or in a worse case scenario, to knock me off? No, that doesn't make any sense at all. I am no threat to anyone at this stage in the game. How could I be, when I have no idea in hell what's going on. Then too, I was a sitting duck in Colston. Yet I came through unscathed. Or if not unscathed, at least unharmed.

After the prerequisite cups of morning coffee, I put through a call to Chemix Labs in Daly City. Inquiring about Frank, I get no further than a cool young receptionist who informs me that all information regarding Chemix employees is classified information. This leaves me no alternative than to make a personal visit to their labs myself.

I rifle through Amy's closets and drawers, piecing together the most conservative combination possible. Which, considering Amy's eclectic tastes, is no easy feat. Heeled and appropriately attired, I hail a taxi and work out my performance enroute.

The Chemix plant is located in a fogged-in no man's land just south of the city. The place looks more like a shopping center than a chemical firm. Right down to the Burger King out back. Arriving at their front office, I pull Amy's hat firmly into place and ignoring the plainly lettered instructions advising me to please knock, walk right in. There are two women seated behind desks at opposite ends of the room. Both look up when I enter, but neither of them speak. I approach the younger of the two women, counting on the vulnerability of her age. My first mistake.

"What are you doing here?" she queries icily.

"Looking for my husband," I reply, planting myself in front of her desk.

"You can't see anyone without an appointment."

"Don't talk appointments with me, Miss. My husband, who has been under your employment for the past two years, has disappeared. And I plan on finding out just where he's disappeared to."

"You don't understand, ma'am. You cannot barge in here

like this, demanding information. It must be done through the necessary channels. Now I'm afraid I must ask you to leave." Her lips press together tightly and her hand hovers ominously over the phone.

"I'm afraid *you* don't understand. I am not about to walk out of this establishment until I find out, once and for all, where my husband has been sent."

The secretary's reaction to my little drama is to pick up the receiver and dial the firm's security police. I glance over at the grey-haired lady opposite and find her regarding the scene with obvious concern.

"Could you possibly help me out?" I ask, Amy's two inch stiletto heels clicking noisily against the finished marble floors as I make my way across the room. "It's about my husband, you see."

She rises, giving a kindly shake to her head. "We aren't authorized to release that kind of information. If he's a past employee, I'm not even sure we would have information on his present whereabouts."

"Frank isn't a past employee. He and his Genco research team have been working for Chemix since 1983. He was their chief director of research down at Paradise, until you closed down in April. And I haven't heard from him since."

"But I'm afraid I don't understand. If you're married to the man, why . . . ?"

"We're divorced. But the fact is, the children and I are utterly dependent on those monthly alimony checks. In the most literal sense of the word. And it's been more than two months now without a single payment. With this month's rent already well overdue," I add, staring down at my feet.

A young man in uniform strolls into the chamber and up to where we stand. "Problem, Mrs. Gaynor?" he asks, giving me a slow once-over which comes to rest at the swooping neck line of Amy's knitted top.

"No, James. Sorry to have disturbed you. We can take care of everything just fine."

"You sure now?" he asks, fingering the exposed butt of his holstered gun. What's the twerp threatening to do? Shoot me?

"Why don't you just go on and have yourself a good

lunch," she counsels agreeably, giving him a gentle nudge toward the door. And after he has gone. "Honestly, Ellen. You needn't have called on security at the drop of a hat, like that. Goodness me."

"Just going according to the book," she sniffs, tossing me a scornful glance before returning her attentions to the colossal word processor which dominates her desk.

"Now, let's see if there's anything we can do for you," she says, directing me to an empty chair at the side of her desk. She brings a two page yellow form out of a wide drawer. The sight of it is enough to make a grown woman cry. I gamely square off, writing in Frank's name, birth date, and other known statistics, including Jennifer's number and home address. I add on my own social security number, then think twice about it.

"I can't quite recall the exact date that Frank's lab team began working for Chemix," I admit, pointing to the first in a long line of questions I am going to have a hell of a time dealing with. "You see, it all happened right in the middle of the divorce proceedings," and I stop, covering my face with my hands in an amateurish but heartfelt attempt at appearing desperately forlorn.

"Now, now," she says kindly. "I'm sure what you have down here will do fine enough. If you can just give me a call sometime later on in the week?" she adds, slipping the form back into her desk.

"Oh. But I had hoped I might be able to get some definite information today. It's. . . . well the situation is terribly unpleasant at this point. To be perfectly honest, we're stone broke. And every day that passes is just another day without . . ." I close my eyes and look the other way.

"I see." She takes the form back out of the drawer for another look.

"If I came back this afternoon? Might you possibly be able to find something out by then?"

"Well this does appear to be something of an emergency, doesn't it now? This afternoon then?"

"How can I thank you," I exclaim, sincerely grateful to this lady for the generosity she is showing me. I take my leave, arranging to meet her back in the office by two p.m.

The next few hours are whiled away in the company's cafeteria, picking over a few rusty leaves of iceberg lettuce and a bowl of watery 'homemade' vegetable soup. The why and wherefore of the Burger King out back has now been explained. Over coffee, I peruse a dog-eared copy of this morning's *Chronicle*, left on the table by a previous customer, and experience an adolescent thrill at coming face to face with Stanley—my Stanley of yesterday's Italian restaurant—center opposite of the editorial page. His name in bold print at the top of his column: Stanley London's View from the Bridge.

So the man's a journalist! With his own daily column, no less. I am duly impressed. And even more so once I have read the piece through: a biting indictment of recent real estate deals being made in downtown San Francisco, with particular attention paid to a highrise soon to be blocking precious sunlight from Chinatown's principal playground, eight to ten hours out of every day.

All which merely confirms my earlier suspicions. That I indeed missed out on a damn good thing yesterday afternoon when I let that man slip through my fingers and out the restaurant door.

I return to the front office a little before two. Mrs. Gaynor shows up at half past.

"I'm afraid we have no record whatsoever of a Dr. Winslow having worked for our firm," she tells me. "And I checked through all the personnel files we have."

"But that's impossible. His research team was working out of Paradise for the last couple of years!" I point out indignantly, waving the *Time* write-up in her face. She is peering over my right shoulder with a look of helpless concern on her face. I turn to find an elderly gentleman there behind me. Pale, portly, and vaguely familiar in a three piece dark blue suit.

"What seems to be the problem?" he asks sternly, looking from me back to Mrs. Gaynor.

"The problem, sir, is that your secretary can find no record of my husband ever working for your firm. While I happen to know that he worked for Chemix Pharmaceutical, out of Paradise, for the last couple of years. I received letters and checks from him out there, for God's sake. Now, *that* is the problem."

He smiles tightly, extending an arm toward the door. "I'm sure there must be some misunderstanding here, Mrs.—"

"Winslow. Mrs. Frank Winslow."

"Mrs. Winslow. Which can be easily resolved. Won't you follow me?"

Most reluctantly, I do. Down one dark corridor and then another, winding up in a large panelled office at the opposite end of the complex. He ushers me in and closes the door behind us. I settle into a cold leather chair while he remains perched on the corner of his desk, looming over me like some doddering bird of prey.

"Let's get one thing straight," I say, hopping back up and pacing to a side mural of the Golden Gate Bridge. Typical corporate tack. "Dr. Winslow, my ex-husband, has been working down at Paradise since 1983. In April the labs down there closed down, and Frank never informed me of the impending move. I'm not interested in any of the details. All I want is my alimony, fair enough? And for that I need Frank. Now where is he?"

"Your husband is a geneticist out of Genco Laboratories, did you say?"

"I don't believe I said any such thing, no."

"Well then perhaps Mrs. Gaynor. . . ?"

"I'm not here to start answering your questions, but to have you answer one of mine. People don't just disappear into thin air like that. Or get sudden transfers without the family being kept informed. I have a legal, not to mention a financial right to know the whereabouts of my ex-husband. And I don't plan on leaving this place until I have learned where he's gone."

"Mrs. Winslow," he begins again, after a weighted pause. Removing his spectacles and buffing them with a light blue handkerchief drawn from his vest pocket. "I'm afraid that somewhere along the line you have been gravely misinformed. It is true that we have contracted out to Genco Laboratories in the past. But the facilities down in Paradise Valley never involved any Genco personnel, at any time

during our stay there. Am I making myself perfectly clear?
We have no record on your husband, Mr. Winslow. For the
very good reason that Dr. Winslow never worked for our
firm. Down at Paradise or anywhere else."

"What are you saying? That I was imagining all the mail
I received from Paradise over the last two years? That I was
receiving mail from an non-existent person? You want me to
get those letters as proof that Frank worked there? Is that
what you want?"

"Whether or not a Dr. Winslow lived in the area is not
my concern. I am simply assuring you that such a man
never worked for our firm. Now if you know what's good
for you, young lady," he goes on, holding his glasses out at
arm's length in order to inspect the quality of his work,
"you will return to your life in San Francisco and make the
best of it. With or without the financial help of your ex-
husband."

There is a threatening undertow to his words and the
manner in which he spoke them. Or maybe it's those beady
blue eyes which, without the benign camouflage of the
bifocals, suddenly appear narrow and menacing to me in
some elemental way. In spite of my brave words of a few
moments ago, I want out. Now. And walk out of that office
without exchanging another word with my blue-suited
predator. Out the door and down the two long corridors,
looking back over my shoulder every other step of the way.

It is high time to make contact with Tom Waters, my
associate over at Time Inc. The one who first clued me in on
Frank's Paradise address back in May. If anyone should be
able to clear up the Chemix-Genco-Frank connection, I can
expect it to be him. As soon as I step back into the
apartment, I put through my call. But all I get is a tape
recording, advising me of the company's office hours. Yes,
of course. Since it is 4 p.m. here in San Francisco, it is
already 7 p.m. back in New York.

I try Genco Labs, located some 150 miles south of here in
Monterey, and am passed along from two different sec-
retaries to a Dr. Bukowski, out of personnel. He proceeds to
inform me that I will need to talk to a Dr. Donald Fawley
concerning all outlying personnel. Unfortunately, Dr. Faw-

ley will be in Japan on business until the beginning of next week. At which time Dr. Bukowski advises that I get back in touch. Seconds after hanging up the phone, it rings in my ear, jarring me out of a muddled trance.

"So where were you last night?" Amy demands, before I even have time to say hello.

"Well now. I suppose I could ask you the same thing, couldn't I?"

"Finelli didn't fill you in?"

"He did, as a matter of fact. But does that really make any sense, Amy? Running off to Mexico with that teenage Troy Donahue under your belt?"

"He's twenty-three years old, Sarah. And I wish you'd stop talking about him that way, okay? Why are you back so soon, anyway? Where's Frank?"

"It's a long story, Amy."

"I've heard that before."

"You don't mind if I stick around here a few more days?"

"No problem. As long as you keep watering the plants and feed the cat. Be back in touch in Baja."

"Where *is* your cat?" I ask. But too late. Amy has already hung up. I ring up Jennifer, in hopes that she's already back from work.

"Lord, am I ever glad to hear from you," she exclaims. "Do you realize I had no idea how to get back in touch?"

"Why? What is it?" I ask, imagining from the agitation in her voice that she has learned something about Frank.

"You know that woman you spoke of? The one Frankie started to see after you?"

"Angelica?"

"I met that woman once. I'm sure of it. In fact, Sarah, I believe she's living right here in San Francisco. I didn't put two and two together until this morning. You referred to her as Mexican, didn't you? She's not Mexican, Sarah. She's from Brazil."

"But how—"

"She stopped by the house one evening, maybe two or three years ago. To give me back a ring, an heirloom in Frankie's family that I'd left with him when Jaimie and I took off for the coast. We only talked a few minutes. All I can really remember from the conversation was that Frankie was still back in New York and that she was going to be living out here."

"Here in San Francisco?"

"That's right. She was joining up with some theater troupe here in town, if I remember it right."

"She's an actress? Wait a minute, are we talking about the same person here? Was this woman tall and skinny, with huge brown eyes?"

"That was her, alright. I rather liked the woman actually. The little I saw of her."

I turn the conversation back to Chemix Pharmaceutical, telling Jennifer about my visit there this afternoon, and apologizing to her for masquerading as Frank's ex-wife. "But Jennifer, not only did they deny any association with Frank. This guy went so far as to deny the presence, now or ever, of any Genco personnel in their Paradise labs. So then I call Genco. And they tell me that Frank's one of their outlying personnel, whatever the hell that's supposed to mean. Outlying? And that I will have to speak with a Dr. Fawley about his whereabouts. Dr. Fawley, of course, happens to be in Japan until the beginning of next week. Do you believe it? Am I getting the run-around, or what? Jennifer, you're absolutely sure Frank worked down at Paradise?"

"Jaimie's been writing to him down there for the past two years."

"Yes, of course. And he never mentioned anything in his letters about an impending move? Or told Jaimie anything about his work?"

"Nothing about a move, I'm quite sure of that. But whether or not he ever referred to his work. . . . Why don't I ask Jaimie about it tonight?"

Before signing off, I suggest that she and I meet for a drink later this evening. But apparently she has other plans. Just as well, I tell myself. Because what I should really do tonight is sit tight and think things through. Trouble is, I'm just not in the mood to sit tight and think things through. By seven p.m. a bowl of cat chow has been left in the middle of the kitchen and I'm heading out the front door. Ostensibly to pick up a few groceries. But au fond, to wend my way back to the little Italian restaurant I chanced upon yesterday afternoon.

Once across the threshold, I look neither left nor right, making a beeline for one of the back tables and ordering the calamari and beer. When I finally do risk a quick survey of the place, my journalist friend, Mr. London, is nowhere in sight. Just as well, I tell myself, starting into the second of the Maigrets I picked up yesterday afternoon.

This particular offering differs significantly from previous ones I have read, in that the illustrious police superintendent, an indefatigable bar hopper if there ever was one, whose every case seems to ebb and flow on the alpha waves of bistros dotting his current beat, has been temporarily grounded. Ordered by his doctor to take a break from the pressures of work and the counterpressures of alcohol, in order to 'taste the waters' of Vichy in southern France.

An hour or so into the book and my ears perk to a familiar voice floating back from the bar. It is Stanley, of course. I shrink into the shadows, overwhelmed by a mousy panic more appropriate to someone half my age. Sensing his approach, my face remains buried in the pages of my book.

"For you, sweetheart," he says, tossing a paperback onto the table. It is a Simenon, of course. And, of course, a non-Maigret.

"Well!" I laugh, momentarily overwhelmed by the gesture. And touched. Not to mention curious as to how he guessed I'd be back here again tonight, when I didn't even know I'd be back here again tonight until walking through that door.

"May I?" he asks, sliding onto the bench opposite.

"Yes, of course. I enjoyed your piece in the *Chronicle* this morning," I quickly add. "Very much, in fact."

"Ah." And he slips a Parliament from my pack on the table.

"You write that column every day, do you?"

"Yep."

"And you never have trouble coming up with decent topics five times a week?"

"Nope."

"So what's your secret?" I ask, willing to give the guy one last chance."

"Secret?"

"How do you come up with the stories day in day out? I haven't been able to come up with any idea lately that hasn't already been covered a hundred times before."

"You write, do you?"

"Yes, I do, as a matter of fact. Freelance. It's the reason I'm out here from New York, actually. On a lead for a story."

He laughs. "All of hair-raising Manhattan at your fingertips and you come out here to find a story?"

"This is no ordinary story I happen to be working on, Stanley. Trust me."

With appropriate encouragement on his part, I go on to elaborate. Touching on everything from meeting Frank at Columbia, to the unexplained telegram, to May's Diner, to Chemix's stance on Frank and the so-called burglary of last Sunday afternoon. When I have finished he nods silently, taking one or two neat sips on his scotch.

"So?" I finally demand. "What do you think?"

"Think. I think. . . . did it ever occur to you, my friend, that you just might be over your head with this thing?"

"From time to time, yes."

"And what do you plan on doing about it?"

"Well for starters, I'm going to verify the Genco-Chemix link down at Paradise. And find out from Genco wh—"

"But you plan on carrying through with this little investigation of yours, do you?"

"Well of course, I do. Up to a certain point, anyway. There may be something very big behind all this. Bottom line, I at least want to find out what has happened to Frank. Where he's gone to. I owe him that much."

"Why do you owe this man anything at all?"

"Well now that's a peculiar question to ask, if I say so myself."

"Look," Stanley says, leaning across the table and covering my hands with both of his. "Genetic engineering has become very Big Business these days. Everyone wants a piece of the cake. The drug companies. Chemical firms. Oil conglomerates. Defense Department. No doubt the Mafia and C.I.A. are tossed in there somewhere. We're talking big stakes here. And one little lady sniffing her nose around the joint isn't going to be allowed to stand in anybody's way."

"Little lady?" I mouth noiselessly, extricating my hands from his grip. "Little lady?" I repeat out loud. A little louder than intended, perhaps. "Didn't that go out with 'chick' and 'girlie' a few hundred light years back? And for your information, Mr. London. I happen to be perfectly cognizant of the stakes involved in recombinant DNA. I wasn't born yesterday, you know."

He is grinning broadly. "I'm well aware you were not born yesterday, believe me."

I'm not sure I like the way he just put that.

"Which doesn't alter the situation any, does it?" he goes on. "Fact is, sweetheart, investigative reporting has hit troubled waters in this land of the free and the brave. You agree with me there, do you not?"

"You mean nobody wants to print the stuff anymore? Look, if we all fall prey to the right wing intimidation going down in th—"

"What I'm trying to say, Sarah, is that a hot story can suddenly get too hot. You get too close to something and you'll be stopped. It's as simple as that. I've had to back down on a fair share of stories in my time, in case you're interested."

"No way I'm throwing this story over yet, Stanley. If that's what you're getting at. Not when things have just begun to get interesting. Someone starts taking potshots at my backside, then I may reconsider."

Stanley looks from me to his scotch. Then back to me again. "What kind of work was your geneticist friend involved in at Columbia?"

"Not AIDS. Not when I knew him. Oncogenes was his area of expertise back then. You know, genes that cause cancer."

"I wasn't aware genes caused cancer."

"Okay, so maybe I'm overstating it there. Not that the

genes actually cause the cancer. But that given the right environment, with a sufficient number of carcinogens in the air, they probably give off the necessary signals to get the tumor-growing process in motion. See?"

"And how did recombinant DNA tie in with his work?"

"That was the technique his team was using to mass produce the genes under study. How much do you know about all this anyway? From a technical angle, I mean?"

He shrugs. "Just what the terminology implies. The splicing together of DNA from different species to form new species."

"Right. Only most current work in recombinant DNA isn't so interested in coming up with new combinations as in mass producing genes that already exist. Which makes it much easier to study them. To learn how they click. Learning to read, as Frank used to put it."

"So they can eventually write?" Stanley suggests sardonically.

"You got it. Ha! To hear Frank and his buddies tell it— and believe me, I heard them tell it more times than I ever care to remember—recombinant DNA is nothing short of the Second Coming. The ultimate fix for all our modern day problems. Famine. Pollution. The energy crisis. Oil spills. Cancer. War. You name it. All solved with a magic flourish of the genetic wand."

"And this piece in *Time?* What did it have to say about your friend's work?"

"No more than what I already told you. That he and his team, working out of Genco laboratories on the West Coast, had come up with very promising results in preliminary testing of an AIDS vaccine. The piece made some hypothetical connections between a workable AIDS vaccine and a general cure for cancer, and that was about it. . . . You take a rather dim view of all this, don't you, Stanley?"

"When they start talking vaccines curing cancer, I sure do. Let's face it, sweetheart. Until we outlaw these death sticks," he says, flicking my pack of cigarettes across the table and into my lap, "and the ten thousand and one other carcinogenic agents thriving in our brave new world, there isn't going to be any cure for cancer. Period."

"I couldn't agree with you more, Stanley. But isn't it getting a little late in the day to be talking about saving our environment? Considering the state of the ozone layer, our ground water, the shrinking jungles, the toxic waste dumps in everyone's backyards. . . . The way Frank saw it, we've already lost the fight to improve our environment. Which means we have only one option left. To improve upon ourselves. You know, turn ourselves into a pollutant-tolerant species."

"You're beginning to sound terribly ominous, Sarah. Are we all to be converted into radioactive-tolerant dioxin eaters? Is that your pitch?"

"Not my pitch, Stanley. Frank's."

"I'm getting very depressed here," Stanley says, swirling the ice around in his empty glass. "I put it to you, sweetheart. Which is worse, sometimes? The problem? Or the solution? Waiter, how about one last round? How about one last round?" he repeats for my benefit.

"Why not? But this one's on me. And if you're looking for the cigarettes . . ." I add, tossing the pack in his direction.

"The problem," he rambles on, "is that these things are sending me to an early grave. These and the booze. The solution is to learn to live without them, of course. But which would be worse, the problem or the solution? Now take Mr. Faccio over there. The guy who owns this place. He also has a problem. His daughter is the problem. Only seventeen years old. Never even been let out of the house on an official date yet. And she's hot to marry some Italian kid just off the boat. Faccio has big plans for his daughter. College. Medical school. The whole shlemiel. And she's hot to marry some illiterate hick who never finished high school and have a slew of kids in the bargain. Faccio's solution to the problem? He's locked his daughter up in her room until she vows on her grandmother's grave that she won't elope with the guy. And his daughter? She's come up with a counter-solution. She's stopped eating. It's been three days now, and the daughter up in her room without a bite to eat. So which is worse here, the problem or the solution?"

"So what are you saying?" I ask with a laugh. "That

problems don't deserve solutions? Or that forced solutions become part of the problem? Or what?'' Since I've been doing most of the talking this evening, I'm unable to pinpoint when the transition took place. But Stanley is definitely tight. For that matter, so am I.

"Deeds done too quickly ripen into thorns that pierce the heart till death," he intones gravely, waving his cigarette through the air. "Catch is, of course, that the very existence of a problem begs a solution. An action begging a reaction. And as we all know, everybody's got problems. Your friend the geneticist. He may have a doozy of a problem. Faccio there most definitely has a problem. You and I—we have a problem."

"We have a problem?"

"Okay. I'll rephrase that. I have a problem."

"You have a problem?"

"My problem? There's this little lady here, who clearly resents being referred to as such, even though that is precisely what she is. And I happen to know that as soon as I leave here tonight, I won't be able to stop thinking about her. The signs are all there. No getting around it. It's going to be a terrible sickness. Something on the order of a mental-emotional bubonic plague. I'll go to sleep thinking about her. And wake up thinking about her. Probably eat breakfast thinking about her. Matters will go on and on like that, getting steadily worse . . .''

"And you could propose a solution to this problem?" I murmur, grinning through a blush that warms me from ear to ear.

"I could suggest—suggest I say—that she—you—join me for dinner tomorrow night. The question, of course, will the solution prove worse than the problem? In the long run, I mean?"

"A deed become a thorn? I suppose there's only one way to find out."

Stanley walks me to the California trolley line. And with a quick peck to the forehead, we take our leave until tomorrow night.

JUNE 15

I awake in the middle of the night, cold and clammy from the after effects of a paralyzing dream. He was in it. That awful bluesuited character from Chemix yesterday afternoon. The details of the dream fade quickly, leaving me with nothing but a vague memory of playing cards with Stanley. Bridge it was. And then looking up from my hand to find that Stanley is no longer my partner but, instead, that hateful iceman, sitting there and cleaning his glasses with the same ominous intent—that steely death glow pouring out of his beady blue eyes.

Now fully awake, I toss about for an hour or so, until it suddenly hits me. An electric shock which I can literally feel passing through my body from head to foot. I have seen that blue-suited Chemix executive before! In May's Diner back in Colston last Saturday afternoon!

I shut my eyes and evoke the images of that day. Walking into the restaurant and taking note of the two businessmen in back. Wondering how the hell they could be wearing suit jackets in that ungodly heat. And yes, it is he! The spectacles. The crepey neck squeezed into a pin-striped tie. He.

Scrambling out of bed, I pace randomly about the apartment, then settle momentarily over a warmed-up cup of coffee from the day before. But I can't keep still, all hopped up on a discomfiting mix of fear and exhilaration. And stranded in here without one lousy cigarette to bring me down, Stanley having smoked up my last one the evening before. I have a sudden urge to call the man and fill him in on the latest development. An urge I immediately squelch, since it is barely four a.m.

Making up a fresh batch of coffee. I mull over the possible significance of the Chemix iceman's presence down in Colston over the week-end. Did his being there have a direct bearing on my own visit to Frank? And if so, was he then well aware of my true identity when I visited Chemix Pharmaceutical yesterday afternoon?

Six a.m. and I put through a call to Time Inc.

"Tom. It's Sarah. Listen kid, this has to be quick. I'm calling from the West Coast. Remember that genetic engineering friend of mine who you hooked me up with a few weeks back? A Dr. Frank Winslow? . . . Come on, Tom! The guy who got that great write-up about his AIDS vaccine in your May issue?"

"What about him?"

"Look. How about if I just hold the line here a second or two, and you go get his file for me." Silence. "I need to know when Frank and the rest of his Genco team moved out to Chemix Pharmaceutical? Because you see, it wasn't Genco labs out at Paradise at all. And Dr. Winslow wasn't at the address you gave me either, Tom. In fact—"

"His file has been classified, Sarah."

"Classified? Who . . . you're telling me that Frank's file has been classified?"

"That's right."

"But I don't understand. How could that kind of thing happen overnight like that? Who classified it?"

"That I couldn't say. All that I know is that the Winslow file was moved out of general and into classified upstairs last week."

"Does this kind of thing happen often? Files suddenly being whisked out of public access like that?"

"That file never was under public access," he reminds me drily.

"Look, Tom. You're going to have to help me here. Something very bizarre may be happening. I never found Frank down at Paradise. And Chemix won't even own up to ever having employed the guy."

"But the man's with Genco Laboratories."

"Maybe. . . . Look, if that file's been classified, there's got to be some pretty interesting information in there. Something which just may lead me to Frank before I blow this thing. . . . Tom," I begin again soberly, "You owe me one." I despise myself for having to bring up a past debt. But the situation is an exceptional one. "If you could just take a peek at that file? My entire investigation could well depend on this."

"Okay. I'll do what I can, Sarah. But I'm telling you right now. I'm not going to hang myself on this thing."

"I don't expect you to. But you must understand that any scrap of information you can leak to me will be exceedingly helpful. How about if I give you a call later on today?"

"No Sarah. I'll be the one to call you."

And that is how we leave it. Tom will be the one to get back in touch with me. Was Stanley right? Am I taking unnecessary risks by pursuing this story? A ransacked motel room. A forged telegram. And a classified file. All adding up to an obliquely sinister situation. So why not drop it like the hot potato it is shaping up to be? Because I don't want to. Simple as that.

Seven a.m. and I'm ravenous. Little wonder, considering the minimal sustenance I've had over the last 24 hours. One mealy bowl of lettuce and a few pieces of fried squid. A quick foray through Amy's pantry turns up nothing more than a stack of sardine tins and the peanut butter and crackers I brought up from Colston Sunday night. Two eggs sunny side up and a crisp order of home fries is more of what I have in mind. Rifling through Amy's closet, I throw on a frenetic pink and yellow striped jump suit which matches my mood, refill the bowl of milk, and head on over the hill into North Beach in quest of the archetypal cafe.

The place is swarming with cafes. Only none of them serves eggs. I suppose it doesn't fit in with the European pastiche. I wind up in a little greasy spoon on the edge of Chinatown, where the cutlery is suspect and the coffee unpotable. But the eggs are done to a luscious sunny-yellow turn.

After paying the bill, I retrace my steps back to North Beach for an honest cup of caffeine. Enroute I pick up a copy of the *Bay Guardian*, some kind of underground weekly with a special 8 page insert cataloguing political and recreational happenings in the week ahead. Over a chocolate-laced cappuccino, I run through the live theater listings, which cover everything from a transvestite ballet company to a political mime troupe performing free in the city's parks. This minimal piece of detectivery—a stab in the dark if there ever was one—is amazingly enough rewarded when I come across the name of Angelica Pescadora, member of the Eureka Theater troupe and currently starring with Steven Coolidge in a production of Sam Shepard's "Fool for Love."

The Angelica? I speculate uneasily. She doesn't seem to be listed in the city's directory. I call up the Eureka Theater and get a tape recording of the week's scheduled performances, then opt for a walk down to the Theater itself, located in the Mission District on the opposite side of town.

I find it rather amazing, how many distinctive and self-contained neighborhoods this city seems able to accommodate. The Mission, for instance, is like no other part of San Francisco I've yet encountered. The area sports some of the oldest and most beautiful Victorians in the city, and is slummy or colorful by turn—depending on the block, one's disposition, and one's point of view.

The Theater itself, located in a warehousey type building off of Mission, is locked up tight. A placard out front announces the production of "Fool" this month, on Wednesday evenings through Sunday afternoons.

Before heading back to the apartment to await Tom's call, I take a stroll along palm tree-lined Dolores street, straight up to the top of Dolores Park, a perspective which affords me an impressive panorama of the entire city, including the silver bows of one or two bridges spanning the East Bay. This city is one continual visual roller coaster ride: terra cotta collage one moment, sweeping vistas of the Bay, the next. One could easily get attached.

Back at Amy's, I read. And nap. And wait. By 5 p.m. there is still no word from Tom. Stanley is expected at 6 o'clock.

I dash across the street for a couple of bottles of decent wine—I can hardly serve up the cut-rate Gallo I have on hand—and a half pound of french brie, then retreat to the bathtub with my latest Simenon and a mugful of chablis. I re-emerge some thirty minutes later feeling a bit on the wild side and opt for one of Amy's more seductive semi-transparent silk blouses and a gaily colored, floor length cotton skirt. A few dabs of her Jovan does the final trick, ripely predisposing me to an evening of scintillating five-star romance.

Stanley arrives on the dot of six, just as I suspected he would.

"How many are you cooking for tonight?" I exclaim approvingly, following the man and his two bags of groceries into the kitchen and gloating over the enticing array of goodies which he sets out on the countertop next to the sink. Red-ripe tomatoes, shiny green peppers, onions, parsley, brandy and butter, garlic and cilantro, as well as a small bottle of extra-virgin olive oil and a crusty loaf of sourdough bread.

"Linguini con Granchi," he announces grandly, allowing me a quick peek at two live blue crabs grabbling up the sides of the ceramic pot.

Stanley does most of the preparing. I open the first bottle of wine and do most of the talking, filling him in on my midnight revelations concerning the man over at Chemix and the possible ramifications thereof. His only voiced opinion on the entire matter is for me to stop jumping to any conclusions about anything until some form of palpable evidence, one way or another, is on hand.

We take the bread, brie, and wine into the livingroom to await the hour long simmering of his Italian crab stew.

"It's really amazing," I declare rather gaily, plopping down on the pile of pillows as he settles on the sofa opposite. "But I somehow feel as if I've known you all my life. You know that, Stanley? Here I met you only a couple of days ago, and yet I feel as if I've known you all my life. How do you explain it?"

"Must be that homely, boy-next-door appeal of mine."

"Ha! Think so? And I've always thought of myself as the girl-next-door. Maybe there's some kind of neighborly affinity working here. What do you think?"

"You are hardly the girl next door, Sarah. Trust me on that."

"Really? You mean I wouldn't be a dead ringer for Debbie Reynolds? Or maybe Doris Day?"

"Afraid not."

"Good!" I declare, raising my glass in a silent toast to Amy's irrepressible wardrobe. "So tell me something, will you?" I ask, spreading some brie on a slice of sourdough before passing the plate back to Stanley. "What actually stopped you from following through on those stories back there? I've been unltra-curious about it ever since you brought the subject up."

"You won't need the gory details."

"Yes, I will."

"Well you're not going to get them. Let's just say that one particularly influential citizen in this city has threatened more than once to have me run off the newspaper, and out of town, if I should reveal certain business matters he's been involved in over the years."

"Aha! What kind of business matters?"

"Mutual accords with a couple of San Francisco's mayors, for one."

"What kind of accords?"

"Profitable ones."

"That much I assumed, Stanley. Good lord, are you always so dreadfully discreet? I loathe discretion. No fun. I happen to be terribly indiscreet myself. Always have been. That said, would you mind if I asked you a somewhat indiscreet question?"

He raises his eyebrows, wary and waiting.

"Why do you always smoke my cigarettes? Not that I mind in the slightest, you understand. In fact, I rather like it. But I'm curious, is all. I mean, you don't seem the type."

"The type?"

"You know. A cadger. A mooch. So?"

He smiles. "This may sound a little on the absurd side."

"Good. I love the absurd."

He clears his throat. "My father died of lung cancer a few years back. From smoking, presumably. He could go through three packs a day. The day of his funeral, my mother asked me to take a solemn oath.''

"Yes?"

"I had to promise her I would never buy another pack of cigarettes again. That was four years ago. I haven't bought a pack since.''

"Ha! You wouldn't care to go into the ethics of the situation, would you?"

"No, I would not," he says, drawing a cigarette from my pack on the table between us.

"Okay. So now it's your turn," I say, settling back against the pillows.

"My turn?"

"Ask me a question. Any question at all. Promise I'll answer it without batting an eye.''

He looks down at me with amusement, placing his feet, first one then the other, onto the table. "Ever married?"

"Nope."

"Why not?"

"This is terribly corny, Stanley. Couldn't you have done better than this?''

"You're batting an eye, I'd say."

"I am not. I never wanted to get married. It's as simple as that. Ever since I was a little girl and would watch my father go off to the office every day while Mom was stuck at home taking care of us kids. I have too much ego for something like that. And not enough love.''

"Being a little hard on yourself, aren't you?"

"Maybe. But it's true, all the same."

"Plenty of wives work these days. Most, in fact."

"Yeah, but there's still an inherent imbalance there. Being someone's Mrs. Changing one's name. Who needs it? Then there's the snowball effect to be taken into consideration, as well.''

"The snowball effect?"

"The kids start coming along and you move to the suburbs, natch. Then comes the station wagon. The power lawn mower. The country clubs. The VCR. The Cuisinart. The microwave oven. The backyard barbecue. I'd suffocate under the weight of it all. I'm a very weird person, actually. I mean I actually like living in one room. Hot water, clean

sheets, a writing desk, good books, and good wine. That, to
me, is luxurious living. Really. Why aren't you drinking?" I
add, nodding at his full glass of wine.

"Why aren't you eating?"

"Not hungry. Never am when I get into these kinds of
moods."

"And what kind of mood is that?"

I smile mischievously, passing a finger across my lips.

"Nope. Definitely not the girl-next-door type, at all,"
Stanley declares, rising from the sofa and bringing the
bottle of wine over to where I sit. He refills my glass and
settles down beside me. I rest my head lightly on his
shoulder, floating off on the lyrics of the Sinatra record he
put on the stereo a few minutes before.

"The bastard sure can sing, can't he?" I murmur, trying
to imagine what it might be like. Stanley's touch. Stanley's
kiss. Stanley's arms. As matters evolve, I don't have very
long to find out. And it is all quite as I could have guessed it
would be. From the very first time I heard one of those
waggish laughs of his, two short days ago.

JUNE 16

8 a.m. Stanley isn't looking so hot this morning. For
good reason, I suppose. Since I kept the poor man up half
the night with my meandering speculations on Frank.

Who were the other geneticists on his research team
down at Paradise and where are they now? Was he in fact
working on an AIDS vaccine, as the piece in *Times*
purported? Or could that have been a cover for other more
covert research? Why does Chemix deny any connection
with the man? And why is Genco classifying Frank as
'outlying' personnel? How much information will this Dr.
Fawley be able or willing to supply me about Frank and his
whereabouts, assuming I ever succeeded in pinning the

gentleman down? And most puzzling of all, why was it suddenly necessary to classify that file at Time Inc, when the same file had been unrestricted information only days before?

"Gotta split," Stanley mumbles, shoving off from the table and dropping his coffee cup into the sink.

"What about your breakfast?" I demur, shoving the plateful of peanut buttered chicken-in-the-biskets his way.

"Yeah, well." He gives the plate a dubious squint. "Maybe next time, sweetheart."

I follow him into the bedroom, bringing up the subject of Angelica, and the Shepard play being staged at the Eureka theater later today. Unfortunately, Stanley has a dinner engagement this evening—an interview with one of the city's supervisors, so he says—but will do his best to make it to the theater by eight o'clock.

Once he's out the door, I refill my coffee mug and retreat to the pillows; passing time with the new Simenon while awaiting the New York call. In time, I drift into a late morning nap. I dream I am playing bridge again. Only this time around, Frank is my partner. And it is apparently my turn to play a card. I hesitate—concerned that whichever card I ultimately choose, it will be the wrong one, and bring Frank's stinging reprovals down on my head. When I finally do turn a card face up on the table, to my surprise and confusion it is a joker. Or to be more precise, not a joker but one of those tarot cards that Amy used to play around with back in New York. The Fool, she called it. Dressed up like some medieval jester and dancing merrily toward the edge of a towering cliff.

I awake to a dizzying terror which cannot be readily explained by the fading image of that dancing clown. Who, in the gallery of my psyche, was The Fool to represent? Myself perhaps? Or Frank? Which one of us is dancing blindly toward the edge of some perilous cliff? Or are we both?

3 p.m. Fed up with waiting around for a phone that never rings, I head down to the city's main library for a little extemporaneous research. Genco is not listed in the library's 1980 edition of *Everybody's Business Almanac*. Perhaps the firm was not established until a later year?

There is ample material on Chemix Pharmaceutical. A perennial 'Fortune 500', the chemical firm began as a gun powder manufacturing plant, set up and run by the four Carrington brothers, back in 1822. By the early 1900's, the company had assured its ascendant position in the American marketplace via a monopolizing interest in the production of explosives used in the First World War. After World War Two, the company merged with an up and coming pharmaceutical firm, changing its name from Carrington to Chemix, and shouldering into the burgeoning antibiotic market as well. Over the last 30 years, company production has branched into everything from napalm to handiwrap. From pesticides to the best car wax in town.

Although no direct reference is made to Chemix' involvement in the field of genetic engineering, I assume that a 1979 decision to expand research and development into the life sciences is an allusion to investment in recombinant DNA research.

An eerie sidelight to the Almanac's sketch of the Chemix firm is the fact that a penetrating biography of the Carrington patriarchy behind Chemix Pharmaceutical, published in 1979, was coerced off the bookshelves and into oblivion less than a month after distribution began. This, in spite of a rave review the book received in the *New York Times,* citing the biography as "a fascinating and revealing look at America's most powerful and wealthiest clan."

By 1981, a suit was pending in the lower courts, with author Philip Kaufman charging that Chemix Pharmaceutical and H. F. Fielding Publishing participated in corporate conspiracy: suppressing distribution of his book and destroying any chance the man had to make a profit from his five years of research. Apparently Kaufman himself bought up some 4000 copies of the unsold and undistributed biography, which he has been selling to interested parties through a New York box office ever since.

I jot down the box office number and address, then head over to the Mission for a quick bite to eat. By the time I reach the Eureka Theater, the lobby is overflowing with tonight's prospective audience. I congratulate myself on having had the forethought to reserve tickets earlier in the day. But clipped on to my two tickets is a short note. A phone message from Stanley, informing me that he will be unable to make it this evening, and asking that I meet him at Verdi's tomorrow afternoon at three.

"Damn," I mutter under my breath, stuffing the note into my purse.

"Be happy to take that ticket off your hands, Ma'am," booms a southwestern twang in my right ear. I look up to find this hulk of a young gentleman peering over my shoulder, short blond bangs framing a beefy, red-cheeked complexion and dark blue eyes. I hand over my extra ticket in exchange for a crisp ten dollar bill, more than a little disconcerted by the idea of sharing my front row seats with this tow-headed monster for the length and breadth of a three act play.

"Second time I've caught this sucker," he informs me, grabbing a program from the usher and slipping his ticket into the pocket of his leather vest.

"Is that so?"

"Yep. This play is real good. Shit, good isn't the word for it. It's great, man. But then, all of his plays are great. America's true native playwright. Its only one, if you want my opinion on the matter."

"Arthur Miller. O'Neill. Mamet. Tennessee Williams," I mumble into my coat.

"Ha! Tennessee Williams shot his wad years ago. And O'Neill's nothing more than a broken record, if you ask me. Drugs and alcohol. Alcohol and drugs. The guy was a crazy drunken son-of-a-bitch, if you want my opinion on the matter. Faggots and drug addicts do not make it as legit chroniclers of American life."

We take our seats. And I utter a silent prayer of thanks when the theater lights immediately dim and the play begins.

The entire scenario of this particular Shepard play is a tacky and claustrophobic motel room. Paradise Lost. The battle of the sexes boiled down to its most guttural and relentless core. And to my mind, Angelica is nothing short of magnificent in her role as Woman, attached at the hip to faithless Man.

The moment the lights come back on, I nod Hercules a

cursory farewell and head back to the main dressing room behind the stage. A large group of well-wishers already surround the two principals of the play. At one point, Angelica herself breaks away from the group, rushing right by me and toward a side lobby door.

"Angelica!" I call out, following her down the hall.

She waves without turning her head and continues on her way.

"Angelica!" I cry again, catching up with the woman and tagging her elbow. She gives me a steely look, causing me to whip the guilty hand behind my back. "You don't remember me, do you?"

She shakes her head, glancing back over her shoulder toward the door.

"Oscar's in New York? One Friday evening, some four or five years back? Frank introduced us, remember? Dr. Frank Winslow?"

"Sarah?"

"That's right. Sarah Calloway," I say, extending my hand once again.

"Well, look. I . . . There's somebody waiting," she explains, gesturing behind her.

"Angelica, listen to me! Frank has disappeared! Vanished without a trace."

Her gaze flickers vaguely. I repeat myself with some variation.

"I'm afraid I don't understand," she murmurs.

"Well I can't very well explain all of it to you right here and now, can I? I need to talk to you, Angelica. At the earliest opportunity."

"I don't see what help I can be to you. I haven't seen Frank in over three years."

"Doesn't matter," I assure her, squibbling out Amy's number on my program and shoving it into her hand. "If you could call me tomorrow morning? Or even later tonight?"

She looks down at the program. Then back up at me with a sultry shrug. The same one she used to such good effect throughout the evening's performance. "Okay. So I call you tomorrow." And with a nod, she turns on her heel and walks out the lobby door.

I head back out the front entrance and onto Mission street, taken off guard by the dramatic change of ambience in this neighborhood: from the sunny-slummy conviviality of yesterday afternoon to the intimidating back-alley murkiness of after-dark.

"So you're acquainted with that actress there, are you now?" My heart skips a beat or two at the sudden appearance of Blondie there at my side. "She's one sexy lady, that broad, if you don't mind my saying so."

"Well I do mind," I say curtly, looking right and left for a cruising cab.

"Be happy to walk you home, Ma'am. If it's not too far. I'd drive you home if I had wheels. But I don't."

"Look Mister—"

"Arnold. Arnold Sax."

"Look Arnold. I'm not in the habit of striking up conversations with strange men. Understand? So if you will just let me get on my way?"

"It's cause I'm such a huge son-of-a-bitch, isn't it?" he suggests, shuffling along beside me. "I scare most women before they even get a chance to know me. It's always been like that. For as long as I can remember."

"I wouldn't care if you were five feet two," I say, stepping up the pace in a vain attempt to shake the guy.

"I'm not trying to pick you up, lady. If that's what you're thinking. I just feel like someone to talk to. I mean, you're kind of old for . . . well you know what I mean."

"Yes, I know exactly what you mean," I hiss over my shoulder, scurrying on down the street.

"Hey! I didn't mean to offend you, Ma'am. There I go again. Always putting my foot in my mouth. What I meant to say was, I just need a little company tonight. Real bad like, you know? Something about that play that got to me this time around. Hey! You hungry? Cause if you are, this place here serves up one heck of a burrito. Huge mothers too, let me tell you. Treats on me," he adds, aware that I am beginning to give way. There's a moment's silence as I contemplate the pros and cons of allowing myself to be corraled into a small hole-in-the-wall of a Mexican restaurant just across the street. "Fuck," he suddenly growls between gritted teeth.

I look up, startled, following his gaze to a cruising black sedan which has stopped at the corner where we stand.

"Why Stanley!" I exclaim in astonishment, running up to the car and peering through the open window. "Whose car is this? How did you know—?"

"Hop in," he says, leaning across the steering wheel and opening the door for me.

I glance back at Arnold, who is scowling at us through the darkness, arms folded across his massive chest, and give a quick wave before sliding into the front seat and closing the door behind me.

"Jesus, what a weirdo," I murmur, rolling up the window and taking another quick look back to where he stands.

"It seems I can't leave you alone, for a minute, sweetheart, can I?"

"Yeah, right. Do you know that guy?"

"Do I know that guy? Do *you* know that guy?"

"Of course not. He just kind of pounced on me the minute I came out of the theater tonight. Funny, cause he saw you before I did. And he seemed to know who you . . . I mean the way he looked was. . . . Well anyway, whose car *is* this?"

"On loan for the night. A buddy from the paper."

"And you came down here just to pick me up. That was really nice, Stanley. You're a good man, you are."

"Sorry I couldn't make it earlier. Did my best. So you enjoyed it?"

"Very much, actually. And it was Frank's Angelica, alright. Recognized her the moment she stepped out on stage. And Stanley, she's a marvelous actress! I was shocked. In some obscure way she reminds me of Marilyn Monroe. Not that she looks like her in the slightest. Or even moves like her. But there's just something there . . ."

There's something here, too. In this car. A pervasive smell of perfume which I find unsettling to the extreme.

"So you told her about Frank?" he asked.

"We didn't have much time to talk. Unfortunately, she hasn't seen the man in a couple of years. So I'm not so sure she's going to be able to help me out. But I convinced her it's a bit of an emergency. At least I hope I did. She promised to call me tomorrow, and I'll have to take it from there. . . . This supervisor you saw tonight. It was a she?"

He laughs. "No, as a matter of fact, *it* was a he. Richard Hongisto. He's coming out strong against Madame Mayor on the Missouri issue. So I'm using him as the spokesman for the opposition in a column next week."

"The Missouri issue? You mean that nuclear battleship Feinstein is trying to port here? So you're going to do one of those pro and con columns again? No offense, Stanley, but I hate that kind of approach. Your column this morning was a gruesome exercise in so-called unpartisanship."

"Nonpartisanship."

"Yeah, well anyway, I just don't go with the 'there's two sides to every issue' approach."

"But sweetheart, there usually is two sides to every issue. Whether you approve of one of the sides, or not."

"There's two sides to apartheid? Really, Stanley? I mean, that's the way your column came off this morning. And I found it cowardly. No really. I mean, you get these two articulate spokespeople—that creepy moral majority minister from Marin, is that where he was from? And that black superintendent—you let them both have their say while you stand back not doing a damn thing. Kind of like washing your hands of the problem. That's avoiding your responsibility, if you ask me."

"My responsibility, as I see it Sarah, is to bring the issues before the people. Not decide the issues for them."

"Stating an opinion, or better, defending a position you honestly believe in by way of hard, cold facts, is not deciding an issue for anyone. It's simply being a thinking, critical-minded human being. That's all. Besides, I honestly do not think there are two sides to every issue. Isn't it possible to say that apartheid is morally wrong, period? That nuclear war is unthinkable? That civil rights and equal rights is where it's at for the human race? Everything's become so damn wishy-washy these days. No rights or wrongs. Just the inevitable 'two sides' to the issue. I mean, that creepy minister actually getting away with claiming he has the black children of South Africa at heart when he defends investment down there. Yuck.''

"Everyone has a right to state their opinions, Sarah. Whether you agree with them or not.''

"So why didn't you state yours? Why did you hide behind those other two extreme opinions—neither which really solve anything—instead of expressing your own view on the matter? London's view from the bridge, right?''

Stanley eases the car against the curb in front of Amy's, keeping the motor running. "Okay sweetheart. Next week I promise you *my* view of apartheid. Is that a deal?''

"A deal. You're not coming up?''

"Promised to get this heap back to Sam by eleven. See you at Verdi's tomorrow afternoon?''

"Yeah, okay. Verdi's at three.'' I get out. Some of that perfume leaving with me. Stanley waits until I have let myself in the front door before giving a couple of soft beeps on the horn and heading on his way.

JUNE 17

I wake this morning to find my elusive ball of calico curled up against my side, its head tucked into the crook of my neck. This kitten's growing trust in me is heartfelt consolation for a lonely body in a strange and lonely bed. It's still dark outside. Why am I waking up so damn early these days? Bad dreams? Unsettling thoughts? Unsettling life? When the first blush of dawn peeks through the venetian blinds, my furry friend stretches and scampers off. Inspiring me to do likewise.

I return to my pile of pillows, a pot of coffee in tow, destined to while away another fruitless morning waiting for Tom's call. It feels like I should be out there doing something. But what? My edginess is compounded by too much coffee and not enough cigarettes. I am eventually reduced to dipping a finger into the jar of peanut butter and calling it lunch.

2:30 and at long last word from Angelica, who sounds as aloof and unapproachable over the telephone as she did last night in that hall. We arrange to meet for a drink in North Beach later in the day. I refill the kitty's milk bowl and slip into yesterday's overalls, then head out to meet Stanley at Verdi's cafe.

"Been waiting long?" I ask, settling in opposite him at what has now become 'our' booth in the rear. In spite of an unaccustomed wariness in our midst, it feels damn good setting eyes on the man once again.

"Forever."

"Ha! No word from Tom, dammit it all. Beginning to wonder if he hasn't decided to chuck the idea of helping me out. It's so frustrating, Stanley. I have good reason to believe the whole key to Frank's whereabouts may lie inside that file. And yet I may never be able to get my hands on a single piece of it. Last week I could have asked Tom to xerox the whole shitload and he probably would have done it for me without a second thought. Red wine," I tell the approaching waiter, hoping a touch of alcohol will smooth out the knots of caffeine at the back of my neck. "Who, in this so-called free country of ours, has the unholy right to classify information like that in the first place? That's what I would like to know. All this incriminating information that gets buried away until the end of time. Even the story behind our dear President's assassination. Incredible. And to protect whom?"

"National Security, woman."

"Yeah right. Did you know that Chemix Pharmaceutical managed to keep a book about its founding family out of distribution, even after it was reviewed in the *New York Times*?"

"I might have heard something along that line, yes."

"You did? Ever hear of the Carrington family? Yeah? Well I sure never heard of them. According to Kaufman's book, they're the world's richest family. Own more cars and swimming pools, more landed estates than any other family in recorded history. Not to mention a swampful of attack-trained alligators stashed away in Costa Rica somewhere. Yet I never heard of these people. Now if that isn't control of the press, what is? Apparently they also own controlling interest in all sorts of our biggest corporations and banks. General Motors. United Fruit. Continental Can. Even a baseball team or two. Now that's pretty spooky, right? God only knows how responsible that one family is for the shape this country's in. Anyway, at least Angelica called. In fact, I have to go meet her at 4 o'clock."

"I see. And I was being so presumptuous as to assume you and I might be getting together for dinner later to—"

"Sounds great," I quickly assure him. "She and I are only meeting for a drink. And tonight's meal will be on me," I add foolishly, blocking out the fact that I have little more than six dollars cash left to my name. God bless American Express.

After finishing off the wine, I head for the Europa Cafe. Which is but a short three block walk away. I arrive some fifteen minutes early. Angelica arrives some fifteen minutes late, breezing through the door and turning the heads of every straight male in the place. In spite of her modest attire, baggy corduroy pants and a light purple turtleneck sweater, the over-all effect is electrifying.

In her first breath she apologizes for her tardiness. And in her second, informs me that she can stay but a few minutes, as she is due back at rehearsal by five o'clock. The waiter approaches. She orders a Perrier. I order another glass of wine.

"You were wonderful last night," I tell her. One of many possible openings I have been rehearsing in the minutes before she came. "That thin line you were able to tread between vulnerability and strength. It was a thrill to watch, Angelica. Really." She nods, looking everywhere but at me as she plays nervously with the thin gold chain around her neck. "Have you been acting for long?"

She gives out a short bitter laugh. "You could say all my life, I guess. My father, you see. He . . . he ran a travelling gypsy show of sorts. Me and my sisters were the gypsies," she finishes off, an ironic smile flitting across her face.

"This was back in Brazil?" I ask, regretting the question the moment it pops out of my mouth.

Her hand moves from the necklace to a watch on her wrist. "We're here to talk about Frank, right? You think he's in some kind of trouble, right? So shoot." Only it sounds more like shit, her latino accent being much more in evidence this afternoon than it was on stage last night.

"Yes, well I . . . You were aware that Frank came out here to work two years back? For Genco labs?"

"I read the papers."

"Yes, well you see I came out here last week to interview him about his work on an AIDS vaccine. That's when I discovered that he's disappeared." I proceed with the story. Then pause a moment while the waiter serves up our drinks. She pushes the Perrier aside but starts to suck on the slice of lime. Arnold was sure on target about one thing last night. This is one hell of a sexy lady here; a raw, effortless sensuality oozing off her with every move she makes.

I take a long sip on my wine and start in once again. I have the rap down by now. And I think I hook her. I can tell by the way her eyes widen at every twist and turn. "And if there's someone jerking me around," I finish off, referring to the forged telegram and my chilly welcome over at Chemix Pharmaceutical, "God only knows what could be happening with Frank."

"Maybe he's hiding out on purpose," Angelica suggests.

"I've thought of that, of course. But why?"

She shrugs. "Maybe he really is close to that AIDS vaccine. They're all so fucking paranoid these days, right? Always looking over the shoulder. So scared their precious research is going to be stolen from under them before they can grab the credit. Or the patent," she adds, rubbing her fingers together to indicate the financial windfalls involved. "Frank was already getting real freaky about it in New York. Wouldn't talk about his work to no-one. Including me."

This last bit of information amazes me. Since the only subjects Frank and I ever did seem to talk about, as I remember it, revolved around developments inside that everloving lab.

"So Frank started working with the AIDS virus back in Columbia?" I ask.

"He was getting the credit for it, if that's what you mean."

"But he wasn't actually wor—?"

"He brought in this woman from Harvard. A doctorate in immunology. Some kind of genius according to Frank. She wasn't much more than a kid. Anyway, she was the one who was doing most of the work with AIDS. It was coming out in all the reports as Frank's stuff—you know, cause he was head of the team—but he wasn't going anywhere with the AIDS thing until she came along."

"You wouldn't happen to know this woman's name?"

"Laurie something. Schwartz? Schwinn? Something Jewish, I think. Wouldn't surprise me none if he brought her out here when he came. She was his bread and butter, as you say. And besides, they were very tight," she adds, a note of sarcasm creeping into her voice.

"Tight?"

She ignores my partially articulated question, checking the time on her watch and glancing around for our waiter, who is presently occupied in a mad flirtation with a handsome young gentleman three tables down. "I really have to be going," she says, rising from the table and slipping a five dollar bill under the untouched bottle of Perrier. "Already I'm late."

"Is there anyway I can get ahold of you if something should come up?"

"What could come up?"

"Well for the moment, I don't know. But—"

"Look. I'm going to be straight with you. I wouldn't want to think Frank's in trouble. But the less I hear or think or know about the guy, the better off I am. He's a no-good, lousy bastard, right?" she adds, giving me the sexiest damn smile I've ever seen. And with that, she turns on her heel and walks out of the cafe.

Another member of Frank's fan club, I think blackly, settling back down in my seat and giving our fawning neighbor an acrid look. The asshole couldn't keep his eyes off Angelica from the moment she came in to the moment she walked out the door. My gaze wanders to the five dollar bill under the bottle, duly ashamed of myself for having allowed her to pay for our drinks. Pocketing the cash, I pay the bill with my American Express and head out to pick up provisions for the evening's meal.

By the time I get back to the apartment, Stanley awaits me on the front stoop, toting a grocery bag twice the size of my own.

"Tonight was supposed to be on me, remember?" I remind him as we trundle up the two flights of stairs.

"This is breakfast, sweetheart. Peanut butter is not my idea of how to begin one's day."

The minute we step into the living room, I regret my too hasty departure earlier this afternoon. The apartment is a pit. The scattered pages of the morning *Chronicle*, dirty ashtrays, empty wine glasses, derelict coffee cups, the open jar of peanut butter on top of the stereo, and the pervasive odor of stale cigarette smoke all living testimony of my slovenly and degenerate ways. Stanley appears not to notice. While he unpacks the groceries, I make an attempt to bring order into the chaos. By the time I return to the kitchen, Stanley is pouring himself a long scotch.

"Since I appear to be making something of a habit of this place," he murmurs, gesturing about the room as he recaps the bottle of scotch and stores it away over the sink. "Nothing territorial in this," he adds, grinning over at me and looking as pleased to be here as I am to have him here.

In adddition to the Black Label, he had brought us a Johannesberg Reisling, a bag of roasted pistachio nuts, and half a dozen poppy seed bagels. The man's a regular Santa Claus.

"Hear the big news?" he asks, nudging me into the living room.

"What?"

"Rock Hudson is dying of AIDS."

"Jesus, that's terrible! I thought he had liver cancer or something."

"Yeah, well the story's changed. He's in Paris trying to get into some special drug program over there, I guess."

"Rock Hudson, of all people. My mother must be having

a fit. He's been her number one heart throb from the beginning of time. I kept telling her he was gay, but she wouldn't believe me. She refuses to believe anybody's gay, when you get down to it. Rock Hudson, yet . . . This could wind up being a good thing, couldn't it? Finally America's going to have to wake up and realize there are actually *people* dying out there. Human beings. And not just faceless expendable perverts. I mean, Rock Hudson's almost as American as apple pie," I add, my tone almost gleeful by now. Not the most appropriate reaction, perhaps, to news of someone's impending death.

Hudson is all over the evening news. Along with a statement from Linda Evans of *Dynasty*, threatening to sue someone or another for allowing her to go through with a love scene with the afflicted star.

"What did he do? Put his prick up your ass?" I scream into the set.

"She can't hear you," Stanley reminds me, pulling me back onto the sofa.

"All these moronic people make me absolutely sick! How many times do people have to be told that AIDS cannot be passed on by saliva before it finally sinks in that AIDS cannot be passed on by saliva! No kidding, Stanley. The public's reaction to this thing totally astounds me. Nurses wearing masks. Bus drivers wearing gloves. It's sick. Sick! The only way AIDS has ever been passed from one person to another is by infected blood, right? So what is everybody's goddamn problem?"

"They're scared, Sarah. This is a 100% fatal disease, we talking about here. With no known cure."

"So that gives everyone the sudden right to turn into half-witted homophobes?" I am beginning to screech. An unfortunate but invariable reaction of mine to the evening news. Leaving Dan Rather to Stanley, I head into the kitchen for a glass of wine and then into the bedroom to prepare for another of those indulgent hot baths.

An hour later and my mood has considerably improved. Stepping out of the tub, I hit upon the brilliant idea of serving myself up to Stanley as the evening's hors d'oeuvre.

Towelling off, I smear on some of Amy's Jovan and slink silently down the hall.

But once around the corner, something feels terribly off key. Stanley is not where I left him, there on the sofa with his eyes glued to the set. Instead, he is huddled over the telephone in a far corner of the room, conversing in a low monotone with some unknown entity at the other end of the line. The obscure, panther-like quality to his stance sets the goose-flesh crawling up the back of my neck. Sensing my presence behind him, Stanley whirls around, smiling—or wincing—in my direction before saying a last few words into the receiver and hanging up the phone.

"Hey Gorgeous," he murmurs lightly, returning the apparatus to the end table and coming over to plant a kiss on top of those goosebumps on the back of my neck.

"Who was that, Stanley?" I demanded warily, taking a few steps back.

"None of your damn business, Ms. Calloway."

"Please Stanley," I say, dodging his caresses. "This just doesn't feel right to me. You coming over here and making secret phone calls behind my back."

"Jesus, Sarah. What secret phone calls? That was my agent, for god's sake. Now come here, woman."

"What do you have an agent for?"

"For the usual reasons."

"You're writing a book, or what?" I ask, all my preposterous suspicions beginning to dissipate into a puddle of self-reproach there at my feet.

"A fait accompli, sweetheart. How delectable you smell this evening."

"So you mean you're about to be published? When?"

"Sooner than you might think," he croons into my ear, tugging gently at the towel wrapped around me and maneuvering me onto the sofa.

"On what?" I ask vaguely, having a hard time keeping my mind and body from going their separate ways. And for the moment, we leave it at that.

Dinner isn't half bad tonight, if I say so myself. Chicken is chicken is chicken, as my grandmother used to say. But baked in white wine and garlic, it is more than a marginal success. Between mouthfuls, Stanley fills me in on his soon-to-be-published-bestseller. Which is actually nothing more than an annotated compilation of his best columns over the last ten years. I find myself feeling almost jealous of the man sitting there across from me, and the incredible privilege he has of speaking his mind to the American public five days a week, fifty weeks out of every year. And now having a goodly portion of his work considered worthy of immortalization within a hard cover text. Jealous and proud.

It is not until we are settled over coffee in the living room that Stanley drops the two-page brochure in my lap. A January 1985 financial assessment of Genco Laboratories written up by E.F. Hutton.

"And?"

"Just have a look."

The first few paragraphs are a general introduction to Genco Labs. The firm was established in 1981, a relatively late start for any company hoping to survive in the highly competitive field of genetic engineering research. Hutton attributes Genco's staying power over the last few years to its decision early on to concentrate on animal health products, which get government approval five to ten times faster than products developed for human use.

A second advantageous factor in the firm's success is its working relationship with Chemix Pharmaceutical. An arrangement which allows the genetics firm to focus all its resources and energies on research and development, with the understanding that Chemix's "vast marketing and sales expertise" will ensure success of any one product once it is ready to go on line.

I skim down to the bottom of the page and flip to the next.

Now that revenues from animal care products, including three vaccines against various livestock diseases and an antibody protecting newborn calves against scours, have begun pouring into Genco coffers, the firm is placing more emphasis on human product research. In the arena of cancer research, the firm has teamed up with a Japanese firm, TechnoGen, in sponsoring the only U.S. trials of an anti-cancer beta interferon. The program, under the direction of Czech oncologist Dr. Zuleika Beerbohm, is—

"My God, Stanley. That man used to work with Frank at Columbia! They shared some of the same lab space!"
"You're quite sure it's the same man?"
"Really Stanley. How many Czech geneticists named Zuleika Beerbohm can one planet hold?" After scanning details of the interferon trials, I proceed to page three and an assessment of a new immunal system support drug Genco is presently working on called interleukin-2.
"So what am I missing?" I ask, flipping back to page one of the migraine-inducing fine print. Stanley directs me to a single paragraph near the bottom of page two:

One of the more promising products in the Genco armory, still in the developmental and testing phase at their Monterey laboratories, is a genetically-engineered viral substance being promoted as a potential AIDS vaccine. The viral mutation, largely the work of the renowned American geneticist Dr. Frank Winslow, has proved to be an effective and lasting repressant of the AIDS virus in a series of animal tests conducted at the beginning of the year. Once government approval is procured, human testing of the vaccine will ensue.

"Very interesting, Stanley. But not much more than a recap of that piece in *Time*."
Stanley pulls a second brochure out of his back pocket and tosses it into my lap. It is Hutton's latest report on Genco labs, published at the beginning of the month, and almost a word-for-word replay of the January brochure. Save for one very important divergence: between the summary of Beerbohm's work on page two, and mention of the interleukin-2 on page three, there is no reference whatsoever to Dr. Winslow and his AIDS vaccine.
"Where did you get these, Stanley?"
"A stockbroker buddy of mine."

"And he explained the omission?"

"Indeed he did. Apparently Genco requested it."

"But why?"

He hesitates, causing me to fear the worse. Though I have no idea what that worse might be. "Apparently, Sarah, you weren't the only one hoping to cop a story on Dr. Winslow's vaccine."

"Oh?"

"The media's been on their backs ever since the piece in *Time* magazine hit the stands. Badgering Genco employees around the clock for news of the vaccine. And that's only the half of it."

"The other half?"

"Genco's been inundated with pleas for help from AIDS victims all over the country. Men even setting up camp outside their Monterey facilities in hopes of getting into human trials of the vaccine. It's turned into a real circus. And all this for a product which—for all logistical purposes—won't be ready for testing until late 1987. Maybe '88."

"1988? Who says? Your stockbroker friend? So why did *Time* imply testing was right around the corner? And that stock report, it damn well implied the same thing."

"A royal P.R. fuck-up."

"What do you mean?"

"An overzealous public relations man down at Genco leaked the misinformation to give the company's investment profile a shot in the arm. Evidently genetic firms are pulling that kind of shit all the time."

"So all this comes down to nothing more than a lousy publicity stunt? Is that what you're telling me? This is very depressing, Stanley. . . . Looks like Angelica may have been right, after all. Maybe Frank did go underground with his research so he could avoid all this ballyhoo above. Jesus H. Christ."

"It's not the end of the world, sweetheart."

"That's what you think. I spent my last red cent to fly out here. And for what? I had such a feeling, Stanley. Such a feeling . . ."

While I stew in place, Stanley returns to the kitchen to boil us up some more tea.

"I'm not buying it, Stanley," I announce when he comes back into the room. "Too much hasn't been clarified here. Like the forged telegram, for one. The incident at the motel. The fact that Frank still hasn't contacted his son about his move. And remember Stanley, Frank hasn't been heard from since April. His disappearance might have nothing to do with that publicity in *Time*. Then there's the classified file. If I had that alone to go on, I'd say there's something wacky going on here. Wouldn't you?"

"Could you be grasping at straws, Sarah?"

"No way. Look, the very least I can do is pin Tom down about that file. And visit Dr. Fawley down at Genco Labs. If he can make sense out of all this for me, well then I'll call it quits. Fair enough?"

I shut my eyes and sink back against the sofa, feeling a lot more discouraged than I'm willing to own up to at the moment. Where in God's name are you, Frank? I ask myself, as a crystal clear image of the man suddenly floats before my mind's eye. Where are you and what the hell are you up to? And why?

"What is it, Sarah?" Stanley asks anxiously, grabbing me by the shoulder.

"I . . . nothing really. Did I jump?"

"You leaped."

"This is going to sound totally off the wall, Stanley. But I just had this razor sharp image of Frank before my eyes, right? And you know what the bastard did? He brought a little hand gun out of his lab coat pocket and shot me! I made no conscious effort whatsoever to create that scenario, Stanley. It just happened of its own accord. Like a movie picture running by me. He drew the gun out of his pocket, took steady aim right between my eyes, and pulled the trigger!"

"So you indulged in a little Freudian fantasy. Nothing to get so excited about."

"Freudian fantasy like hell, Stanley. I could even see the goddamn pearl handle."

"The peanut butter's starting to get to you, Sarah," he murmurs drily, pulling me onto his lap, where I acquiese for a few moments time before sliding right off again. Not being much of a lap person even on the best of days.

"You up for a wedding this week-end?" he suggests out of left field.

"This your idea of a little comic relief? Whose?"

"Faccio's kid."

"You mean the one who's been locked up in her room? But I thought . . .?"

"Pregnant."

"Ouch. You see what happens with overprotective parents? A couple of sweet afternoons with some affectionate lout, and now where is she?"

"Speaking of which, sweetheart. What have you been using for . . . ?"

"For what?" I inquire sweetly, aping the ambiguous, circling gesture he is making with his right hand. In answer, I break into a tap-dancing sing-along of "I've Got Rhythm." Straight into the kitchen for a nightcap swig of wine.

"Does that really work?" Stanley asks skeptically, having followed me into the room.

"Sometimes. Want some?"

He shakes his head. "Then you've never gotten pregnant?"

"I didn't say that."

"So you have gotten pregnant?"

I hold up two fingers while recapping the wine bottle and pushing it back into the fridge.

"Jesus," he murmurs. "And the kids?"

I shake my head. He gazes down at me, broad, deep reproach beaming out of those light brown eyes.

"You disapprove?"

"Just strikes me as a pretty half-assed way of going about things. Especially at your age."

"I see. You mean that at 35 years of age I should know better? Is that it? And what form of birth control have you been using lately, Stanley? Yes, that's what I thought. Look Stanley, dear. For your information, my body has been through the wringer on this thing. I mean to say, I've tried the whole fucking gamut. Rubbers. Pills. Spirals. Shields.

Goo. Coitus interruptus, or whatever the hell they call it.
Every ingenious boobytrap invented by modern man to be
used by modern woman has been stuck up this snooker at
one time or another. Trouble is, every damn one of them
turned out to be marginally ineffectual or lethal. Or both. If
it isn't breast cancer, it's uterine cancer. Or blood clots and
varicose veins. And all sorts of juicy vaginal infections and
hormonal imbalances, and a whole crock of other shit I
can't bring to mind at the moment. And for your information my friend, my first pregnancy happened on a Dalkon
shield," I add for good measure, slamming the refrigerator
door in his face.

"And you've never regretted it?" he asks quietly.

"Regretted what?"

"The abortions."

Jesus Christ, I do not need this. Especially tonight, I do
not need this at all.

"I don't regret not having brought up two kids at those
particular times in my life, if that's what you mean. Wrong
place. Wrong time. Wrong man. Wrong *me*, is what it came
down to. But let me enlighten you on something, Stanley.
Abortion is not something that can be discussed on purely
theoretical terms. The *only* people I will bother discussing
this hairy issue with are those who have had to go through
the same kind of decision-making process as myself. You
know why? Because I experienced first hand, what a
difference a day makes. Before I ever got pregnant, my
whole background and predispositions made me believe that
if anything ever got conceived inside me, I'd have it.
Period. Abortion was somebody else's bloody problem. Not
mine. But the very day, I mean to say the very *second* I
actually learned that I *was* pregnant, then black turned to
white. Or white to black, whichever way you want to put it.
There was no question of going through with either
pregnancy or having the kid. I was having an abortion.
Period. It was as simple as that."

"And you can honestly tell me, Sarah, that you have
never regretted those two abortions?"

"Goddamn it, Stanley. You're not going to give up, are
you? Yeah sure. I may regret them from time to time.

There. Feel better? In some unguarded moment, start conjuring up a couple of healthy children bouncing on someone's healthy knee. But is that truly regret, or delusionary doublethink? Because the truth of it is, Stanley, that if I had it to do over again, I would no doubt make the same decisions I made before. But they weren't even decisions. More like action-reaction. Necessity. Can you understand that? Abortion was simply another form of birth control for me, Stanley. Or life control, if you will. A way to keep my head above water and my life on track. And I don't feel guilty about it, if that's what you're driving at. When a soul is ready to be born, it *will* be born. And nothing I, or anyone else can do, will stop it from being born. I truly believe that," I say, wishing like hell I really did.

We stare at each other a moment or two in studied silence. I make a pantomime of stepping off my soapbox and kicking it aside. Stanley doesn't buy it. His attention is on his coffee cup, which he places oh-so-carefully into the sink before retrieving his trench coat from the kitchen stool.

"What are you doing, Stanley?"

"Heading home."

"But I thought . . ."

He shakes his head. "I have a few things to take care of tomorrow morning before an interview."

"Bullshit. You brought those bagels over here for our breakfast tomorrow morning! You were planning on staying over, Stanley . . ."

"Not tonight," he murmurs, his hand grazing my cheek as he walks toward the living room and the front door.

"Is this it, Stanley?" I ask, following him out. "I mean, are we going to be seeing each other again, or what?"

He turns that damn brooding gaze on me one last time, reaching out to touch the tip of my nose. "Tomorrow at Verdi's?"

"Stanley," I say, catching the door. "Don't leave. This is all so silly, isn't it?"

"Maybe," he says with a quick smile. But heads on out the door, all the same.

I don't feel up to Amy's double bed tonight. Choosing to

camp out, fully dressed, on the living room sofa. A Judy Garland album and a furry kitty cat keeping me company throughout another long and lonely night.

JUNE 18

Six a.m. and I put through a call to Tom in New York.

"Look Tom," I jump in, the moment he comes on the line. "I can't wait any longer. I'm making a visit to Genco Labs Monday morning, right? And I'm going to need some ammunition. Some kind of clue as to what is going on with Frank. . . . Tom?"

"Not a hell of a lot to tell you," he begins, in a low muffled monotone. And then even lower: "Ever hear of the SV40 monkey virus? Or the Marburg virus?"

"SV40?" A vague memory stirs.

"It was mainly packed with news clippings. And what looked like a couple memos from the United States Public Health Service. That's all I got, Sarah."

"The Public Health Service is sending memos to Frank? Is that what you're saying? About what?" Silence. "Couldn't you have made copies of any of this?"

"Not a chance in hell. Promised Tammy and the kids a week-end in the Catskills. And that's what they're going to get. Be with you in a flash, Doll," he adds, off to the side of the receiver.

"You call the women you work with dolls? . . . Look Tom, isn't there anything else you can tell me at the moment? These memos from the Public Health Service, what exactly did they say? You must have picked up a few sentences here and there?"

"Unfortunately no. But give my love to Uncle Harry and Aunt Bell. Tell them I'll be calling in a couple of days. Keep in touch."

"What was that, the Marlboro virus? What?" But he's

already hung up, the bastard. Before I can get in another word.

Uncle Harry and Aunt Bell? Jesus. I toast up one of Stanley's poppy seed bagels and take it into the bedroom. Where I settle down by the kitty cat in a patch of sunshine streaming through the east window, there to mull over what little information Tom has given me. The SV40 monkey virus was just one of many presumed carcinogenic viruses Frank was exposing his oncogenes to. But I certainly can't recall that particular virus being any more or less important in his experiments than all the other carcinogenic shit they were playing around with in that lab.

At some point I return to the living room and put a call through to Stanley. Obviously I have woken the man up. When he finally realizes where he is and who I am, he starts mumbling some kind of apology into the mouthpiece.

"Save it," I interrupt him. "Just tell me, Stanley. Where's the best place in this city to go for information on viruses? There some kind of medical science library around here?" I wait a few moments while he drops the phone, picks it up, drops it, and picks it up again.

"U.C. Med." he finally tells me, after clearing his throat and spitting into what must be some kind of cavernous makeshift spitoon, judging from the echo that comes across the wires. "Just behind Golden Gate Park. Anybody can use it. Even little ladies from Detroit, Mich—"

"Thanks Stanley. See you this afternoon."

I catch a bus over the hill and walk the next ten or so blocks to the University, freezing my ass off in the process, the morning's sunlight having evaporated behind billows of chilly ocean fog. The library itself, located on the second floor of the University's Medical Science building, is pretty much deserted save for a couple of young Chinese-Americans here and there, their heads buried in the pages of thick, intimidating texts.

It doesn't take long to zero in on the SV40. To my surprise there is a considerable amount of material on the subject. It is one of 50 or 60 African monkey viruses which have been discovered over the last thirty years. But it's apparently the best known and most frequently investigated of the lot. I become so involved in the research, taking a few sidetracks here and there whenever they present themselves, that three o'clock comes and goes without having thought about lunch.

I arrive at Verdi's more than an hour late. Stanley is seated before his usual scotch up at the front bar.

"Good news and bad news," I murmur, slipping onto an adjacent stool. "Which do you want to hear first?"

"Neither," he replies, a hand cupping my chin.

"What is it?" I finally ask, taken offstride by the sober look in his eye.

"I want to apologize for last night, Sarah."

"Oh? Well, that's okay. I mean, I under—"

"No, it's not okay. You were being perfectly open with me. Something I should appreciate. And I responded like a first class jerk, clamming up and walking out the way I did. A bad precedent set there."

"Could be," I murmur warmly, smiling at him in the long mirror which stretches across the front of the bar. Moments pass. And all my late night second thoughts begin to dissolve into a fine electric mist of erotic possibility which I can almost see haloing us in that gilded mirror.

Stanley orders me a glass of wine. I fill him in on the morning's phone call to New York and my day of semi-enlightening research. It doesn't surprise me that Stanley has never heard of the SV40 virus. Aside from a small circle of specialists in genetics and virology, who has?

"It's one of the most popular viruses around, Stanley. Because it's carcinogenic. You know, tumor-inducing. And carcinogenic viruses apparently make fascinating playthings in genetic labs. But today I found out where they first detected the SV40. And you're not going to believe this, Stanley. . . . In Salk's polio vaccine!"

"I'm not following you here."

"In Salk's polio vaccine! A carcinogenic monkey virus! All those years that you and I and ten million other American kids stood in line for our yearly shots, little did we know we were subjecting ourselves to a dangerously contaminated vaccine!"

"How in hell did a carcinogenic monkey virus get into the polio vaccine?"

"Because the polio viruses used in the vaccine were grown on monkey kidney tissue, that's how. I guess a lot of viral vaccines are sprouted on monkey tissue. It's the only place the viruses seem to grow."

"So polio viruses for Salk's vaccine were grown on monkey kidney tissue?"

"Right. Which meant that hundreds of thousands of African monkeys were flown into the States during the '50's so we could make the vaccine. All fine and dandy. Until 1960, when someone discovers that all these monkeys, or rather their kidneys, have been infested with a tumor-inducing virus. And as a matter of course, if the monkey kidneys were infested, so was the vaccine!"

"But what does all this have to do with your friend's work with AIDS?"

"I'm not sure yet. But isn't that incredible, Stanley? That the celebrated Salk polio vaccine was contaminated with a carcinogenic virus all those years and yet we never heard a word about it? Some 1963 article in *Science Digest* actually referred to it as the worst mistake in medical history. And yet we never heard a damn thing about it! How do they do it, Stanley? How do they keep something like that out of the mass media and press?"

Stanley drains his glass and grimaces at me in the mirror. "So we're all catching cancer somewhere down the line from a carcinogenic polio vaccine, is that the story?"

"Who knows. There was never any conclusive follow-up research done on the issue. The medical-science party line seems to be that the SV40 isn't carcinogenic for human beings. Only animals. But can you believe them, that's the question. If it can cause cancer in hamsters, why not human beings? There was a '61 article in *U.S. Business Week*, of all places, which drew a hypothetical connection between the contaminated Salk vaccine and the unusual rise in leukemia cases among American children during the late fifties. Now that's downright spooky, isn't it?"

"Yes, it is. But I still don't understand how all this relates to—"

"Well I don't either, Stanley. Not yet. Just give me time. At first I figured that maybe Frank was using the African monkey tissue to grow AIDS viruses, in the same way that Salk once used the kidney tissue to grow the polio virus. But Tom didn't mention anything about monkey kidneys. Just monkey *viruses*."

"So this Marlboro virus—?"

"Marburg. Yes, it comes from monkey kidneys, as well."

"Also carcinogenic?"

"No. Pretty lethal though. Causes some kind of weird hepatitis. So this is what we have here, Stanley. Two monkey viruses. One AIDS virus. And the Public Health Service. We can't forget them, can we? What do you suppose that could all add up to?"

"An overwrought imagination, for one."

"Stanley, I really wish you would stop playing the devil's advocate here. You know as well as I do that something weird could be going on. You said as much the first time I told you my story. Remember?"

But Stanley's attention has been diverted elsewhere. By the cigar-puffing, pot-bellied Italian gentleman who owns and manages this restaurant-bar. After their male greeting ritual has played itself out, Mr. Faccio and I are properly introduced.

"So your daughter is getting married this week-end?" I suggest brightly, for lack of anything better to say.

The man gazes skeptically from me back to Stanley, tapping his cigar butt into the ashtray attached to his right hand. Then muttering a few unintelligible Italian syllables, he jabs Stanley lightly in the chest and walks abruptly away.

"How to win friends and influence people," Stanley murmurs, giving the bartender the high sign and propelling me out the restaurant door.

"Was that really such a horrible thing to say?" I offer on my own behalf. "After all, his daughter *is* getting married this week-end, isn't she? So why avoid the obvious?. . . . How did the two of you become such bosom buddies, anyway?"

"He's my father-in-law."

"Your *what*?" I ask, stopping in my tracks.

"My ex-father-in-law. His daughter is my ex-wife."

"I see . . . So your wife was Italian?" I confirm skeptically, none too happy with the picture that suddenly looms into my mind's eye. Stanley setting up house with some earthy, olive-skinned knock-out who raised hell-fire in and out of the bedroom, and cooked up pot after pot of that incredible linguini-crab stew. "Which means that this wedding tomorrow is going to be pretty much of a family affair? I mean, this young girl who's getting married tomorrow is your sister-in-law, am I right?"

"Right?"

"And your ex-wife, she's going to be attending the festivities, as well?"

"One would presume as much."

"What's she like? Your ex-wife, I mean."

"You'll find out soon enough," he tells me, a smile of one kind or another playing on his lips. For the time being I let it go at that.

Once back at Amy's, Stanley shoves a twenty dollar bill my way, with the suggestion that I pick up fixings for dinner at the Italian deli across the street, meanwhile giving him the opportunity to put through a few calls. It seems I am being dismissed. And I don't like it. Not one bit. What gives this man the right to send me off on his little errands, while he proceeds to make private calls on my telephone, in my apartment?

I should object. But don't. Since voicing objection might mean having to confront certain vague suspicions I harbor about Stanley. Suspicions I'd rather not yet confront.

I take my own sweet time at the deli, eventually settling upon a pint of pesto sauce, some fresh pasta, a half pound of Italian fontina, a bit of the eggplant caponata, a loaf of sourdough, and a couple of bottles of Italian red wine. After adding on a package of cigarettes to the list, I get back twenty-three cents in change. This I pawn off on the middle-aged bag lady who seems to have made a permanent home for herself on the park bench across the street.

By my second or third glass of wine before dinner, I work up enough nerve to ask Stanley a few more questions about his ex-wife. Her name is Maria. And it is no small shock to learn that she and Stanley were divorced but a few months ago.

"You mean to say this thing just happened?!"

"Whatever 'happened', Sarah, happened many years ago. It was only the legal formalities that had to wait until now."

"I see. . . . So what went wrong?"

"Damn nosey little critter, aren't you?"

"Nosey is a poor choice of words, Stanley. Curious would be much more apt a description, I should think. And why shouldn't I be curious about you, Stanley? It's only natural, isn't it? I wouldn't mind in the least if you showed more interest in my own past. In fact, I'd be flattered. . . . Hey look, if you really don't want to talk about it . . ."

"It was all very tediously predictable, Sarah. The usual marital muck-up. Leading to the usual humdrum divorce."

"Come on. No divorce is ever *that* tediously predictable. Otherwise, why would anyone ever bother getting married in the first place?"

"So what is it that you want, sweetheart? The whole bloody story? Is that it? You spilled your guts out last night, so it's my turn tonight." His voice is as subdued as ever. But there is an angry set to his face that hurts.

"Why no. I just. . . ." And I stop.

Stanley rises from the sofa. Walks over to the stereo, where sits the open bottle of wine. And refills his glass. "If you really want to know, Sarah," he begins again, his back to me as he peers through the venetian blinds. "For a time there, it was hell. Pure, unadulterated hell. Separate meals. Separate rooms. Separate beds. Even separate goddamn Tv sets." He pauses, turning to smile wanly in my direction. I shift awkwardly in place.

"There was a hell of a lot of resentment there," he starts up again, his gaze back on the window. "Her resentment of me. Of my work. My resentment of . . . of her youth, I suppose. Our channels of communication weren't the best in those days. I blame myself for that . . . But this is all past history, Sarah. We separated over three years ago.

She's grown up. I've grown up a bit myself," he adds, the wan smile getting wanner; seeming to register a high degree of retrospective pain.

"Do you still love her?" I ask, the question echoing with unintended magnitude in the hushed and solemn ambience of the room.

"I don't know. I suppose we never fall totally out of love with the people we once loved, do we?"

"Speak for yourself. I can look back on every man I ever fell in love with, and see him for the real schmuck he is." Stanley laughs. "But it's true! Which doesn't say a hell of a lot for my past relationships, does it? Whenever I run into some old flame, all I can think is—for god's sake Sarah, how could you ever have fallen for the likes of *him?*"

"Is that what you're going to be thinking about me someday?"

"No doubt."

We're both smiling now. And it hits me, right then and there, now much I really care for this guy. I suspect he's feeling likewise. At least for the moment. And one thing leading to another, we pass the rest of the evening in bed, the goodies from the Italian deli serving as a tasty and festive midnight snack.

JUNE 19

It is sometime after 9 a.m. when Stanley staggers into the room. "You always get up in the middle of the night, like that?" he mutters, sinking against the door jamb.

"Seven in the morning hardly qualifies as the middle of the night. And my, but aren't you looking chipper this morning. Fresh coffee on the stove," I add, hoisting my mug into the air.

He returns with the entire pot, setting it on the floor between us and picking through parts of the morning paper

I've already read. We pass the remainder of the morning in a companionable semi-funk. Stoking up on coffee and exchanging occasional quips on the dismal morning news. I am resolved neither to talk about or even think about the matter of Frank. For one day, at least. In order to give all the parts of the puzzle time to settle and steep.

Around noon I take a shower and make a quick survey of Amy's extensive wardrobe, in a half-hearted attempt at coming up with a winning ensemble for this afternoon's affair. Do I really care what all those strangers today might think of me, I ask myself? Or how I may stand up in comparison to Stanley's previous wife? Unfortunately, indeed I do.

Enroute to the church, we stop off at Stanley's Market street apartment, where he picks up a change of clothes, as well as checking out messages on his machine and rifling through an impressive stack of Saturday morning mail. Or could that be Friday morning's mail, as well. . . . ? While he is so occupied, I make a quick study of his home base—a two room, makeshift affair—hoping to come away with some added insight into this singular human being whom, under the strangest of circumstances, I am beginning to care for and know. But the place offers up no manifest clues. No pictures. No photographs. No mementos of a time gone by. Only one uncomfortable looking Sears-Roebuck sofa bed. A dresser. And a gargantuan oak writing desk, which houses his electric typewriter, a pile of newsclippings, and a half empty bottle of scotch.

"You're actually hungry?" Stanley asks incredulously, catching me with my head inside his refrigerator. "After what we ate last night?"

"Yeah, but we never had any breakfast, if you recall." His ice box looks as forlorn and barren as my own back in New York. "Don't you ever cook in this place? Or eat?"

Stanley grabs a box of Grapenuts flakes from the cupboard over the sink and shoves it into my hand. Not exactly what I had in mind.

We arrive at the church a few minutes late. Just in time to be seated in a back pew and observe the nervous bride make her self-conscious way down the aisle on her father's arm.

Skittish and lovely as a newborn filly she is, with eyes glued tremulously to the red carpet at her feet. One look at the young groom awaiting her up front, and I have little trouble understanding how Faccio's daughter got herself into this mess in the first place. The kid is lean and intense. With a pair of coal black eyes that could burn holes through any young girl's heart. And maybe a few slightly middle-aged hearts, as well.

The ceremony drones on interminably. Punctuated by the innumerable kneelings and risings of a high mass. I plead terminal ennui. Stanley concurs, and we slip noiselessly out of the church and on into a neighboring cafe, where we while away the next hour over a half carafe of the house red. Time enough for the service to have ended and for the reception, being held directly across the street, to have begun.

There are already some 200 guests milling about the hall when we arrive. A five piece combo is warming up on Italian muzak in one corner, and a woman in black is circulating in another, bearing an immense tray of sparkling champagne. I fetch a couple of glasses for Stanley and myself, only to find that the man has disappeared while my back was turned. Which leaves me little alternative than to retreat to a discreet alcove, where I sip anonymously on champagne and observe the passing scene.

It is impossible not to view every woman present between thirty and forty years of age as the potential Mrs. Ex. Twenty minutes or so into this prurient guessing game and I am convinced the field has been narrowed down to a suitable match. She is tall. Statuesque. And in her middle thirties. Attractive, yes. But not overpoweringly so. With a stiff upper-lip demeanor about her. A proud woman. Peacock proud. Sipping on her glass of champagne as if it were a cup of tea and listening with one ear cocked to the gentleman who is gesticulating so dramatically on her right. Turning her nose up at what is being said, I can almost see the feathers ruffling up her neck.

"There you are, woman," Stanley growls, suddenly materializing before me. "Put down the champagne. I want to introduce you to George's wife. And Marie."

He steers us in the opposite direction of my peacock, toward a lively group of new arrivals still gathered about the door. The young bride is among them. As is her father, George Faccio, accompanied by his pleasantly plump, frizzy-haired wife. To one side stands a young woman who bears a striking resemblance to the bride herself. And this woman, to my distress and consternation, is none other than the infamous Marie.

After introductions are made all around, more talk ensues. The general drift of the conversation focuses on the probable whereabouts of the truant groom, who apparently decided to take a quick spin around town in the young couple's newly acquired Datsun 410. A wedding present from the father of the bride. I nod along with the conversation while carrying on furious computations inside my head. This woman beside me, this Marie, couldn't be more than 23 years old. 25 on the outside. Which would her at a tender and nubile 19 when she married Stanley. And Stanley at a well-ripened 39, or 40 years of age!

Stanley eventually offers to dispose of everyone's wraps. While he collects coats, I make my escape back into the main hall. Helping myself to some more of that champagne and settling into my alcove for a discomfiting stew. Stanley London, the worldly wise and clever journalist, marrying a young girl but half his age, The proverbial young-enough-to-be-his-daughter trip. But why?

"Why?" I ask out loud, at Stanley's approach. He obviously has no idea what I am referring to, and cares even less.

"Because," he says with a grin, toasting me with a scotch he just picked up at the open bar.

The combo strikes up a maudlin rendition of "Rags to Riches." We dance. "You're suddenly the silent one," Stanley observes, leaning back and taking a good look into my face. I shrug, and bring my cheek back up to his, in order to hide the mixture of confusion and disgust which must be surfacing there. We waltz on in silence. Until the song grinds down to a melodramatic finish. Whereupon we return to our respective drinks.

"I see it runs in the family," I mutter, apropos to nothing.

"Hmm?"

"Marrying young. It seems to run in the Faccio family, doesn't it?"

We stand there in the corner, having absolutely nothing more to say to one another. Sipping our drinks and staring vacantly about the room.

"Promise you won't accuse me of paranoia?" I suddenly ask, turning my gaze from the array of wedding guests back to Stanley.

"What do you mean?"

"See that man over there? The fat one with the plaid pants? Do you know who he is? A friend of the family?"

"Not that I know of."

"Have you ever seen him before? . . . You didn't notice him in the cafe across the street where we stopped for the wine?"

"Can't say that I did."

"Well he was there, Stanley! Sitting a couple tables down. And giving me the same evil eye he was just giving me a few seconds ago."

"The poor man's besotted with you, Sarah."

"Yeah, right. Listen, would you mind terribly asking Georgey Boy if that's one of his guests?"

"What do you have in mind, Sarah?"

"Don't make me spell it out, Stanley. Please just ask. It can't hurt, can it?"

Shaking his head, Stanley wanders off in search of Faccio. I stay put, in order to keep an eye out for Fatso. Which isn't real hard to do, since he also seems to be keeping an eye out for me. Leering at me over the bottle of beer he swigs from the other side of the room. Finally, I can't take it any longer. And turn my back on the man. Just in time to catch the champagne lady skirting by with a trayful of hors d'oeurves.

"Where is he?" It's Stanley. With Mr. Faccio in tow.

"I . . . he was right over there a second ago. Is he a friend of yours, Mr. Faccio?"

"Who?"

"A tall, fat man," I murmur, glancing frantically about the room. Where the hell did he go?

"You talking about my brother Sid? That who you're talking about? Heh?" And he prods me in the direction of a long buffet table at the rear of the room. Sid is more than fat. He's obese. Some 300 pounds obese. And busy stuffing rounds of salami into his mouth.

"Not him," I say, putting a stop to our progression before the inevitable introductions begin. "This fellow was a little lighter. Bald. Looked like he needed a shave."

Faccio shrugs, giving Stanley a look over my head which is not unlike the look back in the restaurant yesterday afternoon. "Could be somebody's friend, right? I can't keep track of everybody's boyfriends and girlfriends, and husbands and wives, and other such conjugal arrangements, if you know what I mean. Was the guy making offensive advances to you? Is that what you're saying?"

"No, not at all. It's just that I could swear I had seen the guy before and . . . Well, anyway, thanks for helping me out, Mr. Faccio. Sorry I let him slip away."

"Call me George." And with a left hook to Stanley's shoulder, Mr. Faccio takes his leave.

"Hungry?" Stanley asks, thumbing the tableful of food.

"Starved."

"How about if I pick us up some food and drink and you rustle up a couple of seats before they all disappear."

I situate us as far away from the band as is physically possible, though the sound remains deafening all the same. If my eyes do not deceive me, the young man seated at the far end of our table, strumming on his water glass and bobbing his head in time to the ragged calypso beat, is none other than the groom himself. He looks even better at close range than he did back at the church. All those wild black curls and pronounced cheek bones giving him the quintessential gypsy look. The perfect Romeo, if I were casting around for the part. Sensing my gaze upon him, the boy turns, grinning in my direction. Nods. Then turns back to the floor. Looks back again. Grins. Turns away. Looks back. Grins. "You wanna dance?" he asks, his accent thick. His tone suggestively amused.

I laugh and shake my head. "Where's your new wife?"

He nods sideways toward the dance floor, where the

lovely Donna twirls about on the arm of a distinguished grey-haired gentleman, looking as gay and lighthearted now as she looked ill-at-ease earlier in the day.

"So cut in. That's the groom's prerogative, isn't it?"

He shrugs, shaking his head. Making me wonder if he understood a word I said.

"So you like it here in the States?" I ask.

His head bobs back and forth. "It's okay. But my English." And he sucks in through his front teeth while giving a 'Mama-mia' gesture with his right hand.

"You should get yourself a tutor this summer," I counsel him, as if the boy needs my advice. "Meet with him maybe three, four, five times a week. And by September you'll be doing fine."

"Okay," he says, his grin wider than ever, exposing a couple of gold-plated molars on either side of his mouth. "So you wanna dance?"

This kid doesn't know when to quit. "Cha-cha-cha's aren't my style," I tell him truthfully. But no sooner are the words out of my mouth, then the band shifts into a bleary-eyed rendition of "I Left My Heart . . ." Someone in this quintet is a frustrated Tony Bennett. No doubt about it.

"So?" says Mr. Cocksure from the other end of the table. So, we dance. And I get the oddest flash. Like I'm right back at my high school senior prom. Maybe it's the tentative way he holds me. Or the boxy way he moves around the floor. And when he pulls me gently against his chest, I'm ashamed to say that's exactly where I remain. Blame it on all that champagne. When the set is over, we exchange embarrassed smiles—at least I'm embarrassed, I can't answer for him—and return to our seats. Stanley awaits us there. Damn.

"Enjoying yourself?" he asks, eyebrows raised in an unarticulated wisecrack.

The boy mumbles something to Stanley in Italian, grinning over at me as he plops down in the chair next to him, meanwhile helping himself to the glass of wine obviously intended for me.

"Is that so?" Stanley asks, turning to me.

"Is what so?"

"He tells me you're going to be teaching him English this summer."

"Yeah sure," I mutter, swooping the glass out of the young groom's hand and settling on Stanley's other side. "And since when do you speak Italian?"

"She don't like me," the boy whispers loudly in Stanley's ear.

"Tell him to go dance with his wife, for God's sake."

"You heard what the woman said."

"Okay! Okay!" And the groom staggers to his feet. Suddenly beginning to act a lot drunker than he really is.

Stanley and I sip our drinks in silence, while picking away at a hefty plate of Italian antipasta.

"Don't let me keep you from your friends," I say. "No, I mean it, Stanley. Just because I'm not in a particularly sociable mood this afternoon, shouldn't stop you from—"

"You looked pretty sociable back there on the dance floor, I thought."

"You think so?"

"I think so, yes."

"Look Stanley. I might enjoy dancing with someone half my age. For all I know, I might even enjoy fucking someone half my age. But I sure as hell wouldn't marry him."

"Is that what all this is about, Sarah? Are you insulted because my ex-wife happens to be a good many years younger than yourself? Is that it?"

"Younger than me? Younger than you! At least twenty years younger, right? I'm not insulted, Stanley. Just disgusted. Disappointed . . . Disillusioned," I add for good measure. "Men who go around marrying little girls have serious psychological problems. That's the way I see it, anyway."

"Even if one happens to be deeply in love with the girl?"

"That makes it ten times worse," I hiss into his ear, as another couple settles down at our table. "How can you possibly fall in love with someone who can't possibly understand the half of what you try to say to her. I don't care how smart she is. At 19, or 20, or whatever, her eyes aren't even open yet, for God's sake."

"Just the other night, I seem to recall you referring to

Bogart and Bacall as the most romantic couple in cinema history. Or something to that effect. I suppose Bogart had these psychological problems you refer to, as well?"

"He doesn't count."

"Oh?"

"Shit, I don't know. It's possible that I don't know what the fuck I'm talking about. Okay? So let's just drop it." And I jump up to replenish our plate.

When we finally get back out on Columbus street, it is after eight p.m. Fatso is nowhere in sight. Which doesn't stop me from looking over my shoulder every other step of our twenty minute walk back over the hill.

I'm feeling damn good, in spite of the occasional prickle at the back of my neck. Which must have something to do with all the champagne I consumed back there. And something to do with the loving affection Stanley proceeded to shower on me the rest of the afternoon. If he was out to prove a point today, he succeeded. Enough to make me stop and ponder where all this is going to end.

JUNE 20

I wake up to an overpowering aftertaste of garlic in my mouth. Echoes of that incredible marinated eggplant I found impossible to resist yesterday afternoon.

"Where are you off to?" Stanley murmurs, reaching out to grab my arm as I slip out of bed.

"To brush my teeth, for one thing. And throw a few gallons of water down me, for another," I answer, tossing Amy's terry cloth bathrobe over my shoulder and shuffling out of the room.

The woman staring back at me in the bathroom mirror is not someone I particularly care to identify with. All that champagne on top of the brandy Stanley and I took to bed with us last night, has certainly left its mark. When did it happen, I ask myself forlornly, burrowing under an ice cold shower in a futile attempt at scrubbing away all those bags and wrinkles. When did I get so old?

Out of the bathroom and into the kitchen, I put a pot of water to boil on the stove and settle at the breakfast table with a pile of newsclippings xeroxed at the library a few days before.

"You know, Stanley, Something doesn't quite add up here," I muse out loud, when he finally joins me there at the table, a few hours into the day. "Why ever did the Genco-Chemix collaboration get involved with an AIDS vaccine, in the first place?"

"And why not?"

"Because, the majority of pharmaceutical firms—in fact, almost every one of them except Chemix—are avoiding the AIDS question like the plague. None of them want anything to do with an AIDS vaccine."

"I would have thought—"

"So would I. But most of the private firms are claiming that any commitment to AIDS research would be too great a financial risk. That the AIDS virus is too mutable to ever be worked into an effective vaccine. Critics of these firms claim that the problem isn't financial risk at all, but indifference. That the corporate bureaucracies heading these private companies just don't give a damn, either about AIDS or about developing a vaccine. For the obvious reason that most AIDS victims are still homosexuals or drug addicts. You know, officialdom perverts."

"You mean why bother saving what's better off dead?"

"Something like that, yes. So why is Chemix bucking the tide? Why is Chemix the only private drug firm of any account taking up the cause of the AIDS vaccine? There's certainly nothing in their past to indicate latent humanistic tendencies, that's for damn sure. They were the main dealer in napalm, for God's sake. So why . . . ?" I temporize. Hoping Stanley might come up with a brilliant suggestion or two. But I hope in vain. This man is *not* a morning person. A fact which becomes more obvious with every passing day.

"And there's something else that bothers me," I go on,

after refilling our cups. "All these news stories and profiles on Frank. They get decidedly vaguer after 1982."

"Vaguer?"

"For instance, the later pieces don't carry any direct quotes. While the earlier pieces are full of them. Frank loved his soap box. And there aren't any descriptions of his lab in the later stories, either. None of the little details that tell you the reporter was actually there on the spot. Even this photo of Frank out of the May issue of *Time*. It didn't strike me until this morning, Stanley. But this picture is at least four years old! That's his Columbia lab in the background. I'd recognize it anywhere. Now you tell me why, if you're doing a story on Frank's work out here in California, they were forced to dredge up a four year old snapshot of the man taken back in New York? I'm beginning to wonder who has actually seen Frank in the last couple of years. Was this AIDS research as secretive as all that?"

Stanley reserves comment for the time being, beginning to thumb through some of the newsclippings on his own. "She's a lovely woman, your friend's wife," he murmurs, taking a good long look at their wedding picture. One of four or five snapshots I took with me from New York.

"His *ex*-wife. And that picture was taken years ago," I remind him cattily. Then divert his attention to the photograph which follows: five men in white lab coats gazing soberly into the camera lens. "Frank's team back at Columbia. Also taken quite a few years back. There's Dr. Beerbohm," I add, pointing out the tall, nervous looking gentleman on the far left. "Nice man. Only one in the bunch I could ever feel comfortable with. Including Frank. Ha! And that's Dr. Joseph Walters. The pudgy one next to Frank. We never got along too well, Joe and I." An understatement if there ever was one.

Stanley flips back to the wedding picture, seemingly transfixed. I am reminded of my duty to get on the phone and inform Jennifer of my trip down to Genco tomorrow morning. Since I will once again be pawning myself off as Jennifer Winslow, Dr. Winslow's ex-wife. Does Jennifer object? After a moment's hesitation, she assures me that she does not. We chat awhile longer, making plans to catch Angelica at today's Sunday matinee. We will meet at the theater at one o'clock.

Angelica disappoints this afternoon, her acting jagged and tentative as compared to the sharply delineated performance she provided a few nights before. But her slack highlights the other performers' strengths. And the strength of the play as a whole. A vivid, absorbing drama, which is tense and surprisingly comic by turn. After final curtain, Jennifer suggests we go backstage to give the woman our regards. We are the only ones from today's audience to do so. She is seated in the back corner, tearing make up off her face. Catching sight of us in the mirror, she spins around abruptly, flashing accusing eyes in my direction.

"Who are you? What do you want with me?" she demands spitefully, dragging me toward a tiny bathroom to our left. This woman is a lot stronger than she looks.

"I don't understand," I stammer. "You know who I am. I . . . we . . . This is Jennifer Winslow, Frank's ex-wife? I believe you already met?"

She ignores my introductions, yanking me into the cubbyhole and slamming the door behind us. "This man! He's been calling every hour on the hour the last two nights. Saying nothing. Just heavy breathing into the phone. So finally I ask the bastard what he wants. And you know what he says? Ask Sarah Calloway! That's your name, right? Sarah Calloway? Ask Sarah Calloway, he says in this slimy whisper. Ask Sarah Calloway. Shit lady, I don't want any trouble. You hear? Not now. Not ever."

"My god, I don't believe it," I murmur bewilderedly. "So they must be up to something after all."

"Who?"

"I'm not sure, Angelica. You probably know about as much as I do about this thing. Maybe more? Something important, Angelica? Something they don't want me to find out! Otherwise, why the intimidation?"

"Who is they?" she beseeches me frantically, her hands tightening into fists she waves in my face.

"You tell me. Chemix? Genco? Maybe the FBI, for all I

know. Angelica, is there anything about Frank or his work that you could have forgotten to tell me? You never once talked to him after he got out here to California?"

"I haven't seen the guy in three years! Believe me! I have no idea where he is or what he is up to. And I don't give a damn, you understand? I just want to be left in peace. That's all!"

"Look, Angelica. None of this is going to go away, just because you or I may want it to. I'm sorry if I got you involved in this thing against your will. But the fact is, you've been involved all along. We all have," I add, shoving open the door and gesturing toward Jennifer. "Simply because each of us, at one time or another, was involved with Frank . . . Why don't you join Jennifer and me for a drink? Maybe together, the three of us can tie up parts of the puzzle we wouldn't be able to tie up apart. What do you say?"

Angelica looks from Jennifer back to me, tugging at her necklace so fiercely I'm sure it's about to snap. "Not tonight. I can't."

"When then?"

She shrugs indifferently. "Maybe Thursday night. Maybe."

"Thursday at seven then," I jot down Amy's address on a scrap of paper and push it into her hand.

"You seem strangely buoyed by this latest turn of events," Jennifer observes drily, once we are settled over some acrid coffee at the hole-in-the-wall Mexican restaurant across the street.

"I do? Well, maybe I am. I mean, I think it's terrible someone's been hassling Angelica like that. But at least it's proof positive that something strange is going on here. That I'm on the right track."

"They must be following you, Sarah."

"I know. Pretty creepy, right? Maybe keeping watch on us this very moment," I add, making a quick survey of the deserted dining room. "But the thing is, why? What is it they don't want me to know? And why are they being so circumspect about it? Why not simply threaten me with imminent annihilation unless I mind my own business, and leave it at that?"

"Maybe they need you."

"Need me? For what?"

Jennifer shrugs, shifting in her seat to have a look around the dining room herself.

"You know I can't help but feel Angelica is hiding something from me," I continue. "Can't explain why I feel that way, but I do. And you should have seen her face when I mentioned the FBI back there. God only knows why it slipped out of my mouth. But when it did, she went as white a sheet. Never seen anything like it."

"The poor girl's spooked. Those kind of phone calls could put anyone on edge," she says, taking another surreptitious peek over her shoulder. "I have to be heading home, Sarah. But I wanted to tell you that I read Frank's letters. The ones out of Paradise."

"And?"

"There is absolutely nothing in them about his work down there, if that's what you're thinking. A few references to workers in his lab. Or whom I presume are workers in his lab. But that was the extent of it. As if he had been living in a vacuum for the last couple of years. All the same, he comes off pretty melancholy in those letters. Which is not at all Frank's style. You must be aware of that as much as I. It frightened me reading them. Gave me the feeling that if something has gone wrong in his life, it started going wrong a long time ago. And something else . . . I don't know if this would mean anything. But in the last letter he ever wrote to Jaimie, Frank mentioned something about taking a trip."

"Where?"

"He didn't say. Just asked Jaimie if he'd be up for a spot of traveling this summer, and left it at that."

"What was the date of this last letter?"

"Late March. Around the 28th."

"About three months ago. . . . Would Jaimie mind if I took a couple of those letters down to Monterey? If Genco starts playing possum with me, it would be real nice to have that kind of evidence on hand."

"Jaimie doesn't know anything about all this. And I prefer to keep it that way, Sarah. At least for the time being."

"You couldn't slip me one or two letters behind his back? I'll return them to you the moment I get home."

I accompany Jennifer back to her wooden framed bungalow on Vallejo. And get snared into a game of Trivial Pursuit with Jaimie and two of his buddies from school—coming off the first class idiot, as I always do when I play that stupid game—before I can make my escape with three of Frank's letters tucked away in my purse. Ten paces from the house and I take a peep. Struck not so much by the melancholy tone Jennifer had alluded to earlier, as by the genuine affection which the man apparently harbors for his son. An affection which causes me to look at Frank under a slightly different light.

As I'm fumbling with Amy's keys, the phone begins to ring. Four, five times. Then stops, the moment I step into the room. I settle on the sofa and read through the letters one more time. Determined to ferret out some invisible clue.

If you don't make the team this summer, son, how about you and I taking off on a little trip? Just the two of us. High time we got reacquainted, I should think.

Dr. Frank Winslow, the workaholic's workaholic, and on the brink of developing an all-important, Nobel-prize-winning vaccine, actually considering taking time off to go traveling with his son? The same man who once refused to take off a lousy three hours on New Year's Eve until I acted out a veritable epileptic fit outside his laboratory door? The same man who considered *Casablanca* to be a 'puerile soap opera' and reading fiction 'a waste of time'? The same man who started crawling walls with deprivation fever after twelve hours away from his lab? This same man was suggesting an extended vacation so as to become reacquainted with his teenaged son?

Again, the phone. "Hello?. . . . Stanley? . . ." A

cool, cottony silence is all I get from the other end of the line. Hanging up, I throw on Amy's parka and head straight out to Verdi's Cafe.

"Can you move in for a few days?" I ask Stanley, the moment I finally get him alone at the far end of the bar.

"Is this a proposal?"

"I'm serious, Stanley. Can you?"

"I was under the impression I already had."

"Good. No chickening out now." In so many words, I tell him the latest developments. And before I can take a single sip on my beer Stanley is hauling me out the door and flagging down a passing cab.

In five minutes we are back at Amy's. The apartment feels completely different now. One lousy phone call did it. Sabotaging the natural homey flavor of this place. Poisoning the air with its eerie, intimidating spell.

"Your goddamn phone's been tapped!" Stanley mutters savagely, bringing the receiver up to my ear. All I hear is a dial tone. He hangs it up, then hands the receiver back to me one more time. And this time I pick it up. A faint, distant echo a moment after putting my ear to the phone. I hang up and try again. And again, that unearthly echo, setting my teeth on edge.

"How do you tap a phone?! Did they actually have to come inside this apartment to do it?"

"That depends who did it and what they have access to."

"But this is horrible! How long do you suppose it's been tapped? All the way back to Friday morning? Back when I called Tom in New York? . . . What are you doing, Stanley?"

"Checking for bugs."

"You don't think. . . ? If you find any bugs in this place, Stanley. I'm going to drop this case right here and now."

Stanley doesn't appear to be listening, as he proceeds with an exhaustive shakedown of the entire flat. Nothing escapes those probing, sentient fingertips of his. From curtain rods to top soil. From picture frames to table lamps to the innards of Amy's stereo and the bindings of every book on her library shelves.

"The Sensuous Woman," Stanley murmurs, ticking off a few of her choicer titles. *"You and Your Vibrator? How to be a Real Woman with a Real Man?"*

"Yeah. Amy's really into self-improvement, 80's style. Ha! Or is that 70's style? Found herself one hell of a Real Man, too. The character even surfs, if you can believe it. . . . No bugs?"

He shakes his head and moves into the bedroom, emptying out Amy's closets and drawers, and tossing the mass of clothes and other personal belongings into a flowering, chaotic pile on the double bed. "You certainly seem to know what you're doing," I observe speculatively as he so expertly frisks the backing of the dresser drawers. And so he does.

A hour of such ferreting about turns up nothing more interesting than aforementioned vibrator and a couple of kewpie doll snapshots of Amy in a transparent red negligee, licking a candy cane and giving the camera a salacious grin. Leftover Christmas cards, perhaps?

"So who do you think did it?" I query Stanley, between bites of a congealing pizza we ordered from a restaurant down the street. "FBI? CIA? NSA?"

Stanley laughs. "Think you're big stuff, do you?"

"Well who else goes around tapping phones like that? Tricky Dicky? Mr. Hunt?"

"Everybody taps phones these days, Sarah. No corporation in America is worth its salt with a battle array of Intelligence men and security forces working on its behalf. Our entire capitalist system is shored up by a crisscrossing network of spies and counterspies devoted to snuffing out creeping radicalism wherever it starts raising its nasty head. There must be ten thousand wire taps done every month. At least. You're just one of many, sweetheart. So don't go getting a swelled head about this."

"Are you serious? Ten thousand a month? And what do they do with all the information, for god's sake? Store it in some fancy computer until the Second Coming or what?"

"I have my theories."

"Like what?"

"Isn't this getting off the subject at hand, Sarah?"

"Which is?"

"This trip of yours down to Genco Labs. How about postponing the visit until Thursday morning and I'll keep you company down there."

"Thursday? That's too long to wait, Stanley. I have a sense of urgency about this thing. Don't give me that look. I mean it! Look, how much can happen? I'll drive down tomorrow morning, have a talk with this Dr. Fawley, and be back in the city before tomorrow night. It will be as simple as that."

JUNE 21

Tooling down Highway 101 in a canary yellow '71 Datsun—by odd coincidence the same yellow Datsun 'Rent-a-Wreck' meted out to me the week before—I'm pumped high on paranoia-laced adrenalin. Shades of an LSD tripping breakdown some fifteen years before. A night when the enemy was everywhere. Everywhere! Under every lampshade. Peering through every window. Oozing out of every electrolysized molecule popping to life before my acid-wired eyes.

This morning, the rear view mirror is my only line of defense between such pitiful vulnerability and the omnipresent enemy camp on my tail. Why didn't I listen to Stanley? Why didn't I have the fucking patience to put off this trip a few more lousy days? I could turn back now, of course. And make it into the city in less than an hour's time. But the fickle-hearted cowardliness of such a move goads me on down the line.

A fire-engine red Pinto has been following me for the last fifteen minutes or so. Maybe longer. I speed up. So does the Pinto. I slow down and it passes me by. Only to be supplanted by a menacing looking black four door sedan. I slow down again, this time to a crawl. The driver behind me leans on his horn, screaming out some international obscenity—'fuck you' in German perhaps?—as he zips on by. And so it goes for the next hour or so. Until the pure repetitiousness of my panic, not to mention the incredible beauty of the scenery, work together and separately to whittle my hysteria back down to human size.

This has to be one of the sublimest examples of coastline in America. If not the world. Ragged, pearly white beachhead bordering a limitless emerald sea. And all of it set on fire and sanctified by the sheer brilliance of an early morning light.

By 10:30 I arrive at the outskirts of Monterey. Where I stop at an oceanside cafe for a quick cup and directions to Genco Laboratories, located on the southern edge of town. The firm is a cluster of low-level pink stucco buildings set within a prettified industrial park. Four or five tents are set up smack in the middle of the complex. The desperate AIDS victims Stanley's stockbroker friend alluded to? Hoping for a crack at the elusive vaccine? And how is it that Genco Labs is tolerating such flagrant squatters in its midst?

I drive around the complex once. Twice. Finally, I locate Building A where the personnel office is to be found. After parking the car, I stay put for a moment or two, checking out the area for my phantom tail. But the only movement in the entire lot is a woman in a flapping white lab coat stepping quickly toward a squat, L-shaped research facility on my left.

"Dr. Fawley has been abroad for the last two weeks," the red-headed receptionist informs me when I ask directions to his office or lab.

"So I was told. But I was also told that he would be back today and that I might be able to speak with him. Today. It's a bit of an emergency, you understand."

"And your name?"

"Mrs. Jennifer Winslow."

I could swear the little woman jumps a millimeter or two at the tidbit of information. Could she be one of Frank's past or present conquests? She certainly looks the part.

"And whom did you speak to about seeing the Doctor?

"A Dr. Bukowski. Last Thursday afternoon."

"I see. Well, if you could please take a seat, Mrs. Winslow. I'll look into the matter."

The seat I am directed to is a long leather divan on the other side of the office. Far enough away from the receptionist's desk to make eavesdropping an unlikely possibility. After two or three low-decibel conversations on the phone, the receptionist informs me that Dr. Fawley will be with me in a few minutes time. Would I care for some coffee while I wait?

In seconds she is serving me up a cup, with two shortbread cookies tucked discreetly onto the delicate china saucer. I am duly impressed. Both with the plush courteous ambiance of this office and the unusual accessibility of Dr. Fawley, who has consented at such short notice to give me a few minutes of his time.

But after an hour, and then an hour and a half pass by, with no sign of my Dr. Fawley, first impressions begin to fade. The receptionist initiates another brief conversation on the phone, only to inform me that the doctor has been unexpectedly detained. "He will be available later this afternoon, Mrs. Winslow. But if it suits you, tomorrow morning would be much more convenient for the doctor."

"I'm afraid that's impossible. I really must see him today."

"Well then. Shall we aim for four o'clock?"

Four o'clock it is. Which leaves me three and a half hours to fritter away. I opt for a brief tour of the premises. It is very brief indeed, as there are few buildings in this research complex open to non-specified personnel. Passing by 'tent city', a young man who is playing cards with two of his friends smiles and waves in my direction. I wave back, tempted to approach. Then decide against it. My growing appetite leads me back to Building A and the company's spacious cafeteria.

Picking up an orange plastic tray from the stack at the door, I secure a place in line, all the while keeping an eye out for Fatso. Or any other unsavory looking characters in the general environs. A vaguely familiar figure crosses my line of vision, dropping refuse into a garbage bin at the far end of the room.

"Why Dr. Beerbohm," I murmur, following the man through the revolving turnstile and out the swinging glass door. "Dr. Beerbohm!"

He turns, cocking his head to one side. Looking very tired and very old.

"Doctor, it's me! Sarah Calloway. Frank's friend from Columbia?"

"Good heavens, Miss Calloway is it? Aren't you a long way from home?"

"Yes. Well you see, I'm out here working on a story and thought I'd look up Frank while I'm here."

"How is he?" we inquire of one another at precisely the same moment in time.

"You don't stay in touch?" I ask, my brief spot of hope quickly undone.

"I'm afraid we've both been much too busy to keep up the contact, Sarah."

"Frank doesn't work here in Monterey?"

The doctor pauses, pulling at the loose skin under his chin. "I'm not the person you should be querying about this matter, my dear. The head office should be able to help you out much better than I. Do pass my regards on to Frank when you see him. It's been much too long."

"And how are your beta interferon trials coming along?" I ask, putting a temporary halt to his retreat.

"As well as can be expected," he answers. Registering mild surprise at my question.

"And your wife? I trust she's well?"

Another pause. "Edith died of cancer last year, Sarah."

"Doctor, I'm so sorry to hear that! She was a very special lady, Mrs. Beerbohm," I add lamely.

"That she was," he murmurs, tugging at the sagging pouch and smiling vaguely at something above my head. "Now I'm afraid I really must be on my way."

"Dr. Beerbohm!" I call after the slowly retreating figure. "I don't mean to keep you. But would you happen to know of a young woman who joined Frank's team a few years back? This was back at Columbia . . . ?"

"You're speaking of Dr. Schoenberg, of course. A fine young lady, Laurie Schoenberg. Even a finer geneticist.

One of the best. It was a real loss to genetics when she dropped out of the field."

"You mean she's no longer working for Frank?"

"She apparently came out here with such intentions, but . . ." He shakes his head. "I've always wondered what happened there."

"Is she still with Genco? Or did she join some other lab?"

"She left the field entirely, Sarah. Last I heard, she was working in some cafe up in San Francisco, if you can imagine. Such a tragic waste of talent," he adds, as if to himself. And with a final nod, he continues on his despondent way down the hall.

A cafe in San Francisco? This last bit of information triggers off tiny implosions inside my head. To think that Jennifer, Angelica, Laurie, and I—all with our respective and varying connections with the missing leading man— have landed in the same crazy city. San Francisco as the swirling vortex and core of a particular network of relationships, in a particular space of time.

The significance of such a coincidence lessens somewhat, when I stop to consider the hordes of Americans who have been making their way out here to California in recent years. But nonetheless . . .

By the time I return to the cafeteria, the line has doubled in size. My appetite has dwindled proportionally. Besides, it's a perfectly lovely day out. So why waste my spare time in some corporate dining hall slurping up canned chicken-noodle soup?

Heading out the front door, I am obliged to pass tent city again, as it stands between myself and the car. The same three men are playing cards. While a fourth is hanging up wet laundry on a makeshift clothes line. And a fifth is rubbing tanning oil onto his slim, lovely limbs, looking about as sick as Robert Redford in the *Electric Horseman*. Which is to say, not too sick at all. All these handsome young men going gay on us. It's a crying shame.

The young man with the baseball cap gives me another wave, beckoning me over to the group. I stop, waffling in tentativeness.

"Come on, Beautiful. We're in dire need for a fourth for bridge," he calls out cheerfully. Quite as if I were some long-time buddy of theirs from down the street.

"How did you know I play bridge?" I ask, walking up to the edge of their blanket and smiling down at the three of them. What a motley crew.

"It's all in the walk," he says, pushing the extra hand my way. "That air of purposeful decisiveness we bridge players carry around with us."

"So if I'm so decisively purposeful—"

"Purposefully decisive."

"Purposefully decisive, why would I have anything to do with this silly game in the first place," I point out. Settling down on the blanket and taking a look at my hand, I spot three aces off the bat.

"Your bid."

And I bid, never having been one to pass up a decent bridge game when it comes my way. Which—in this age of video, Trivial Pursuits, and VCR—it rarely does. In fact, my last good game was back in Detroit with Mom, Gran, and Aunt Gracie this past New Year's Eve. The four of us pulling off a glorious all-nighter on popcorn, sherry, and keen-edged, competitive play. One of the real highlights of 1984. Which might say something about the level of our game. Or might say something about the level of my year.

After the first hand or two, introductions are made. My partner, the impish Joel Grey look-alike who cajoled me over here in the first place, is Gary. Philip, your basic blue-eyed skeleton, is to my left. He doesn't look as if he's going to make it through another day. And François. With an accent that sounds as delicious as his name.

I can't bring myself to ask any of the questions on the tip of my tongue. Oddly enough, they don't ask me questions either. As if fourths for their little bridge parties drop out of the sky every day of the week. Well for all I know, maybe they do. Media hounds such as myself who can't get through Genco's first layer of defense and wind up at Camp Desperate, feeling as discombobulated and perturbed as I'm beginning to feel at this particular moment on this unusually bright and beautiful California day.

Are all these young men dying? Every last one of them? They certainly don't act like they're dying, what with the fast-paced amusing patter they maintain through hand after hand. But as one hour stretches into two, I begin to pick up the tell-tale slips. The mention of a mutual friend, followed up with a weighted pause or exchange of looks. The reference to some future plan, quickly negated by a bitter laugh or a wan, devastating smile.

Strange how the essential tragedy of AIDS has never come home to me until this very moment. The arbitrary cruelty and inevitability of the disease. All these men, in the prime of their life, falling victim to an alien virus which neither they, nor anyone else, really know a damn thing about. Neither where it came from nor where it's going. Nor how to stop its deadly parade.

But that's not exactly true, is it? There are ways to stop its deadly parade. Presuming that one has not yet been infected. There's condoms, for one. And celibacy, for another. All the same, the disease pounds away at the very heart of an entire way of life. How would *I* feel, realizing I could never make love again for the rest of my life, without the specter of death sitting by the bedside, coloring and anesthetizing every ounce of desire and joy into a pervasive dread.

Suddenly, it's ten to four. "Got to go," I tell them, before another hand is dealt. "Have an interview at four."

"Inside?" Philips asks. As if 'inside' were the inner sanctum of some sacred temple where the answers to all of life's problems were benevolently bestowed.

"Could you do us a favor, love?" Gary asks quietly, his eyes on Philip's face. "And ask them when those damn vaccine trials are going to begin."

"Of course," I murmur after a flustered pause. Still amazed these young men could be hanging onto such a thin thread of hope. But then again, if that's all there is between life and death, what other choice does one have? Taking my leave, the image of that dancing clown flashes before my eyes.

When I arrive back at the personnel office, it is not Dr. Fawley who awaits me there but Dr. Bukowski. The gentleman I spoke to on the phone. The man is a great deal younger than I would have guessed from his gravelly voice over the wires. And wreaking of an antiquated aftershave— English Leather perhaps? Shades of Tommy Winters and Bloomsdale High.

He informs me that Dr. Fawley will be indisposed until tomorrow morning at ten, due to unforseen developments in the laboratories while he was away.

"You surely understand how these things are, Mrs. Winslow. From the contact you had with your husband's work. Time is money. Especially when dealing with such intricate, potentially ground-breaking research as we are at the moment."

"On the contrary, Doctor. Frank led me to believe a high school graduate could do the work of the men and women in your labs. And as for this myth of ground-breaking potential. It still has to be shown, has it not? And speaking of my husband . . ."

"I have no information on his whereabouts, Mrs. Winslow. I told you that over the phone."

"But this Dr. Fawley does?" He nods. "So why couldn't Dr. Fawley have relayed the information to you, and you to me? I'm asking a simple question here. Where is my husband? And no one—*no one*—seems willing to tell me where he is. What is it? What are you hiding?"

"My good woman. What makes you think we're hiding a thing? It's simply that I am not informed of your husband's present position while Dr. Fawley is."

"And why couldn't you have passed the information on to me?" I demand heatedly. I'm definitely losing my cool here. Something the real Jennifer Winslow would never do.

"We have certain policies here, Mrs. Winslow. Which it might be difficult for outsiders to understand. It's a matter of routine procedure to isolate certain projects from one another. And even from the world at large. For security's sake, you understand."

"Whose security?"

"The company's. And the country, I might add."

"The country?"

"That's correct. Don't think for a minute that the high-tech industry in Silicon Valley is the only target of Soviet infiltration these last few years. Our genetic engineering firms are under siege, Mrs. Winslow. Under siege. This isn't common knowledge. And I depend on you to handle the information with discretion. But we are fairly certain of the presence of an extensive network of Soviet spies working to get inside the industry. Which forces us to maintain a very cautious and confidential approach to our work here. I'm sure you understand."

"Let me get this straight. You're telling me that because of alleged Russian spies running rampant in your laboratories, you can't tell me where my husband is? Is that what you're telling me?!"

"Not at all, Mrs. Winslow. I'm simply trying to explain why Dr. Fawley might have access to information which I do not. And why he might be reluctant to pass that information on. Do you understand?"

"What other choice do I have. How can I even be sure Dr. Fawley will see me tomorrow?"

"Trust me, Mrs. Winslow. He'll be there. We wouldn't think of asking you to come back here if we weren't planning on keeping our part of the bargain. Until tomorrow then?" And with a syrupy, ingratiating smile, he ushers me out the door.

Too late, I remember the forgotten question concerning trials of the vaccine. And to avoid the agitated, questioning looks of my bridge playing friends, I skirt around the back of the building to my car.

The idea of wasting another day—or more specifically, another night—in this town, is less than a pleasant one. To be holed up in some strange motel room all night long, with my omnipresent tail lurking behind every shuttered window and blind. But then again, it's become fairly obvious that my bodily harm is not what they are after. At least, not yet. What they are after, only time will tell.

"No Vacancy" signs flash from every motel I pass. After considerable inquiry, I dig up a room in a trailer-like travel lodge in the very center of the city. A tacky enclave in the middle of yuppie heaven. It makes me feel right at home.

After a quick shower I place a call to Stanley at Verdi's. Exactly where I guessed he would be at this time of day. I ask him to keep a watch on Amy's place, and after reluctantly hanging up hop back in the Datsun for an early evening tour of Carmel, just a few miles south of town. The place has little of the quaint charm I had been led to expect. Too overrun with gift shops and super chic boutiques to carry it off. I find myself oddly nostalgic for the arid desolation of Colston. And the greasy down-homeness of May's.

In order to get matters back on a more even keel, I stop at the first bookstore in my path for another Maigret, then wend my way back to Monterey and a seaside restaurant called the Itinerant Pelican, recommended by the elderly innkeeper's wife. Settling on their open-air deck in back, I linger over a half carafe of the house red while the evening sky transmogrifies itself from blue to pink to orange to purple to velvety inkwell black. The waters change accordingly. And I begin to wonder why it is that the ocean is such an intrinsic aspect of California. Part of one's vision. Part of one's view. While back in Manhattan, I am barely conscious of water being anywhere at all. Even though the city is surrounded by river and ocean on three of its sides. Or is it four?

Cool offshore breezes eventually chase me back indoors where I install myself at a booth in the rear corner of the room.

"Holy shit!"

The voice sends cringes up my shoulder blades. I turn to see Arnold Sax, my favorite Texas theater critic, bounding across the room and coming to rest before my table. Grinning down at me from his muscle-bound tower high above. A friendly paw is waved in my face, giving me little alternative than to give it a tepid shake.

"What brings you to these parts, Ma'am? Catching another play?"

"What are you doing here?" I ask in return.

"Killing time. The rig's in repairs. They put us on comp. Figured it was a good a time as any to get to know the territory, right?"

"Rig?"

"Oil," he tells me, pumping his arm up and down. "Off Santa Barbara. You wouldn't be looking for a little company, would you?"

"Actually, Arnold. I was just about to call it a night."

"Aw come on, Ma'am. You can't be as anti-social as all that. Just a few minutes company?" he barters, meanwhile helping himself to a seat at my table. "Some frigging coincidence, right? The two of us running into each other like this, two times in a single week."

Wrong, a voice inside me speculates. Maybe not so coincidental, at all.

When the young waitress approaches, Arnold orders a half pounder all dressed and three glasses of milk. I succumb to the circumstances, ordering some soup and salad, and another half carafe of the house wine. Arnold proceeds to fill me in on a play-in-progress he is working on, while I nibble away at a complementary bowl of tortilla chips and ponder on the antic incongruity of some struggling playwright striving toward fruition inside the frame of this Nordic Gunga Din.

"It all takes place inside this laundry mat, see? Laundry mat as the universal symbol of the human condition."

"A laundry mat?"

"Yeah sure. Think about it. Like, all these frigging machines are on the frigging blink, see? Washers flooding the floor. Dryers that don't even spin or get warm. Change machines with no change. Soap machines with only bleach in them. Who ever uses bleach in a laundry mat? Get the picture? And then there's these three people in there doing their laundry, see? Representing, you know, the different parts of society. Three suckers whose clothes get shot to hell in that place. But with nobody to complain to about it, see? That's always how it is in those places, right? You never see any of the owners. Never see anybody you can actually bitch to when things start going wrong."

"And that's how you see the world today, is that it?"

"Yeah. Sort of."

"Not bad, Arnold. No really! I kind of like it."

"Yeah? Trouble is, the third act is turning into a real bear.

I want it to end upbeat, natch. You know, for these people to start solving the problems on their own. You know, fixing up the machines themselves. Sharing each other's detergent. Things like that.''

"Sharing the assets. Sounds great! Revolution in the laundry mat. Marxism and the dialectics of cleaning ones clothes.''

"Marxism? There's nothing communist in this. No way! I see it more like getting religion. The whole thing could turn into a goddamn celebration, see? Someone bringing in champagne. The whole bit. Could even have it take place on Christmas Eve. Maybe. Christmas Eve at the Laundry Mat, I could call it. Marxism? No way, man. Shit.''

"Why not just turn it into a single act?'' I suggest. But Arnold doesn't appear to hear me as he breaks ground at the table for the huge platter of food and drink coming our way.

"So what brings you west?'' he asks, after shovelling a good third of the hamburger into his mouth.

"From where?''

"From . . . I don't know. New York, I guess.''

"And what makes you think I'm from New York?''

"That accent, Ma'am. If you don't mind my saying so. A dead ringer. Pegged you from Brooklyn the very first moment you opened your mouth. Possibly a member of the Jewish faith?''

"Presbyterian. Detroit.''

"No shit. Gee, I don't miss much either. So what brings you out here?''

"Visiting a friend. Which is none of your business to begin with, is it?''

"Have it your way, lady,'' he says with a shrug. Popping a couple of french fries into his mouth. "Bet you can't guess what famous personage I saw in a restaurant here today?''

"Jimmy Hoffa.''

"He's dead, man. Come on.''

"Marlene Dietrich? Marilyn Chambers?''

"Come on! I'm serious, man. And he wasn't with his little wifey neither, in case you're interested.''

"Then who, for God's sake.''

"Woody Allen.''

"I don't believe you. He hates California.''

"It was him, alright. Scrawny little bastard, too."

"But Woody Allen isn't even married."

"No? I thought he was shacked up with that skinny, frizzy-haired broad he used to put in all his movies."

"Diane Keaton?" I suggest, my stomach beginning to curdle.

"Yeah, right. The lady he was with today was even skinnier than her. Straight out of Dachau, if you want my opinion. Not hard to figure why he picks such skinny-minnies, though. If they had any more meat of 'em, they'd squash him flat as a pancake. Ha! Ha!"

"Does Woody Allen threaten you, Arnold?"

"Threaten me? What the hell you talking about? That peanut couldn't threaten a mouse."

"But he does threaten you all the same, doesn't he?"

"No way! What put that crazy frigging idea in your head, lady? Ha! I just have a tough time figuring why so many people dig the guy, that's all. He's nothing but a Jewish Mama's Boy. A whiny, circumsised prick."

"What does circumcision have to do with any of this?"

"No reason to get so hot under the collar, lady. Is he your lover boy or something?" Pushing aside his finished plate of food, he draws a packet of photographs from his jacket and tosses them my way. It's Woody Allen, all right. And Mia Farrow. Looking perfectly exquisite. Her long blond hair swept into two braids which crown her lovely head. The two of them are in shot after shot. In bowed conversation over lunch.

"How did you manage to get these?" I ask, well aware of Allen's publicity shy ways.

"I got my methods."

"Like what?"

He digs into another pocket and brings out the tiniest camera I've ever seen. And clicks it in my face.

"Give me that!" I shout, lunging across the table for the camera.

"Jesus, lady. What are you so afraid of. It's only a lousy picture. It ain't going to kill you. Never saw anyone get so uptight over a lousy camera before."

"Yeah, well we all have our quirks, Arnold," I say, shoving away from the table.

"You're splitting? But you didn't even eat yet! Hey, come on, Sarah. I didn't mean nothing by it."

Like hell he didn't, I think darkly. Tearing out the front door. And trying to remember if I have ever mentioned my first name to Arnold before. Possibly during that first night at the theater? Unfortunately, I can't really recall.

Once back in the car, I regret not having confronted Arnold directly. Not that it would have done any good. He would have denied everything, of course. But it might have given me a clearer clue as to his involvement or noninvolvement in the entire affair. A moment ago, I was totally convinced he was one of my elusive tails. I'm no longer so sure. The guy just seems too stupid to be involved in any kind of intelligence work. Too slow. Too dumb. Coming right out and taking my picture like that. It's very difficult to imagine some CIA spook writing moronic plays about getting religion in "laundry mats," that's for damn sure. My rampant paranoia might just be getting the better of me at that.

I can no longer see myself spending the night in some lethally lonely motel room. How I ever considered it as a feasible possibility this afternoon is beyond me. But if not the motel room, then where? Driving past Genco labs, I hear music and see lights emanating from the cluster of tents in the middle of the grounds. And make a split second decision to stop in.

There are a few more campers visible this evening than I took note of earlier in the day. And everyone but Philip and Gary is dancing it up in the middle of the campsite to an old fifties tune—"My Boyfriend's Back." Philip is watching the goings on from the sideline, seated cross-legged with a blanket over his shoulder. And looking no better this evening than he did earlier today. Gary, squatted over a hibachi full of hot dogs, is the first to take notice of my approach, the others being a little too far gone on a pitcher of purple passions making the rounds to be overly concerned with an extraneous person in their midst.

"What's the celebration?" I ask, accepting the glass of vodka and Welch's Gary passes my way.

"Phil's birthday," he murmurs, nodding in the direction

of a large chocolate layer cake there at my feet. "Happy Birthday Tootsie" is written across the fudge icing in green and yellow script. "Any news for us?" he asks offhandedly as he begins to stuff hot dogs into the rolls and line them up on a large piece of cardboard.

"If you mean the trials. I didn't get a chance to bring it up this afternoon. As it turns out, I didn't even have my interview this afternoon. They put me off until tomorrow at ten."

He nods as if he expected as much, passing me along one of the hot dogs before circulating the group with the rest.

"Haven't you asked them yourselves?" I ask, when he returns to throw another batch on the grill.

"Of course. We've tried everything. Even picketing the grounds."

"And?"

"Nada. Kaput. Always the same stinking reply. They can't release any information on the progression of research because it's all classified crap. And even if trials were to start tomorrow, we wouldn't automatically be participants. That isn't the way they choose them. Et cetera. Et cetera. Shit piled on more shit. So high."

"What do they think of you guys camping out here?"

"What do you think they think?"

"So why haven't they kicked you out?"

"They have. But some of us keep coming back." And he gives me that impish grin of his. For someone who most probably is dying of a fatal disease, this fellow sure keeps himself in a positive state of mind. "About a week ago they stopped hassling us. Something's up, maybe. Who knows." He refills my paper cup with some more of the purple Kool-aid, as they call it. Which is exactly what it tastes like. And exactly what it feels like going down.

By the third glass, Gary has me out there dancing my ass off and roaring out the lyrics along with the rest of the crew. It's not a radio, as I had originally presumed, but a tape deck. And one hell of a tape. All the memorable, fadeless, deathless hits of the late fifties and early sixties. The ones us baby-boomers grew up on, went to our first dance on, sweated out our first date on, had our first kiss on, fell in love on, and experienced our first heartbreak on. "Be My Pretty Baby." "Runaway." "I'm Sorry." "Heatwave." "When I Fall in Love." "Do You Want to Dance." "Put Your Head on My Shoulder." "You've Lost That Loving Feeling."

And then it hits me. Somewhere between "I Want to Hold Your Hand," and "The Way You Look Tonight." These couldn't be the songs that this particular group of baby-boomers fell in love on. Or if they did, then it must have been a very confusing and agonizing state of affairs. After all, what must it have been like growing up in the make-believe, "Father Knows Best" atmosphere of the fifties with totally 'unsuitable' homosexual longings in one's gut? It must have been hell, that's what. So how is it they all seem to be getting such a kick out of these songs? Songs that surely resound with the frustration, ambiguity, and pretense of those early years. Not only for these fellows here. But for thousands of other gay men and women in America, who must have grown up feeling a little twisted and out of shape until the maturity of years, and the support of Gay Liberation, began putting things back on track.

That's the real tragedy of all this. Just when 'being gay' had begun to lose its reprobate ring. When men and women by the thousands and from all walks of life—doctors, lawyers, politicians, teachers, celebrities and local librarians—were feeling free to step out and proclaim their gayness with pride and self respect. Along comes AIDS. And the attendant AIDS paranoia. Pushing everyone right back into their closets once again. A very tragic turn of events for us all.

The cake, with its 36 candles melting into the frosting, is finally brought into the proceedings. Philip stands in the middle of the circle, eyes closed as he works out a wish. And then, with a little help from his friends, all the candles get blown out on the very first try. Dear Philip, will your wish come true?

Gargantuan slices are meted out and more dancing ensues. For another hour or so. Until around one a.m., when the party begins to break up. Finally Gary, François, and I are the only ones still up. As I huddle up to the hibachi for a little reflective warmth, Gary and François do "The Stroll" up and down the middle of the camp.

"You fellows mind if I stay here for the night?" I ask Gary when he comes over to douse the coals from the grill.

"You serious?"

"It's like this, Gary. I don't really want to be alone tonight. See I . . . This is going to sound crazy. But I think someone may be following me. It's been like this ever since I got started on this story."

"Tell all!" he encourages me, settling us down on the blanket in front of his tent. The guy is obviously intrigued. So I tell my entire tale, adding a few embellishments here and there for the sake of my attentive audience.

"I knew something was up!" he exclaims excitedly, bouncing to his feet and pacing circles around me. "Knew it. Knew it. Knew it."

"Why?"

"Because we've been bugging the heck out of these guys, that's why. Trespassing on private lands. Heckling workers. Making general pain-in-the-asses out of ourselves. Practically begging on hand and knee to be dragged off to jail. But as often as their security guards have herded us off the property, nobody's ever been sent over to arrest us. Ask me why."

"Why?"

"Why? Because they don't want the publicity, that's why. Ask me why they don't want the publicity."

"Why don't they want the publicity?"

"You know what I think? I think this buddy of yours has absconded with the family jewels. Taken off with the formula for the vaccine! And now they're trying to get it back!"

"But you don't understand how these things work, Gary," I say, grinning at the young man's breakneck, total involvement in the case. "Frank had a whole team of lab assistants working with him. He wouldn't be the only one to know how to put this thing together. Not by a long shot. And even if he was, why the hell would he run off with the information? Doesn't make any sense. Developing the AIDS vaccine is going to make him a very famous man."

"Maybe he's selling it to the highest bidder."

I laugh. "It just doesn't work that way, Gary."

"Why not? Just leave it to me. I'll figure this thing out," he says, spreading out a couple of extra blankets on the other side of his tent. My intended bed?

"Okay if I sleep out here?" I suggest, indicating the space right in front of the door.

"Yeah. Yeah, sure," he murmurs, the shutters suddenly coming down, sardonic glaze over the eyes and cool indifference in the voice.

"It's not what you're thinking, Gary. Really. I just can't stand sleeping in tents. Never could. Too stuffy and claustrophobic, I guess. Need the stars overhead."

"Sure," he murmurs again. Tossing the two blankets out of the tent and letting down the flap.

"Goodnight, Gary," I say brightly, after lining up the blankets and crawling in. Silence is my only response.

Sleep refuses to come as I toss and turn for what seems to be hours, amidst a shitload of my own scruples and regrets. Thinking about Frank. Thinking about Stanley. Thinking about Philip. Thinking about Gary and my own hesitation to sleep in his tent tonight. And cursing the hell out of my stupid thoughtlessness in opting for the open air. If I didn't have so much damn pride, I'd crawl back in there this very minute. Give the man a grateful hug for offering me safe harbor through unsafe times. And fall asleep by his side. But I do have too much damn pride, and never make a move, drifting instead, in and out of a fitful sleep on the cold hard ground. Under cold hard stars overhead.

JUNE 22

I'm up early. The air crisp and delicious. The ground digs into my shoulder blades as I watch the last of the morning stars fade away in the early light. Someone else is up as well. Philip. I can tell by the old-mannish way he drags himself around the camp. Lighting up coals in the hibachi and putting a pot of water on to boil. The smell of fresh brewing coffee brings me out of my cocoon.

As the two of us sip on our coffee, I bring up a subject or two for conversation. But he seems to prefer his silence. Cross-legged and shivering inside his blanket like the night before. "Guess I better be heading on," I finally say, after folding up the two blankets and leaving them in front of Gary's tent. "Say good bye to the others for me. I'll be back if I get any news," I add, nodding in the direction of one of Genco's labs.

Philip nods blankly and turns away. What happened to all that naive optimism of the day before? Or did he have such a bad night last night, that nothing seems to matter anymore? Even a few magic words about imminent trials of a magic vaccine.

I'm not the slightest bit hungry; my digestive system is still working on last night's hot dogs and hunk of dense, double fudge chocolate cake. So I opt for a visit to Carmel's one Spanish mission, which looked so intriguing when I chanced by it yesterday afternoon. Apparently I am a few minutes early. But one of the gardeners out front is kind enough to let me in, all the same.

Being their first visitor of the day, I am afforded the full benefit of the mission's cool, tranquil setting. A timeless, landscaped courtyard surrounded on three sides by a wooden veranda and white adobe walls. The kind of out-moded enclave of spiritual resonance a lot of us would still love to call home. After a tour of the gardens, I head inside. Past the dining room and reception area to the small bedroom where Junipero Serra, the mission's founder, apparently passed long stretches of his time, year after year. Reading. Writing. Meditating. And sleeping. Which is about all you could do in this tiny cell of a room. It's the real thing, alright. No doubt about it. The narrow, hard looking bed. The single desk and straightbacked chair. The pen and paper. Two or three books. And nothing more. No fri-volous diversions. Not even a picture on the wall to

distract the man from his singular goal of inner spiritual
resolve.

I suddenly panic, as if I were in the inside looking out,
rather than the outside looking in, and I return to the
veranda out back. How long do I stand there, gazing at the
sculptured water fountain in the center of the yard, before
the vision materializes before my eyes? The fountain is
supplanted by two figures in long grey robes, books in hand
and bowed in conversation, as they stroll leisurely across
the flagstone walk.

I blink, and it's gone. Both the vision and the overwhelming smell of freshly harvested corn which accompanied it.
The fountain back where it belongs. But what am I to make
of it? I saw those two monks! I would stake my life on it.
Walking across the center of this square.

What the hell is happening here? In 35 years of an
essentially predictable existence, I have never once been
visited by anything of even a remotely paranormal cast. No
flashes of ESP. No mind blowing coincidences. No so-
called 'out of the body' experiences such as a few of my
friends have owned up to in recent years. No ghosts or
clairvoyant dreams. Until these last few days, that is. When
suddenly I begin to sense a crack in the cosmic egg. Or is
the crack in me? Am I the one who is slowly breaking apart?

There are footsteps behind me. Muffled and discreet. I
turn, locked in place by a strong sense of aura. Of a
presence which just streaked back around the corner of the
adobe wall.

"Arnold?" I call out warily. Two healthy looking
grandmother-types, with walking sticks and guide books in
hand, appear around the corner and smile questionably in
my direction.

"Did either of you happen to see anyone—a man—just
run through that door?"

"Why yes," the taller of the two replies. Looking back
over her shoulder. "Surely you can catch him, dear. If you
hurry right along."

"A large, muscular man with blond hair?"

"Why no. He was quite a slender young man. Wasn't he,
Dorothy?"

I do not wait around for the other woman's response before dashing past them and back through the mission's interior, to the parking lot out front. Just in time to see a canary yellow sports car screech off the gravel driveway and onto the road leading to Highway 101.

When I arrive at Personnel, the receptionist directs me to Dr. Fawley's office in Building C. The doctor's premises seem cramped and disheveled. On the order of my apartment back in New York. Dr. Fawley is a bit on the disheveled side himself. A harried, likeable looking, middle-aged man with an over-the-belt paunch that sits awkwardly on his otherwise tall and slender frame.

"Why the masquerade?" he demands, after settling me down in a chair by his desk.

"What do you mean?"

"Who are you?"

"Who am—? I'm Jennifer Winslow. Dr. Winslow's ex-wife. I assumed they already told you. You see, I ha—"

"Cut the crap. You're not Mrs. Winslow. So who are you?" Every question couched in the same calm, mildly curious tone of voice.

"How do you know I'm not Jennifer?" I ask stupidly.

He smiles. "We have our ways. That's rather serious business, my friend. False representation and impersonation is fraud. A criminal offense. We could prosecute if we were so inclined . . . What are you up to here?"

"The truth. That's all I want, Dr. Fawley," I say, squirming in my seat as I struggle to recover a little of my sangfroid. "Where is Dr. Winslow? How can I get in touch with him? That's all I want to know."

"And you're ready to tell me who you are?"

"Sarah Calloway. Free lance writer out of New York."

"And what is your interest in Dr. Winslow?"

"He's an old friend, for one thing. For another, I had hoped to get a story together on his work with the AIDS vaccine."

The doctor smiles, blinking lazily as he shakes his head. "And who were you going to be writing this story of yours for, if I may inquire?"

"*New York Magazine*."

"I see. Well it would have been worth your while, Mrs. Calloway—"

"*Miss* Calloway."

"Miss Calloway, and that of your magazine, to contact us before coming out here. All representatives of the press have been temporarily barred from our AIDS research project. What our team needs right now is time. And *not* a rash of sensationalist articles aimed at misleading the public as to the nature and potential of an as yet unrefined vaccine."

"But at the very least, you can tell me where Dr. Winslow may be located? I need to talk to him. It won't involve any story. I give you my word on that." He only smiles. "Doctor. The real Mrs. Winslow doesn't even know where Frank is. Now why is that? And neither does his son. They're very concerned. As a matter of fact, so am I."

He takes a deep breath. Exhales. And I brace myself for another commie spy routine. "We have no information on Dr. Winslow's whereabouts," he tells me quietly. "He left the firm in May, and we haven't heard word from him since. For P.R. purposes, we've kept his departure under wraps until now."

"I don't believe you."

"That, my dear woman, is your problem. Not mine," he says, eyes narrowing as he moves to usher me out of my chair. I stay put.

"Why on earth would Frank desert a project he was directing? And one on which he was making so much progress, to boot? What could possibly have made him do such a thing?"

"There had been some long-standing differences of view within the team. Concerning certain scientific procedures. Testing approaches . . ."

"Between who?"

"Particularly between Dr. Winslow and his chief lab assistant."

"So why didn't the *assistant* leave?"

"This is all off the record, Miss Calloway. You understand? It was Dr. Winslow's decision. We had nothing to say about it. We were very sorry to see him go, of course. But I'm obliged to add that the project is running much smoother since his departure. Dissension is not always a productive ingredient in these matters. Come back in three or four months. Then you might have yourself a real story. And a real vaccine.''

I leave Dr. Fawley's office a mass of befuddled agitation. And a rather deflated mass, at that. The doctor came off sounding so forthright. So basically sincere. Is it conceivable that the man was being straight with me? That Frank has in fact taken off for parts unknown, like the doctor said? Dissension was certainly a common enough element in Frank's laboratories. At least back at Columbia, where he was such a dominating bastard. Always determined to run the entire show. But to leave a project of such phenomenal importance? To hand over his fame and fortune to some assistant in his lab because they couldn't come to terms on how to work together? No way. Frank would never have been the one to leave. Never. At least not the Frank I once knew. So persistent and driven. So obsessed.

But then there's the melancholy tone of those recent letters to be taken into account. And his mention of a trip. For all I know, the Frank Winslow of today bears little resemblance to the Frank Winslow of yesteryear. Time, stress, and pressure having wrought a changed, mutated man.

Though none of this would explain who the hell is busy tampering with my phone.

Camp Desperate is deserted. The fellows must be out for lunch. I leave a note in Gary's tent:

Four months, so they say. But I don't trust this place. Which means I'll probably be back. Forgive me. And thanks for the bed and company last night. You'll all be in my nightly prayers.

Sarah C.

Back on Highway 101, my dismal meanderings on the relative failure of clarification down at Genco labs, are cut short by the sight of the bright yellow sports car in my rear view mirror. I panic. And begin weaving in and out of expressway traffic, nearly sideswiping a dilapidated VW van in the process. The yellow coupe swings into the adjacent lane, its driver honking angrily it would seem, and fluttering something out the open window. I take a quick and cringing peek, ready to see some gun pointed at me, shades of *Easy Rider,* modern day Manhattan, and one crazy week in time. And can't quite believe my eyes when I see Frank! Waving madly and shouting something across the lane of traffic. Looking a bit weary for wear, what with the scruffy beard and all. And a bit on the desperate side, perhaps. But Frank, all the same. Handsome and whole.

The next thing I'm aware of is a sickening crunch, as I jerk forward in my seat belt, my head hitting the steering wheel and whipping back against the seat. I have just rear-ended a sleek, grey-toned Rolls Royce.

"Thank God you could come!" are the first words out of my mouth as I spring out of the back seat of the police car and up to where Stanley stands, by his friend's jalopy Chevrolet. I wave back to the two coppers and crawl into the car. "Let's get out of here, Stanley," I hiss. Trying to jar him out of his catatonic trance. Must be all those flashing red lights.

"What the hell happened?" he finally asks me once we are safely on our way.

"Frank! I mean, Stanley! Stanley, I just saw Frank! Can you believe it? He rode right up alongside me on the highway. Probably has been following me around for some time."

"And you're all in one piece?" he asks, testing out the bump on my forehead. Which is already beginning to turn a smarmy yellow-grey.

"Except for this. And my neck. Otherwise, I came out okay. The car, less okay."

"Where *is* the car?"

"They towed it away."

"Jesus."

"Wouldn't start. Water dripping out of the radiator. The

whole bit. At least it's insured. . . . But can you beat that, Stanley? How did Frank know how to find me? And why couldn't he have approached me right out in the open instead of on the highway like that? Why is he even trying to get in touch?"

"Where is he now?"

"God only knows. The police were swarming all over the place as soon as the accident occurred. You should have seen the mess I made out of the expressway back there. Traffic was backed up for miles. It was awful. All these people creeping by and rubbernecking me in the back seat of that police car. Felt like I was in jail. Like I was some kind of criminal or something. No kidding. And that was exactly how the police treated me, by the way. Checking my license through their damn computer. Asking me all sorts of weird questions. I bumped into some hot shot out of Sacramento, if you can believe it. A Senator Wellington? His car hardly got a scratch . . ." Stanley's expression remains as stony as ever. "Stanley, you don't seem to be taking in the import of what I just told you back there. Frank tried to make contact with me! Now why?"

"And I don't think you're taking in the seriousness of what just happened on the highway back there, Sarah. You could have been murdered, for God's sake. And taken a couple of other innocent people along with you."

"Murdered? What do you mean murdered? No one was bumping me off, Stanley. I bumped into somebody else. *I* caused the accident. It was just the shock of it all, you know? Suddenly seeing Frank like that. After all these days of tracking him down."

"Had dinner yet?" are the next words out of my mouth, some two hours down the road, just as Stanley swings the car into a rare empty parking space in front of the apartment. I'm ravenous. Also sweaty, gritty, and a wee bit unhinged.

"When could I have eaten?" he asks, clinching me with that same stony stare.

"Okay. So how about some fat, juicy hamburgers? And a couple of stiff drinks?" I suggest, having delayed fantasies about that half-pounder Arnold wolfed down the other night. Not the other night. *Last* night, I remind myself, startled by the way time has begun to warp and telescope these last few days. Yesterday feeling like last week. Last week, like last month. And last month like a lifetime ago.

The moment we step into Amy's front hall, a disgusting, hauntingly familiar odor stops me in my tracks. "Stanley," I whisper, motioning him silent. And then dragging him back into the corridor. "That god-awful smell! You noticed it? Stale cigar smoke, right? The exact same smell that was in my motel room after the break-in. I'm positive of it!"

"What your finely tuned olfactory nerves have detected, Miss Drew," Stanley drawls, prodding me back into the apartment, "is a rare, five star handrolled cigar." And he walks over to the stereo to present me with a large, partially smoked sample.

"Since when do you smoke cigars?"

"Whenever George gets a new shipment of these babies in."

"Jesus, Stanley. The average cigar smells bad enough. But these things are the absolute pits."

"Twenty-five dollar Cuban plums you're slandering, sweetheart," he informs me, drawing the putrid item under my nose. I push it away and make the rounds of the apartment. Opening up every window I pass. Then take a much needed shower and shampoo.

Over a late night dinner at Bruno's down on Mission street, we cool down and mellow out over scotch and soda. Finally getting back in touch. I tell Stanley about Arnold. Genco. And Frank. And we come to the same inevitable conclusions about this affair. One: Frank, for some as yet unclarified reason, is trying to make contact with me. Two: It is for this reason that I am being tailed all about. I'm a possible link-up. Through me, someone out there hopes to hunt down Frank.

But how Frank came to know I was on his trail is another question entirely. He is obviously well aware that someone is on mine. Which would explain the oblique approach he's taking in trying to reconnect.

By the time the two of us finally hit the sack, it is well past one a.m. I'm exhausted. But once again, I have trouble falling asleep. Leery voices mentally pacing the floor by the bedside. It is the cigar smoke that rankles, of course. The fact that my Colston burglar and dearest Stanley happen to have gotten their hands on the same foul smelling Cuban cigar. I dig back furiously to that first day here in San Francisco. That Sunday afternoon when I headed down to North Beach in quest of a late lunch.

Is it possible that Stanley followed me into the restaurant that Sunday afternoon? With the intention of picking me up as he did? Is it in fact possible that he followed me all the way back from Colston on that Saturday night? . . . . But such a theory is patently absurd. The man's a renowned journalist, for god's sake. And Verdi's is his regular hang out every night of the week. In fact, I was the one to come back to Verdi's the following evening looking for him. Not the other way around. So how could he be anymore than what he seems to be? An intimate stranger with whom I'm beginning to fall in love.

That much resolved, I force my body against Stanley's warm back. Oddly enough, once in visceral contact with the man, all the tiny pin-pricks of doubt melt away. The basic comfort of flesh on flesh cut through all the paranoia to a simple truth on the other side. In a matter of seconds, I fall into a deep and grateful sleep.

JUNE 23

Once Stanley is out the door, I pour myself a third cup of coffee and mull over the situation at hand. As much as I would like to consider myself a self-activating entity in this affair, with every passing day I become more convinced that I, and everyone else involved, including Jennifer, Angelica, Stanley, and Frank, are nothing more than pawns to some grander design. Some immutable game plan which got set in motion over five years ago, when I first set eyes on Dr. Frank Winslow in that damp and crowded university hall.

The kitty crawls out of her hole, meowing plaintively for breakfast. With Stanley now sharing the bed on a regular basis, I've lost my furry midnight visitor. In fact, I rarely see her at all anymore. Except when she's hungry. And even then, only after Stanley has left the house. I fill up her bowl, pile dirty dishes into the sink, and head out into still another foggy San Francisco morning to scout out still another of Frank's erstwhile woman friends.

Like Angelica before her, Laurie is not listed in the directory. Which leaves me little alternative than to trust Dr. Beerbohm's information implicitly, making an exhaustive survey of every cafe in town. Going on percentages, North Beach is the first neighborhood on my list. But some 20 cafes and two cappuccinos later, I am no closer to the woman than when I first got out of bed. I move on to the upper Polk. Then over to the elegant Nob Hill. (Snob Hill, I see scribbled across an alley wall). Across the city to the yuppie-chic waters of the Marina. And then down to the post-hippie déja vu of the Haight. By three o'clock, my nerves jangle on an excess of caffeine and the feet point homeward. Toward the usual soothing antidotes. But I resist, opting for one last shot in the Mission district, a neighborhood which, in spite of its occasional grubbiness and grime, is becoming my favorite part of the city. San Francisco's black sheep.

The Clarion is the first cafe I stop in. Then Picaro's and Gitanes. The Artemis. Nipal. And finally, on the unlikely corner of Mission and 24th, La Boheme. I ask my timeworn question of a mohawked free spirit who works the expresso machine up front.

"Hey Shoo!" he yells over the back counter. "You got company."

In seconds, a young woman, tall and slender, with straight, almost waist length blond hair, steps out and gazes hesitantly about.

"Laurie? Laurie Schoenberg?"

"Yes?"

"You once worked with a Dr. Frank Winslow, is that correct?"

She doesn't respond immediately, folding her arms against her chest and giving me and the purple golf ball on my forehead a quizzical squint. "Who are you?" she asks.

"Sarah Calloway. An old friend of Frank's. I was hoping you might be able to help me track him down."

"He's working down at Genco Labs. In Monterey."

"According to the people down there he left the firm a few months back."

"Shoo!" her co-worker calls out again, snapping a couple of sandwich orders onto the lazy susan over her head. She edges back behind the counter, tossing a couple of slices of rye into the toaster.

"When's the last time you saw Frank?" I ask.

"A year and a half, two years ago. He left Genco Labs? I can't understand that. His work there was so important to him."

"Shoo!"

"Could we talk privately, Laurie? Maybe later tonight?"

"I just came on shift."

"Tomorrow morning, then? Say around ten? I could meet you right back here, if that's what is most convenient for you."

"Okay," she agrees, smiling briefly in my direction before sliding back behind the counter. Where in hell does Frank dig up all these gorgeous females, I ask myself in disgruntled wonder, giving her a final salute before heading out the cafe door.

By the time I hear Stanley's key playing in the lock, I am blissfully submerged in that bath I had promised myself and deep into the Maigret picked up in Monterey.

"Howdy!" he greets me, sticking his head into the room and giving me his own particular version of a salacious wink. He ducks back, presumably to change into that old sweater of his, pour himself a scotch, and relax before the MacNeil/Lehrer evening news. Our short life together has already settled into a most satisfactory routine.

"You have more goddamn cafes in this city of yours, Stanley!" I call out through the open door.

"Which is precisely the charm of this place," he tells me, stepping back into the room minus his trench coat and

shoes. "The only city in America where the art of leisure
and conversation still count for something."

"Maybe. But there's a decadent side to it, all the same.
Never in all my life have I seen so many grown-up people
sitting around doing nothing! How are all these *artistes*
making a living? That's what I'd like to know."

"I hear New York talking."

"Ha! Could be. Alright, so one thing I'll admit. Which is
that I'm going to miss all these lovely cafes when I'm gone.
I'd quite forgotten what a simple pleasure it is, lingering en
masse over cups of caffeine. What do you think you're
doing, Stanley? Stanley!"

"Are cafes the only thing you're going to miss, sweetheart?" Stanley croons, stepping over me and into the tub.

"There's not enough room for the two of us in this
thing," I protest. But as matters develop, there is more than
enough room, after all.

After our bath, Stanley informs me he has an appointment tonight. A rendezvous with a couple of reading
experts in Menlo Park, to discuss the growing literacy
problem here at home. I wish I believed the man 100%
about these kinds of evening activities. But I don't. There's
still that irritating smidgeon of doubt. The situation is
becoming ludicrous to the extreme. If I'm not suspecting
the man of spying on me, then I'm suspecting him of two-
timing me. Which just goes to show how unstable my sense
of self has become.

After Stanley heads out the door, the apartment changes
color. From a pleasing yellow-orange to a threatening
purple-gray. It's the first time I've been in this place after
dark and alone since the phone was tapped. And for some
dumb reason I can't stop looking at the damn thing, sitting
there on the end table and sending me out its malicious
vibes. I can't use it, either. For the same reason. Which
means putting off contact with Jennifer until tomorrow
afternoon.

After watching a re-re-rerun of *Mash*, which still beats
most other stuff on the set, I start wandering about the
apartment in hopes of smoking out my elusive cat. A map of
San Francisco sits on the breakfast table. The map I carried

around with me all day long. I open it up, curious to check
out the mileage I covered today. And a piece of paper
flutters out of the folds and down to the floor. I pick it up
and read:

Sarah:
  Meet me at Caesar's Palace. 8 p.m. Get out on the
  dance floor and show no sign of recognition when we
  meet.

Frank

I stare at the words swimming before me. Stunned and
baffled as to when he possibly could have slipped the paper
into this map without my being aware? On one of the
occasions I stopped off for a cappuccino and the use of a
cafe's restroom? Those being the only times I can remember
leaving anything unattended throughout the day.

It's already 7:45, I realize frantically. And where the hell
is Caesar's Palace? I throw on one of Amy's silk blouses and
flowered skirts, dig into Stanley's other pair of pants for a
few extra bills, and tear out of the apartment, flagging down
the first free cab that comes my way. Enroute to this
Caesar's Palace, located back in the Mission district
according to my driver, a hundred different questions
bombard my frazzled state of mind. What made me walk
over to that map as I did this evening, and open it up? How
close did I come to never receiving Frank's message at all?
Am I being tailed down to this club? More than likely. Is
Frank being tailed down, as well? How does he plan to
make contact tonight without being discovered? And what
on earth does he have to say?

It seems to take forever for the cab to reach our
destination, and it is well past 8:30 when I finally make my
entrance into the loud and crowded hall. Now what? I ask
myself, suddenly feeling a thousand predatory eyes upon
me. As any woman stupid enough to walk into this place by
herself would feel. I head straight for the long bar which
borders on one side of the room, settling on a stool at one
end and ordering myself a glass of wine. Then two. And
finally three, without one of the million and one stag males

milling around this place bothering to ask me to dance. Where are the predatory eyes when you need them? I am finally reduced to carrying on an outrageous flirtation with a short stocky latino gentleman across the way. In a few moments, it does the trick. My friend escorting me gallantly to the floor and his blood-shot cocker spaniel eyes speaking passionate love songs as he propels us around the hyper-animated room.

I am totally inept at following his complicated goose steps all over the goddamn place. But he doesn't seem to mind. Or even notice. His hips sashay effortlessly to the three four salsa beat as he circles around me like some unctious erotic whale. The interminable number finally draws to a finale with no sign whatsoever of Frank. I plead terminal dehydration and return to my bar stool with Jose Greco in my wake. I order another glass of wine. My friend orders nothing, seemingly content just to stand there beside me, smiling his cosmic expectant smile.

"May I feel free to talk freely with you, *señorita*?" he begins, edging closer and playing suggestively with the napkin by my drink. Before he can say another word, I drag him back out on the floor and prance around like a raving lunatic in hopes of forcing Frank to play his hand. And suddenly the heat, light, and wine all blow over me, seeing him weaving through the crowd from a far corner of the room. Arms crossed over his chest. His thin chest, I think automatically, wondering when was the last time the guy had a decent meal.

"Run," he hisses, grabbing me by the elbow and steering us quickly toward an emergency exit at the rear of the room. "Run!" As if I have any choice in the matter, as he yanks me down an alley and into what appears to be an underground garage. Then up a clanging iron fire escape—two flights worth—and out onto a gravelled roof. He leaps a two foot abyss. I hesitate one cowardly moment before following suit. Hopping onto a lower roof and down another fire escape which leads to still another alley below.

I'm hobbling by now, having parted company with the left heel of Amy's sandals on one of those iron steps. Coming out of the alley, we land on a quiet side street. I follow Frank through a narrow hole in broken wooden fence and into the backyard of what appears to be a deserted Victorian. Overgrown dry vines throttle an eerie green fountain in the center of the yard. We scramble under a back porch, a three foot high overhang which stretches back some twenty feet. The air under here reeks of mildew and rancid grease from a Kentucky Fried chicken outlet somewhere down the street.

Pulling a flashlight from a back pocket, Frank leads us, crawling, to a back corner, where we settle on a pile of musty army blankets. This gaunt, wild-eyed creature now before me is hardly the version of Frank Winslow I was expecting to see tonight. Whatever vague dangers I may have been skirting these last few days are obviously puppy play when compared to what he's been going through.

"How did you find me, Frank? How did you even know I've been looking for you?"

"That waitress in Colston," he tells me, still trying to catch his breath. "You've been showing my picture all over the goddamn place, it would seem."

"Yes, but—"

"Listen, Sarah. We've got no time for small talk here. I want you to get a hold of some papers for me. Pass them on to a friend."

"Papers?"

"They think I took them with me. But I left them back in Paradise, Sarah. I need you to go down there and pick them up for me. Pass them on to a Philip Kaufman in New York."

"You mean the guy who wrote that book on Chemix Pharmaceutical. *That* Philip Kaufman? But how—"

"I left the file in my house at Paradise. It's obvious they never found it, or they wouldn't be hunting me down like this," he repeats. For his own benefit, not mine.

"Frank, what papers! What is this all about?"

"I can't explain it all to you now."

"You must tell me something, Frank. I can't stand being in the dark like this any longer!"

"It's a military file, Sarah. June Mail. But the less you know about all this the better off you'll be."

"June Mail?"

"Intelligence term for top secret, eyes only information."

"What kind of information?"

"Military experiments conducted in Haiti a few years back."

"What kind of military experiments? . . . . Frank, I wish you would stop being so goddamn paternalistic about all this. If you want me to help you out on this thing, I need to know what this is all about. I have that right."

"I see you haven't changed any," he says, smiling slightly and touching the bump on my forehead. "Sorry about that mess yesterday. I played it all wrong."

"Frank, tell me!"

He takes in a few deep breaths, sounding hollow inside. And sick. "In 1976 the Defense Department—with the assistance of Chemix Pharmaceutical—set up a covert germ warfare research laboratory in Haiti . . . The result of certain recombinant DNA experiments conducted down there inadvertently spawned the LAV virus. The virus for AIDS."

"The AIDS virus? Let me get this straight. Military genetic research down in Haiti created the virus for AIDS?!" I stare at him a moment, as the gravity of the situation sinks in. "How did you learn about this, Frank?"

He doesn't answer me immediately, rubbing his forehead and looking so totally exhausted that I feel protective toward the man. Something I have never experienced with Frank before. "Kaufman," he finally murmurs. "He came snooping around the premises and we had a couple of talks. . . . Things began to fall into place."

"But how was Kaufman able to guess the AIDS connection?"

"Internal documents his lawyers subpoenaed out of Chemix. He's taking the fuckers to court. Look Sarah, I can't—" And he stops. Listening intently to the sounds of traffic and voices somewhere beyond the yard.

"But why me, Frank?" I whisper. "You know as well as I do that they have me under surveillance. My phone's even been tapped. By whom? The Pentagon? Chemix? How am I ever going to get down to Paradise without someone on my back?"

"I'm coming out of hiding, Sarah. No one else is going to matter to them anymore. I'm the one they're after. And the file. I'll do my best to stall them. Give you two, three days. . . . I don't know who to trust on this, Sarah. Two men on my team have already fucked me over. Guys who I thought were with me on this."

"So why didn't you just release the information to the press yourself?"

"Blackmail. Threat. Counterthreat."

"What do you mean?"

He smiles grimly. "They held up funds. I threatened to leak the file. They threatened to have me thrown in prison as a Soviet spy."

"What?! Frank, there's no way a crazy charge like that would ever stick!"

"Like hell it wouldn't. Listen, kid. I don't stand a chance against these fuckers, you understand? They're in a position to manufacture whatever witnesses, whatever official affidavits they could possibly need to lock me up for life. My only hope—" He stops again, his grip on my arm tightening into a vise. I am shoved down on my stomach, tasting slimy mulch and dry leaves. But hearing not a thing.

"I'm depending on you, Sarah," he whispers, helping me up to my knees. "Tell no one about this meeting. Do you understand? No one. Now get."

"But Frank, I. . . . Will I be able to get back in touch? Where are you staying?"

"Get!"

And I do. Taking one last look at the man before dashing out from under the porch and through the hole in the fence. And onto a wide boulevard which turns out to be South Van Ness.

When I finally get back to the apartment, Stanley awaits me there. Sipping a cognac and smoking one of those damn cigars.

"What the . . .?" he murmurs, when I walk through the door. Looking like some refugee out of WW III.

"I went dancing," I say preposterously. Trying to make a

quick decision on whether to trust Stanley with Frank's message or not. Somehow I hadn't expected him to be home as yet.

"And someone raped you on the dance floor, or what?"

"Stanley, I met with Frank tonight! I can't tell you what he had to say. He made me promise not to tell anyone for a couple of days. It's not as bad as I thought it was. And at the same time, it's much much worse. Anyway, he was a mess, the poor man. Like he's been on the run for weeks."

"Where in God's name did you meet?"

"Well, we started off at Caesar's Palace. Ha! But then he dragged me off to some hovel near by. Obviously he'd worked the whole thing out. The guy's getting even crazier than I."

"And he didn't draw any pearl handled gun from his pocket?"

"No way. In fact, he wants me to help him out," I blurt out. Then wish I hadn't.

"And you are?" he asks quietly.

"Do I have a choice?"

"It wasn't much fun waiting for you to come home tonight, Sarah. Wondering if you were dead or alive."

"Hey, come on. Things haven't gotten as bad as all that, have they?"

The phone rings. I'm not sure who jumps higher. Stanley or I. I pick up the receiver and wait.

"Sarah . . .?"

"Amy!" I cry out, rolling my eyes in Stanley's direction. "Where the hell have you been?"

"The Yucatan. Listen, would—"

"The Yucatan? I thought this was going to be some little week-end jaunt to Carmel? What the hell is happening with you, Amy?"

"Wouldn't you like to know. Listen, sweetie. When are you going back to New York?"

"Well I don't. . . . I can't really say as yet."

"So you could stay put for a few more days? Take care of the cat? We're thinking of going further south. Maybe checking out Nicaragua."

"You're going to try reaching Nicaragua on a fucking

motorcycle? Are you out of your mind? El Salvador and
Honduras are fucking death camps." Before I can say
another word, the line goes dead. Amy has hung up on me
again.

"As if I don't have enough to worry about," I groan to
Stanley after putting down the phone. "Now I have to
worry about Amy getting raped and tortured by some El
Salvadorean death squad. They're taking a joy ride through
Central America, if you can believe it. Like it was
Disneyland or something. And I still forgot to ask her about
the damn cat."

"You'll find the cat curled up inside the vacuum cleaner
out back."

"Where?"

Stanley unwinds, rises, and returns seconds later with a
small, portable vacuum cleaner in tow. I peer down into the
dust bag, slung low and unattached at the top, to meet two
sleepy yellow eyes peering back up. My mind is made up.
I'm taking this precious animal back to New York with me,
whether Amy ever returns to San Francisco or not.

JUNE 24

Breakfast is somewhat of a strained affair this morning.
After all Stanley has been my principal collaborator and
mentor throughout this entire crazy venture. The ready ear
into which all my little exploits, tidings, and suspicions
have been so readily poured. And now to be under
obligation to keep the clincher under wraps. To Stanley's
credit, he doesn't press. Only giving me long, speculative
looks now and again between sips of his coffee and reading
of the morning news.

He leaves earlier than usual this morning. I leave with
him, no longer willing to spend time in that apartment alone
unless absolutely necessary. By 9 a.m. I am settled into a

window seat at Cafe La Boheme, sipping an incredibly creamy cafe latte and carrying out an inner debate between my paranoid alter ego and Frank's paranoid alter ego, as to the wisdom or recklessness of letting Laurie in on last night's rendezvous with Frank. The truth of the matter is, I would feel a lot better about this trip down to Paradise today if at least one other person knew where I was headed. And when I was expected back.

Laurie arrives promptly at ten, acknowledging my presence with a nod before heading on to the rear of the cafe to collect some breakfast. She returns, looking the veritable image of willowy sunshine which I have a difficult time matching up with some genetic genius out of Frank's lab. Which goes to show my stereotyped frame of mind.

I ask her if there's a more private place for us to talk. And she leads me to a back room piled high with every imaginable kind of pastry and dessert. Two months in this place and I'd be a walking, talking advertisement for their principal supplier. No doubt about it.

Once we are settled, I ask Laurie how it was that she first began working for Frank.

"It came about in a matter of hours," she says, smiling slightly as she slides lower in her chair. "He attended a seminar I was giving on T-cell therapy. Saw how my work tied in with his research. And convinced my supervisor at Harvard to allow me to finish off my doctorate under his direction at Columbia."

"And you were happy with the move?"

She slips still lower. "As a graduate student, I considered it a great honor to be working with Frank. Anyone would."

"So why didn't you join up with his team out here?"

"What's with all the questions?"

"Look, Laurie. There's a lot I want to tell you. But I think it's better if I hear your side of the story first. Okay?"

"What do you mean, my side of the story? Have you talked with Frank?"

"I'll tell you everything. But first I just want to know what stopped you from joining up with Frank's team at Genco. Why you're working in this cafe for five dollars an hour when you could be earning 50,000 a year in some lab.

According to Beerbohm, you were one of the true geniuses in the field before you left."

She smiles wryly at this last remark, while stirring cream into her cup of tea and carefully setting the spoon aside. "Frank's whole project was under some kind of confidence umbrella when I got out there. They wanted us to sign this secrecy contract. A 'compact of voluntary collusion' was their term for it. What it really amounted to was a five year vow of silence concerning all the work we would be involved in out here. I couldn't see my way to signing that thing. So I left. . . . Now why don't you tell me what this is all about."

"I saw Frank last night. He's in real trouble, Laurie. I can't go into all the details. All I can tell you now is that he needs someone to pick up some confidential papers for him and deliver them to a friend in New York. Papers somehow connected with the work they were doing on an AIDS vaccine. I said I'd do it. Would you be willing to tag along?"

"Where?"

"Paradise Valley. In Central California. Maybe 250, 300 miles south-east of here."

"How did you get involved in all this?"

I start from the beginning, where I have started so many times before, giving her a tidy synopsis of my adventure up to date save for Frank's spooky revelation of the evening before. She is a careful, discerning listener. Her questions insightful. Her judgement razor sharp. And she agrees to accompany me, on the provision that a replacement can be found for her afternoon shift.

I am concerned that somebody may still be on my tail and as an extra protection, hand my American Express card over to Laurie and ask her to pick up a rented car for us. We are to meet on the corner of Market and Van Ness at one o'clock. After going our separate ways, I call Stanley at the office and leave a message in his machine. The next two hours are spent trying to lose whatever spook, or spooks, may be on my tail. Just like in the movies. The truth is, I'm beginning to feel like I'm in the movies. Hopping last minute subway cars criss-crossing the city. A cab here. A street car there. Into Macy's for a rendezvous in their crowded deli. Until the overpowering smell of chopped liver sends me back out on the streets again. Another subway. Another bus.

And at last, dropping into the Kodak hut off of South Van Ness, where I pick up some photographs for Stanley. Did he actually request that I pick them up? No, he did not. But I came across the retainer stub amongst the heap of bills grabbed out of his pocket last night, and cannot resist this unforseen opportunity to get a peek into another side of Stanley's life.

Will I see evidence of other women in these snapshots? Past loves? Romantic trysts or ongoing affairs? When the young sales clerk finally locates the packet for me, my perverted curiosity must remain temporarily unwhetted. For it is already some five minutes past one o'clock. I toss the pictures into my purse and dash the two blocks down to our corner of assignation. Laurie is parked in front of a Zim's restaurant in a scarlet red Toyota sedan.

Once on the road, the engine's steady purr quickly lapses into syncopated pandemonium, giving off signs of an imminent breakdown. Laurie takes the first exit off Highway 5, parking the car on the shoulder of a service road and digging into her backpack for a set of tools. She proceeds to poke around under the hood like she actually knows what she's doing in there.

"Where the hell did you learn to do that?" I ask, once we've started up again. Something worked somewhere, because it's smooth sailing once again.

"My Dad. I had to know an engine inside out before he even let me drive a car."

"Yeah? That's great, Laurie. I don't even know how to change a tire. . . . For that matter, it took me three years to get up the nerve to start using self service gas pumps."

"Females," she murmurs, smiling across at me.

"Hey, we're not the only ones with problems. My brother has never once done his laundry in his entire life. Hard to figure, right? A computer programmer who can't see his way to sticking three or four quarters into a coin slot and pushing a button. Just not part of his script."

"My parents tried bringing us up without any scripts at all. My two brothers were in the kitchen as much as I was outside mowing the front lawn."

"That's great!"

"Not so sure. I can't even boil an egg."

"So what? Neither can I. Can't cook. Can't sew. God knows I can't keep house. What *can* I do, is the question?"

Laurie laughs. "You write, don't you?"

"Yeah. But about what? My last published piece was on pooper scoopers, if you can believe it. A worthy cause, I won't deny it. But all the same . . ."

"It beats making five hundred and sixty cappuccinos every day."

"Ha! You may have a point there. . . . Why did you leave, anyway? I mean, I know why you left Genco. But why not join up with some other lab?"

"Seems like all the reasons I went into the field in the first place—to help mankind and all that rot—got lost in the shuffle. Genetic engineering has become a business like any other business. And I'm not interested in business. . . . It's all become a little more insidious than that, of course."

"What do you mean?"

"Let's just say the handwriting is on the wall."

"What are you talking about, Laurie?"

"More and more funding for recombinant DNA research is coming out of the Defense Department. And less and less out of the National Institute of Health. Priorities have definitely shifted over the last five years. My Dad used to say that World War One belonged to the chemists, and World War Two to the physicists. The way I see it, World War Three could very well belong to the biologists. Or geneticists, to be more precise. It's so ironic, too. Here my Dad switched from physics into biology after the War, because physics seemed so clearly to be about death, while biology seemed so clearly to be about life. And now, thirty years later, and I'm dropping out of biology for the same reason he dropped out of physics. . . . You're going to tell me anything about these papers of Frank's we're picking up?"

"Well, I. . . . it sounds like you might have already guessed."

"A lot of people have guessed, Sarah," she murmurs.

"Wait a minute. Guessed what?"

"That the AIDS virus is a casualty of genetic engineering research."

"You serious? I thought everybody was assuming it came out of Africa, or something."

"Convenient, isn't it? Blaming it on Africa. On underdevelopment, rather than overdevelopment? Look carefully at the scientists who are pointing a finger at Africa. They're the very ones with the most to lose if the finger is pointed back at us."

"But if a lot of people are already suspecting the real origin of AIDS, how come we never hear anything about it in the press?"

"Because no one wants to face the facts. Especially the very scientists who are in the position to suspect the worse. Which is why they go around spouting off their crazy theories on natural mutation. All a bunch of bull, of course. No virus in the history of medical science has ever naturally mutated and caused an epidemic of any kind. Ever. It's quite obvious that AIDS is the result of manmade mutations. And for all we know, only the first in a long line of genetically engineered diseases to come."

We continue on in silence for the next hour or so. Until somewhere in artichoke country, when I suggest a stop for coffee. Returning to the car with a couple of styrofoam cupfuls, I find Laurie playing solitaire with a deck of tarot cards spread across the front seat.

"You believe in that stuff?" I asked incredulously. She doesn't answer. Taking each of the four piles before her, spreading them out one by one, studying them methodically, and then bringing them back together again.

"That's it!" I exclaim, picking the top card off one of the middle piles. "The Fool, right? I actually dreamed about this card a few nights back. Of all the cards in a tarot deck for my subconscious to zero in on, it would have to be The Fool, wouldn't it?"

"How much do you know about all this?" Laurie asks,

gathering the deck together and putting it back into her pack.

"Not a goddamn thing."

"She's a very strong card, The Fool. Maybe the strongest in the deck."

"Yeah? Then what's she doing waltzing off some monstrous cliff?"

"We all have to take the leap now and again, don't we?"

"Ha! I prefer solid ground, thank you."

"You wouldn't be here if that were entirely true," Laurie points out matter-of-factly. "Neither would I." She heads off to the restroom, leaving me behind with my ambivalent thoughts.

Upon her return, she suggests taking the wheel again. I gladly accept her offer, since I'm still fighting off a late afternoon snooze. In fact the minute we hit the expressway, I drift into a semi-conscious stupor. With Frank's face looming onto the horizon. Not the face of yesteryear, but the face I saw in the haunting yellow glow of his flashlight last night. Those once handsome features distorted by terror and exhaustion into a sagging mask of nervous desperation. A steely-hearted general in the process of coming undone.

It was that uncommon steeliness which had first attracted me to the man, of course. That impregnable aura of self-assurance and power which emanated from every pore of his lean and wiry frame. Even when he began to turn the steel against me—which as our relationship deteriorated, he was prone to do more and more of the time—it continued to hold an unhealthy attraction for my semi-adolescent and neurotic heart.

A sexual fantasy unreels before my eyes. Frank is seated on the sofa in my apartment back in New York. Sipping wine and watching me, his gaze icy and intent, as I slowly strip for the man. And ah, the delicious inglorious pleasure of it all. As I proceed to expose myself, body and soul, to this cold-eyed stranger. More electrically tuned into the moment than I have ever been before. I at my most vulnerable, while Frank remains his usual invulnerable self.

He then proceeds to instruct me on how to sit. And move. As if he were piecing together some telepathic porno flick.

Telling me where to place a leg. Or how to touch a thigh. A breast. Or wet a lip. In order to achieve the most desired effect. And I do exactly as I am bid. Totally immersed in this erotic little power game of his. (Mine?) Tuned up and turned on to the point of no return. And it is at this precise moment, when I am burning up inside and filled with desire for the man, that he suddenly stands up, takes a last long draught of wine, and walks out the apartment door!

I jerk awake, speculating sourly on how the sado-masochistic core of that fantasy so aptly reflects on our relationship as it once stood. A tidy, consummate echo of what two people had come to mean to one another. With all the attendant resonance or lack thereof.

It is approaching dusk when we finally swing off the exit ramp and see the familiar road signs ahead. One pointing east to Colston. The other west to Paradise Valley and Chemix labs. We take a quick spin around the deserted subdivision, checking out for any possible watchmen or lingering residents in the area. A man is jogging his dog around the idle laboratory facilities. Nothing more. We pass by Frank's musty yellow bungalow. Now boarded up. Which it hadn't been last time I was here. And then head back to Colston to wait until dark.

I recommend May's Diner for a quick bite to eat. The place looks so damn familiar and welcoming in the fading light of day that it's almost like coming home. But the coming home feeling eases up real quick. As soon as we walk through the doorway and catch one of May's jittery looks our way. Something's up. I touch Laurie's arm and we move back out of the cafe.

Our only option, unless we return to the car, is a sleazy looking tavern kitty corner to the post office. It's darker inside this place than out, with vague anthropomorphic shadows playing off the ceiling and walls. I order a cold beer. Laurie, a V-8. And we discuss the problem at hand. Trouble is, until we get back with May, there's not a whole lot to discuss. Obviously someone has arrived here before us. But who? And for how long? If the truth will out, the idea that we might actually get into Frank's bungalow tonight unobserved, pick up the papers, and deliver them safely to this Philip Kaufman in New York with life and limb still reasonably intact, is beginning to look hopelessly naive.

"We could get a room somewhere here in town," Laurie suggests quietly, doodling serial parabolas on the cocktail napkin between us. "Leave the car behind as a decoy. And slip back to Frank's in the middle of the night."

"Are you aware how far the closest motel is from Paradise?"

"Do you have any better suggestions?"

"We could always wait it out a day or two. Until . . ." Until what? And what am I doing playing the devil's advocate here, anyway? That's been Stanley's role in this affair. Not mine. The thought brings to mind the packet of photographs sitting at the bottom of my purse.

"Where did Frank hide the papers?" Laurie asks.

"What do you mean where? In his house."

"Yes, but where in his house?"

"He didn't say," I murmur incredulously. "Isn't that ridiculous!" Even more ridiculous, I didn't think to ask.

The diner closes at eight. 8:05 and I put through a call to May on the public phone behind the bar.

"Why didn't you tell me you were in such hot water, young lady?" May demands, the moment I say hello. "Good lord, all the questions they've been asking. Where you're from? What you're after? Who you been talking to?"

"Who?"

"Two gentlemen from the F.B.I. They come down here last week, flashing their badges all over town in exchange for your life story. Told them I didn't know a thing about you. As a matter of fact, I don't know a lot about you, do I now? I suspect Lucy and Sheriff Kelly might have been a bit more generous with their opinions."

"The F.B.I. . . . ?"

"You didn't know you were so popular, huh?"

"So that's why you headed us out of the diner tonight?" I whisper.

"What's that?"

"The F.B.I. was in there?"

"In where?"

"In your diner!"

"When's that?"

"Tonight, May! The F.B.I. was in your diner tonight!

"They was?"

"They wasn't? Weren't?"

"Not that I know of, honey. Not tonight."

"So they left? They're gone?" Abbot and Costello couldn't improve on this conversation if they tried.

"Far as I know, they have. Come up one day and were gone the next."

"So why did you give me that look in the diner tonight?"

"It's Kelly I'm concerned about, the old coot. He don't know anymore about your troubles than the rest of us. Which hasn't stopped him from stringing those government folks along as far as he could hook them. He figures you may be some kind of anti-nuclear terrorist."

"Jesus."

"Well, that's his theory, anyhow. Me, I don't much care what trouble you're in, young lady. Just think you'd be better moving on, before somebody spots you and hauls you in."

"Anti-nuclear terrorist? Isn't that some kind of contradiction in terms?" I can't help but point out, in the mood to shove Sheriff Kelly and his worse case scenarios into the Carrington family's alligator-infested swamp.

"You wouldn't be planning anything foolish now, would you?"

"Nothing more than a good night's sleep. We'll be heading back to the city as soon as it's light. But I want to thank you for everything, May. Really."

"You just take care of yourself now. And come back and visit when things get back to normal around here. I'll be looking for you."

I promise to do so, feeling morbidly pessimistic about things ever 'getting back to normal', here in Colston or anywhere else, ever again.

The issue of surveillance—whether Laurie and I are under it or not—must remain an open question, though my gut feeling is that we're in this alone. We stick to her original plan of hoofing it from some motel, on the premise that entering the subdivision on foot will cause considerably less commotion than driving through in our car. After booking a room in a travel lodge some four miles due east of Paradise, we make do with a couple of burritos from a drive-in taqueria before returning to the motel to prepare for our midnight hike.

We had planned to slip out of the room long after the other patrons in this pasted together flop house had turned off their lights and gone to bed. But there is a party going on above our heads that won't quit. Shrill talk, shriller laughter, breaking glass, scuffles, and a continual train of tight-eyed inebriates stumping up and down the staircase out front in quest of sodas, ice, and some of that fresh desert air. One a.m. and we can wait no longer. Climbing out a side window, we scout out a brush trail which skirts Route 99, taking us west toward Paradise through a hushed and moonless night.

My pessimistic state of mind is gradually undermined by the excruciating perfection of the landscape before us. The desert sky, desert air, desert silence, and Laurie's dauntless presence there by my side, all acting on me like some kind of aphrodisiac. Getting me drunk on danger, as it were. I begin reaping an almost erotic pleasure out of this impossible venture of ours and the attendant risks involved.

In an hour's time, we have reached the tacky Grecian columns which herald one's approach to Paradise. The desolate subdivision stretches out before us like some modern day black hole of Calcutta. No lights shine from any window. No sound breaches the eerie hush, save an occasional semi-trailer swishing down Route 99. We begin wending our way through the deserted streets, with many a backward glance over our shoulders. Arriving at Frank's back door step, Laurie hauls a screw driver and wrench out of her back pack. With quiet concentration she wrestles the four pieces of plywood off the aluminum frame.

Once inside the bungalow, we risk turning on the flashlight. The place has been sacked from end to end. Disemboweled might be a more accurate description for it. A dismantled nightmare, with papers, books, sofa stuffing, splintered furniture and clothing strewn about the room.

Laurie begins scrutinizing a pile of papers at her feet. I

move into the bedroom, shaken anew by the raw violent cast of the disorder before my eyes. The mattress lies in two pieces on the floor. Doubled over upon itself like some ghostly, bloodless corpse. I rummage through the wreckage—bedclothes, towels, papers, socks—coming up with nothing more interesting than a three or four year old snapshot of Jaimie, grinning into the camera with a puppy in his lap. The walk-in closet has been stripped of everything save a broken tennis racket and an ancient Hoover vacuum cleaner I haven't seen the likes of in some twenty years. I linger there a moment or two, smitten by that familiar blend of Old Spice and formaldehyde which still hovers in the air.

A quick survey of the kitchen proves equally fruitless. A few cans of Frank's liquid protein drink. Some tea bags. An empty bottle of cognac. Nothing more. Returning to the living room, I find Laurie perched on the edge of the ravaged sofa, paging through a spiral notebook in her lap.

"Well?"

"Some kind of a journal. Interesting. But not what we're looking for," she says. Dropping the notebook into her backpack, nonetheless. We retrace our steps through the bungalow, wading and rewading through all the crap in our unwillingness to believe the journey out here has all been for naught. Frank himself had been so convinced the precious file had not yet been found.

"Laurie!" I whisper, inspired by one last impossible brainstorm as I yank the flashlight out of her hand and tear back into the bedroom closet. Dragging the massive vacuum cleaner out of its corner, I unhook the heavy cotton bag and thrust my hand into a cloud of palpable dust. "Yes!" I cry out, my fingers closing around what feels to be a manila envelope. And indeed, it is a manila envelope.

We stare at it a moment in dread expectation before I tear it open and pull out ten or so pages of typewritten notes. I read aloud:

MEMORANDUM FOR THE RECORD   3/3/76
SUBJECT: Meeting at OCB's office concerning HJKINGO

1. At 10:30 a.m. this date, Senator Hellsley convened
   in his office the DDP, the D/S, and the C/CI Project
   to report on recent action concerning the HJKINGO

"What the hell?" I murmur. But Laurie's attention is
elsewhere. On a flashlight beam which is scaling the front
window right to left. Then left to right. My hand tightens
around Laurie's arm as the two of us steal slowly toward the
kitchen. Stumbling over a pile of books, it is only Laurie's
steadying grip which prevents me from falling flat on my
back. At which point we drop all pretense of stealth,
making a mad dash out the back door.

"Hey? What's going on around here?" a man's voice
demands heatedly from somewhere inside the bungalow,
just as Laurie and I careen around the corner of the house
and across a series of overgrown front lawns, dash down
one street and then another, and back through the Grecian
columns toward Highway 99.

Our pursuer appears to be alone. Heavy, slow, and
lumbering. Some 40 yards to our rear. Neither of us dare
take a look behind us. Waves of hoarded up adrenalin pump
us on down the highway and across the desert brush. East.
Toward our seedy motel room and the soft orange whisper
of another day. The watchman fires a round or two. The
bullets give off a surrealistic echo in the still, early morning
air. My only appreciable reaction is one of indignation; that
this strange man should be aiming his lethal lead in our
direction without having the slightest inkling who we are.
Or what, if anything, we have done.

Thank God for the new moon. And the desert darkness.
Enshrouding us in her dry, crusty womb. We jog along
tirelessly, having managed to shed our trigger-happy
shadow, but having no apparent reason to slow our pace.
Could he be phoning ahead? Apprising contacts in Colston
of the break-in and the two scrawny females to whom he
gave chase? We had purposely avoided the Colston area
when seeking lodgings for the night. Which doesn't mean
they haven't caught on to our whereabouts, all the same.
But when we edge up to the travel lodge, nothing appears to
be amiss. No signs of life anywhere save for a couple of

well-stewed leftovers from last night's blow-out, sharing a bottle of spirits on the front steps.

"Hey girls!" one of them calls out drunkenly, as we slip into the waiting Toyota. "Join the party, will ya?"

Laurie backs the car off the tarred-over drive. Tires squeal as we shoot out onto Route 99.

"Goddamn it, Laurie. We actually pulled this thing off!" I exclaim incredulously, whacking the dashboard with our precious booty.

"Not so fast," she reminds me. Her cautious tone belied by the gleeful grin creeping across her face.

I bring out the pages again, by-passing page one, along with page two and three, riddled through with cryptic scientific notations Laurie may be able to decipher, but not I. And begin reading page four which, like the three pages before it, actually has TOP SECRET/EYES ONLY stamped across the top and bottom of the page.

To: Mr. R. K. Wilson
From: K. L. Hanes

SUBJECT: RESEARCH SURVEILLANCE RE-
QUEST FEDERAL BUREAU OF IN-
VESTIGATION

In accordance with the Director's meeting with the President on 5/8/82, the results of the very sensitive coverage requested by the U.S. Chemical Corps were personally delivered by liaison to Dr. J. B. Walters on 5/12/82 . . .

"Wait a minute, Laurie! That couldn't be *Frank's* Dr. Walters, could it?"

"Who?"

"Joe Walters. Jackass Joe, we used to call him. At least I did. You never worked with him?"

She shakes her head, eyes glued to the rear view mirror.

"Then he must have left Frank's team just before you came on. Lucky you. I never could figure out how Frank could stand the guy."

I read on:

Dr. Walters advised Liaison Supervisor K. L. Hanes
that this material, at Director's specific instructions, be
handed over to him personally. In the event of his
absence, it was to be given to his assistant liaison, to
be held unopened, for Attorney General Mace.

"Don't panic, Sarah," Laurie interjects quietly, her gaze
still riveted on the rear view mirror. "But I think we're
being followed. . . . Pontiac station wagon. Left rear.
Every time I switch lanes, he does the same. Been going on
like this for the last three minutes or so. Dig into the front
pocket of my backpack," she adds, edging into the right
hand lane. "There's a roll of stamps in there somewhere."

"But who the hell can we possibly mail this thing to?" I
ask, coming up with the said roll and frantically pasting a
dozen or so first class stamps across the top of the envelope.
"We don't dare send it off to Kaufman. If they can intercept
Frank's mail, they certainly can intercept his. And I can't
very well send it off to myself, right? Maybe to you,
Laurie?" I suggest, my mind going off in three different
directions at once.

"If they catch up with us, what good am I going to do?"
she points out, cutting across another lane of traffic and
veering onto an exit ramp. The station wagon tries a similar
maneuver, but is stopped short by a pick up truck sticking
too close to its right front fender.

"We lost them?"

Laurie shakes her head, gunning the car up a steep incline
and down around a hair pin turn, into a town called Canyon
Lake. No lake in sight. Ignoring distant thunder, I address
the envelope to Mr. Stanley London: Apt. 607, Fox Plaza,
Market Street, San Francisco. In seconds, we are into the
center of town. Laurie stops at the first mail box we see. I
hop out and drop the envelope in. Wondering all the while if
we aren't making a terrible mistake here. Problem is, there's
no time to think. Only time to act.

We continue down the main street, following road signs
back to Highway 5. Taking a right turn, we nearly collide
head-on with our station wagon turning left. The other car

spins into a screaming U-turn as Laurie cuts a sharp left.
Then left again. Right past the entrance ramp and back, via
a service road, toward the direction of town.

"What are you doing," I demand bewilderedly, my mind
flashing back on that face. Those eyes. Which for one
horrific moment as we took the turn back there, were only
inches from my own. The face of a vicious, determined
thug. Alias beer-swigging Fatso of the Italian wedding some
five days ago. "They're going to figure us getting back on
the expressway," Laurie whispers hoarsely, crouching low
in her seat. In my heightened panic, Laurie and the steering
wheel she is gripping so tightly seem to fuse and become
one. A supranatural hybrid of woman/machine out of some
futuristic fairy tale, I think absurdly, bracing myself against
the dashboard as we lurch down the road. We hit a red light.
She runs it and hooks a right. Over the expressway and
down another road pointing toward a town called Weston.
We turn left and left again. Beginning to breathe a little
easier as three, then four minutes pass with no further sign
of our menacing tail. We hit another light. And it is then
that we catch sight of those distinctive head lights turning
right onto the roadway some two or three blocks back.

"This thing must be bugged," Laurie mutters furiously,
making a sharp right which throws me into her lap. "We're
going to have to make a jump for it, Sarah."

"What are you talking about? Jump? Jump where?"

"I'm taking us back up to the summit of that canyon.
Once over the top, I'll lock the wheels. We'll bolt as soon as
it starts downhill."

"We could kill ourselves jumping out of a moving car!"

"We'll hardly be moving at all. Just remember to tuck
and roll and you'll be okay."

Tuck and roll? All too soon she's pressing the accelerator
down to the floor as we soar up the incline leading to the top
of Canyon Lake. "I can't believe this is happening," I
mutter dolefully. Also futilely, as Laurie edges us over the
crest of the hill.

She opens her door. I do likewise. "Now jump!" she

cries out. And having little other choice, that's precisely what I do.

The next thing I'm conscious of is an explosion. Like a fair sized stick of dynamite going off inside my head and echoing in triplicate of the canyon walls below. Then a dull throbbing ache in my right shoulder. Hide! I'm supposed to hide, I think frantically, as tires tread stealthily up the gravel road. My eyes close down in a frozen panic as the car creeps slowly over the top and on down the other side of the hill.

"You okay, Sarah?"

"Yeah. Yeah, I think so. Jesus, I think I blacked out. . . . They're gone?"

She nods, bringing me to my feet. "But we better split before they bring back the police." For a moment or two we stand mesmerized by the mass of burning steel and rubber raging in the canyon below. Then head off in the opposite direction. Over boulders, gravel, and prickly desert weeds to the bottom of the hill. Any sense of victory has been more than neutralized by the dull pains shooting through the various parts of my person. And by the budding certainty that I shouldn't have dropped the all-important envelope into that wretched mailbox a few minutes ago.

As day breaks, we arrive at a fairly untraveled road somewhere east of Canyon Lake and try our hand at hitchhiking, eventually getting picked up by a kindly looking farmer hauling a truckload of hay. "Only going as far as Canbey," he says, sending looks of unbridled curiosity our way. But he asks no questions. And we offer him no answers.

In Canbey, we're fortunate enough to cross paths with a Greyhound express, leaving for San Francisco in a matter of minutes. Laurie must pay for our tickets. I'm broke. She also offers to buy me lunch. Or breakfast. But I'm not the slightest bit hungry. Head, heart, and soul all focused forward on the becalming oblivion of a long, hot bath.

I conk out as soon as we find our seats. Only to come to again when the bus is easing into its berth at the grimy Greyhound station in downtown San Francisco. What's going to happen now? I ask myself, with no small degree of morose trepidation. How long did it take those guys to realize I wasn't part and parcel of that flaming wreck back at Canyon Lake? How long will it take them to snap back onto my trail and the trail of the June Mail file? They have no proof whatsoever that I actually found the stuff. And that's going to have to be my trump card, should I need one in the days to come. My insistence that I never dug up the missing file. As a chancy and unpremeditated back up, I slip three quarters into one of the foot lockers stacked against a far wall of the bus station, extract the key, and drop it into my purse.

It is already three o'clock. Incredibly enough, Laurie is planning to go straight to work at her cafe. She wants to know what I plan on telling them over at "Rent-a-Wreck" about the car. Damn if I know. This is the second heap in less than a week that I've managed to total for that outfit. What can I tell them, after all? On that dismal note, Laurie and I part company. Promising to reconnect by tomorrow night.

Back at Amy's, I am sharply disappointed to find that Stanley isn't there waiting for me. But then, why should he be? I never told him where I was going. Or even hinted at when I might be back. He is no doubt over at Verdi's, where he can generally be found at this hour of the day. Sipping scotch and sodas and talking shop with the rest of the boys. I make a beeline for the bathroom and start up the hot water for my bath. Then take a good look at myself in the mirror. Flabbergasted by the bugged-eyed sorry soul I see staring back at me there. The yellowing bump on the left side of my forehead is nothing compared to the new black and blue monster over my right eyebrow. Why in god's name didn't Laurie tell me what terrible shape I was in? The Bride of Frankenstein comes to mind as I stand there grimacing at myself. And an impoverished one, at that.

I dig Stanley's packet of photographs out of my purse and toss them on to the bath mat. Then head into the kitchen for the bottle of Gallo and a glass. After a few quick, salutary gulps of cold white wine, I step greedily into the waiting tub of hot suds. Sipping mindlessly on a second glass of wine as I enjoy a much needed nap.

By my third glass, I begin to glean an enormous comic

thrill out of successive push-button replays on the last crazy twenty-four hours in time. Was that really Laurie and I back there in Paradise Valley, breaking into Frank's boarded-up flat? Racing through the desert night with live bullets whizzing toward our backs? Not to mention our flying leaps from a moving automobile which burst into flames only seconds after we jumped ship. No small feat we pulled off, all things considered! What with the F.B.I. and God knows who else hot on our trail and the trail of the 'June Mail' file. And yet, two greenhorn amateurs out of nowhere somehow managed to prevail. With a little help from Frank, of course. And that precious, evanescent cat.

I put aside my wine glass and turn to the photographs, waiting for me there on the bathroom mat. I finger the packet gingerly, reluctant to have a look. What is it I'm so afraid of? How bad could it be? Even blatant signs of another woman in Stanley's life should be something I can handle with a stoic grain of salt. After all, we only met but a few week-ends ago.

Biting through the tape, I take out the pictures and toss the envelope with its negatives aside. The first shot is a ruralish small town setting. A restaurant, with a few cars parked in front. A diner, I realize after taking a closer look. May's Diner. . . . And my rented yellow Datsun parked there in front? I stare at the snapshot an undeterminate amount of time as the various parts of the puzzle pick themselves up, shuffle themselves around, and settle back into place. All my worst suspicions instantly confirmed. Stanley, the man whom I have been sharing the last ten days and nights with, the man whom I have even allowed myself to fall a little in love with, is one of them.

Snapshot /2: The Datsun parked in front of Frank's yellow bungalow. But where am I? And how is it that I had no sense of another human being in the general vicinity when I was out there? Or did I?

Snapshot /3: Me standing in front of the green bungalow adjacent to Frank's.

Snapshot /4: Me coming out of the post office.

Snapshot /5: Another one of the diner. This one a closeup. I can just make out Miss Lucy behind the counter, scarfing down her apple pie.

Snapshot /6: The postmistress and I in conversation at the side of the jeep.

Snapshot /7: Me climbing out of my Datsun in front of the Motel Six.

Snapshot /8: May and I in front of the post office.

Snapshot /9: May, Sheriff Kelly, and myself walking towards the ransacked motel room.

Snapshot /10: Woody Allen and Mia Farrow in bowed conversation over lunch.

What?! I ask myself over and over, brushing the winey cobwebs out of my line of thought. Arnold was the one who took pictures of Woody and Mia. Not Stanley. So how to explain. . . . ? Maybe Arnold took these pictures and then passed the retainer stub on to Stanley the following day? Arnold did appear to recognize Stanley the night of Angelica's play, now that I recall. But he sure wasn't any too happy to see him there. If they are working together on this thing, why would Stanley's appearance have annoyed Arnold so?

The sound of a key in the lock of an adjoining apartment jars me out of these inner speculations. Stanley could be returning any time now. I have to get out of this place and quick.

I am dressed and halfway out the door before I remember the kitty. I balk at the idea of leaving her here unattended. And rush back to the kitchen to scoop her out of her nest, bundle her into a towel, and cart her off to Jennifer's Winslow's place, only a twenty minute hike away.

"You heard the news?" Jennifer murmurs incredulously, ushering me into the back room without a second glance at my forehead or the creature under my arm.

"What is it? What's wrong?"

"It's Frank! They're saying he's some kind of double agent. A Soviet spy!"

We stand there mute and horrified before the MacNeil/Lehrer news hour, watching a solemn Judy Woodruff watching us, as she relates the alleged activities of Dr. Frank Winslow. A former C.I.A. 'consultant' who F.B.I. officials believe to have helped Soviet authorities in tracking down a Soviet official, who has since been arrested by the

KGB as an American spy. A photo of Frank flashes onto the screen. A strangely atypical shot. He looks angry. Even a little drunk. Ms. Woodruff tells us that Dr. Winslow has apparently fled the country. Possibly to Mexico, although officials remain vague and uncertain of his whereabouts at this time.

"You think it could be true?" Jennifer asks bewilderedly, sinking into the sofa. A pained, drawn expression on her face.

"No way, Jennifer! But God, these people work fast. Look, I just saw Frank on Wednesday night! And he hinted to me that they just might try to pull off some crazy scheme such as this."

"You saw him Wednesday night?"

"Yes! You see, Frank—well I—shit, how do I explain all this? The crux of it all is—Frank got hold of some top secret papers which link American military germ-warfare research up with AIDS."

"What are you saying, Sarah?"

"I'm saying that recombinant DNA experiments, conducted on certain monkey viruses in the mid-seventies, created the virus for AIDS! That's what I'm saying. And now certain powers that be, obviously scared shitless that this incriminating tidbit might break into the press, are trying to cover their tracks. You see? They're using Frank as their sacrificial lamb. Well now, that's not quite how to put it. Anyway, they're obviously out to discredit Frank. Which, in turn, will make it that much easier to discredit whatever freaky story Frank might manage to go public with in the days ahead."

"Who do you mean by 'they'?"

"Everybody, as far as I can figure. Chemix. The Pentagon, anyway. The C.I.A. F.B.I. Maybe even Genco. Though I really can't tell if they are directly aware of this cover-up or not. . . . What I don't understand is that bit about Frank having fled to Mexico. His plan wasn't to flee at all. At least I didn't think it was," I hedge, a myriad of possibilities springing to mind.

Jennifer is more confused than ever. And exceedingly distraught. I do my best to clarify the situation. Giving her a

straightforward account of the last few days. From Genco.
To Caesar's Palace. To Paradise and back. Saving the worst
for last. The fact that I may have mailed the all-important
file straight into the hands of the enemy. In the person of
Mr. Stanley London, my presumed confidante and friend.
Not to mention lover and soul-mate over the last few weeks.

I go over the set of photographs with Jennifer, working
through the only feasible theory I can come up with: Arnold
shooting the pictures and passing the Kodak stub onto
Stanley later in the week. Jennifer looks from the pictures
back up to me. And from me back to the pictures. A
vaguely censurious cast to her eyes.

"What's to become of Frankie?" she finally murmurs,
setting the pile of photographs on the table between us.

"I don't know, Jennifer. I really feel awful about this.
Frank was depending on me to pull this thing off. . . .
You know Jennifer, in spite of everything I still find it hard
to believe that a journalist as well known as Stanley London
could be hooked into some kind of U.S. Intelligence racket.
Don't you?"

She shrugs despondently. "According to that book—
what was the name of it? *The Company?*—The C.I.A. has
plants in every major newspaper in the country. People who
will write the news like the C.I.A. wants them to."

"But Stanley's stuff isn't like that at all! You've read his
columns, haven't you? He's too damn liberal to be involved
in all that shit." And too damn nice, I add to myself. Too
damn nice.

"Where did you say you met him?"

"Stanley? In a cafe in North Beach. We found we had a
favorite author in common . . . and kind of took it from
there."

"Do you do that kind of thing often."

"What kind of thing?"

"Meet strange men in cafes. Or at parties. And
then . . ."

"And then what? Hop into the sack with them? Is that
what you're getting at?"

"Doesn't it ever enter your mind to be wary of these men,
Sarah?"

Who exactly is she referring to now? Stanley? Or Frank? Or both?

"Well of course it enters my mind to be wary, Jennifer! Good God. But you've been out there on your own the last four years. You must know what it's like. I mean, there are men and there are men. Right?"

"I haven't the slightest idea what you are talking about," she says, getting to her feet and piling some kindling into the hearth. Whatever may be the implications of her last remarks, I don't care to go into the subject any further. I'm more than a little relieved to have Jaimie interrupt our conversation with his spirited entrance into the room. Apparently he has yet to hear the news about his Dad. And Jennifer prefers to keep it that way for the time being, perhaps hoping for some miracle of faith; that the spy story will die a quick and painless death before the break of another day.

I go into the den and make a collect call to Sandy Willis, a neighbor and good friend of mine back in New York. I give her Philip Kaufman's box office number, as well as the Manhattan publishing company which had originally put out his book. And ask her to make contact with the man as soon as possible—in person, rather than over the phone, on the assumption that his line could be tapped as well—passing along the message to make immediate contact with me in San Francisco concerning the matter of Frank.

One way or another, I must eventually confront Stanley with my suspicions and evidence thereof. I have no other choice, since the envelope is going to his address, whether I like it or not. But given the options, I prefer the confrontation to take place in the light of day. So, I readily accept Jennifer's invitation to spend the night. The three of us share a pot of spaghetti in front of PBS, watching a wonderful documentary on Laurence Olivier. And then all hit the sack. The two of them upstairs, and I on the downstairs living-room sofa. The kitty, who buried herself in their Baby Grand piano most of the evening, eventually joins me there. Purring sonorously in my right ear. A fortuitous sign, I think—grabbing at straws—that, in spite of all evidence to the contrary, things are going to work out okay.

JUNE 26

The cat and I leave Jennifer's apartment by 7 a.m. Before either she or her son are out of bed. I stop off at a cafe to bolster my confidence with a couple of quick cups, meanwhile giving myself the opportunity to work through a feasible approach with Stanley, should he be waiting for me at the apartment when I return. A young Vietnamese boy passes the table with a armful of morning papers. I buy one up and rifle through it, hoping against hope to find no confirmation of yesterday's story within.

But the confirmation is there alright. Page four. Upper left. A picture of Frank, this time in suit, coat and tie, under the heading: FBI Combs the World for Ex-CIA Man. According to the article, every FBI office worldwide is participating in the manhunt! Although the search is centering in Mexico. With a few agents following leads back to his home town in Iowa. And others on a trail which leads into Finland, enroute to the U.S.S.R. Once again, there is mention of that Soviet official who Frank allegedly fingered for the KGB because of undercover work the man was doing for the United States. They certainly are covering all their tracks.

The article is more interesting for what it doesn't say than for what it does. There is no reference throughout to the services Frank might have been rendering for the C.I.A. Nor, oddly enough, is there any mention of his scientific background in genetic engineering or his recent work on an AIDS vaccine.

I walk back to Amy's, feeling heavy in limb and heart. And stand there in front of her door for five minutes at least, listening for sounds within. I hear nothing but the muffled ticking of her alarm clock. Maybe Stanley passed the night back at his own place, after all?

I stick my head through the door, hear myself scream, then jump back into the hall. The place has been pillaged! Sacked. Shades of Frank's Paradise bungalow. And I could swear I spotted a large, lumpy entity—a body?—lying in the middle of the floor. I look again.

"Stanley!" I cry out, running up to where he lies there in front of the sofa. Looking so pale. And so deathly still. "Stanley!" I cry out again and again. Shaking him wildly and pounding his chest. His eyelids flutter. A low moan escapes his lips as his head moves weakly from side to side. Thank God in heaven, the man's alive.

I dash for a glass of water. Return. Support his head in my lap and bring the glass to his lips. "Take a sip, sweetheart. Just a sip," I murmur, taking note of a cruel gash over his right eyebrow and a gummy clump of blood and hair at the back of his head. "You okay, honey? Are you alright?"

He gulps down the entire glass before making another sound. "Shit," he finally mutters, a hand going to his head. A grim smile on his lips as he takes note of where he is and who I am.

"What happened? How long have you been lying here, Stanley?"

He comes to a sitting position, letting his head flop back on the sofa behind him. "Think I could use a couple of aspirin," he murmurs, taking my hand for a second. Then letting it go.

"Right." I rush about everywhere looking for that bottle of aspirin, but come up empty-handed. For lack of a better idea, I come back in the room with a bottle of scotch.

"God, no," he moans, waving the bottle out of his line of vision before hoisting himself up on the couch.

"Are you able to talk, Stanley? Can you tell me what happened here?" I ask, daubing a wet wash cloth over the gash above his eye.

"Not really sure," he mumbles, taking the wash cloth out of my hand and pressing it to the back of his head. "It all happened so damn fast," he adds a moment later, his gaze taking in the damage wrought about the room. "Sometime early this morning. Three, four o'clock? I thought it was you. Walked right in here like a damn fool. One of them whacked me over the head and that was all there was to it. I didn't play a particularly heroic role in all this, I'm afraid."

"How many were there?"

"Two, that I saw."

"What did they look like?"

He shakes his head. "Stockings over their heads. God those things are ugly."

"Did one of them look at all like that guy we saw at your sister-in-law's wedding? You know, the fat man with the plaid pants?"

"Couldn't say. Two men. Average height," he adds, squeezing his eyes together against a wave of pain and moving the wash cloth back to his eye. "What did they come here looking for, Sarah?"

"The papers, I assume."

"What papers?"

I start to answer. Then stop. Moving to the edge of the couch.

"I see you ran into a bit of trouble yourself," Stanley adds, with a nod to my forehead. "You want to tell me about it?"

"Right here? But what if they come back?"

"Why would they come back?"

"I don't know. Maybe now that they realize I'm here?"

"What's up, Sarah?"

I take the snapshots out of my purse and toss them onto the table. Then stand and move to the middle of the room. He goes through the pile, one by one. "Who took these?" he finally asks, going back through the pile.

"You tell me."

"How in hell should I know? It's your trip down to Colston, I assume? How did you get ahold of these, anyway?"

"Your ticket stub . . . Kodak . . . remember? Which

I unintentionally dug out of your pocket on Wednesday night."

He stares at me in a thoughtful silence.

"Are you working for the other side, Stanley? Is that it? Did you pick me up at Verdi's a couple week-ends back in the line of duty? Pure and simple?"

"What the hell are you talking about, Sarah?"

"What else am I supposed to believe? *Can* I believe? The ticket was in your pocket, after all. The ticket for those photos. . . ."

"I found that ticket right here in the apartment, Sarah."

"Where?"

"On the kitchen floor."

"When?"

He closes his eyes again for a few moments, head resting against the back of the sofa. "Wednesday evening. Came home. You were in the tub, as usual. Remember? I went into the kitchen to fix myself a scotch and picked the stub off the floor. Figured it was probably yours."

"So why didn't you mention anything about it?"

"I had every intention. In fact, I believe I went into the bathroom for that very purpose. But . . . seems I got distracted," he adds, the vaguest of smiles playing on his lips. I think back to that afternoon, just two days ago. Stanley walking back into the bathroom and joining me there in the tub.

"Convenient story," I mumble.

"So if I'm in league with those goons of yours, how do you explain this?" he says, patting his eye.

"I haven't figured that out yet. Maybe this is all a set up. They did that to you so I would assume you're innocent."

His eyes close as he lets his head drop back against the cushion. He's right. That theory sounds patently absurd. Even to me.

"Stanley," I murmur, rejoining him there on the sofa. "You don't know how many times I've had to go back and forth on this thing! I want to trust you. Good God, I want to trust you."

"So trust me then," he says, eyeing me solemnly. If it were only that simple.

"How do you suppose that stub got into the kitchen?" I

finally ask, re-establishing a little distance between Stanley and myself.

He shrugs. "An earlier break-in? Less thorough than this one, obviously."

"And obviously involving Arnold. What an unlikely spook that guy is. I mean, he comes off such the bird brain."

"Why assume it was him?"

"That picture of Woody Allen. He already told me about running into Allen somewhere. Do you suppose Arnold was the one who tapped the phone?"

"What about these papers, Sarah? You're going to tell me more about them?"

"Yes, well you see, that was the favor Frank asked of me on Wednesday night. That I go down there, to his house in Paradise, and pick up some top secret papers he had hidden there. And that's what I did. Laurie and I. Only we were followed out of town and panicked. And decided to mail the stuff off before we got caught."

"To who?"

"To you."

"To me," he repeats. In a monotone that tells me it hasn't quite hit home.

"You're the only one I could think of, Stanley. The only one I thought I could trust. Ha!" Ah, the irony of it all. "Anyway, you should be receiving it by this afternoon. Or Monday, at the latest. Then we have to get it to a connection of Frank's in New York."

"This is all beginning to sound terribly complicated, Sarah. Especially when considering all the people who seem to be watching your every move."

"Yeah, well I'm afraid it's gotten more complicated still. . . . You watched the evening news last night, didn't you?"

He shakes his head.

"You didn't? Why not? I mean, you always watch the evening news."

"Not that it's any of your business, sweetheart. But I had dinner with my ex-wife."

"Oh. . . . Well then, you didn't hear it. It's about

Frank. The United States government is accusing him of being . . . of being a Soviet spy."

Stanley just sits there looking at me. His eyes blinking every five seconds or so. Looking.

"Are you alright, Stanley?"

"Sarah, do you have any idea what this could mean? Any idea!" he repeats, his voice picking up a decibel or two with every word.

"But none of it's true, Stanley. It's all trumped up hogwash. You know, to cover up our defense department's link up to AIDS."

"To what?"

"Oh yeah, that's right. You don't know anything about that, do you. I keep forgetting whom I told what. Ha!" Stanley isn't seeing the humor in the situation. "See, remember these papers Frank asked me to pick up? They expose certain military experiments carried out in the mid-seventies—germ warfare research—that inadvertently, so Frank says, gave birth to the AIDS virus! See?"

"Where's the bottle of scotch?"

"You serious?"

"I'm serious."

"I put it back in the kitchen."

"I'm going in there to make myself a tall drink. Understand? And when I come back here, I want the whole story. Everything. Is that too much to ask?"

He waits there. Looking at me. Like he expects an answer. "No," I finally squeak out. And then a little louder, "Make one for me while you're at it."

When Stanley returns to the room with two glasses and the bottle, he's looking deadly serious. As well he should be. The fact of the matter being—as he is so quick to point out—that he and I could be socked into prison right along with Frank, if it ever came down to it. Unwitting accessories to the crime. Fellow agents in the game of espionage, and all the other rot. But as the minutes pass, and my story amplifies and expands with every sip of scotch I take on an empty stomach, he too begins to derive a certain truant pleasure out of the manic series of events. Which no doubt has something to do with scotch on his empty stomach, as well.

"You what?" he snorts, some thirty minutes into my tale.

"Drove the cliff over the car! I mean, the car, ha! over the cliff. You know, because we just couldn't lose these guys. We jumped out first, of course. Would you stop giving me those looks, Stanley! Look, we did it, didn't we? Actually outwitted those characters at their own game."

"And what exactly do these top secret memos have to say?"

"I didn't see much more than a lot of scientific notation and intelligence coded double-talk. But it would appear that everyone's involved in this cover-up from the Attorney General on down. I also suspect one of Frank's former lab assistants is mixed up in it someway or another. Remember the short pudgy guy in that picture of Frank's Columbia lab team? Him. . . . Have you ever heard of the U.S. Chemical Corps?"

"Has a vaguely familiar ring to it."

"Yeah? Well, it seems this Chemical Corps, whatever that is, passed some top secret material on to Dr. Walters. This was back in 81? 82? Senator Hellsley's name came up somewhere, as well."

"Hellsley?"

"Right. Funny, isn't it? All these so-called Right-To-Lifers who are so obsessed with death?"

"And where does your friend fit into all this?"

"Frank? What do you mean?"

"If one of his own lab assistants is implicated in this research, doesn't it stand to reason—"

"What are you saying, Stanley? That Frank was some-how involved in the monkey virus research down in Haiti? No way. At least, I don't . . . No, that's impossible. Why would he be leaking such incriminating evidence if he himself had been involved? Besides, don't you think I would have known if he had been mixed up in something like that? . . . . Look, Stanley. That research took place back in the middle seventies, right? I met Frank in 1980. By then, he'd already been working at Columbia for seven straight years. He couldn't very well have been working in two places at once, could he?" Stanley doesn't answer me. "What time does your mail usually arive?" I finally ask.

"Eleven, twelve o'clock." He tosses the wash cloth onto

the table and takes another look around the room. "Why don't I help you clean this place up and then head on over."

"I'm coming with you," I say, following him into the kitchen.

"Wouldn't it be a little smarter if I went on my own?"

"Because of my tails. . . . ? What will you do with the stuff if it's arrived?"

"Bury it. Until we make contact with your Mr. Kaufman. Sarah, you've got to trust me on this. There's no halfway here."

"I do, Stanley. I do. . . . So you're coming straight back here afterwards? No wait. Why don't you meet me over at Verdi's? That's where I told Kaufman to get in touch."

An hour or so later and Stanley is out the door. I take a good look at that banged up mug of mine in the bathroom mirror and decide that emergency measures are called for. Bangs. Retrieving a pair of scissors from a kitchen drawer, I set to work on my shoulder length locks. A little here. A little there. . . .

The result is catastrophic. An unmitigated disaster. Something in the square set of those bangs highlighting an unsuspected square and jowly set to my face. A vague bovineness which has been lying graciously at bay all these years. Until now. If I had the time, I'd no doubt sit myself down for a good cry. But it's already past eleven o'clock. Making a futile attempt at camouflaging the damage under one of Amy's wilder hats, I fill up the kitty's bowl and head out to Verdi's cafe. Wondering idly, enroute, if I'm being tailed by Arnold or Fatso, or any facsimile thereof. Not that I give a damn at the moment, because I don't.

"Have I received any calls?" I ask of George Faccio, as he drops a dollop of whip cream onto my double espresso.

"No calls, Miss Calloway. You have changed, no?" he adds, punching his stubby cigar into my face. "What is it?"

"Can't imagine. If anyone should call, I'll be in back," I add, before making my escape with the espresso and a hard boiled egg. I read. And wait. And get distracted by a Giants-Mets game on the TV set over the bar. Not so much by the game itself as by the characters watching the game. Men and sports.

Sometime around twelve-thirty, a waiter informs me I
have a phone call up front. I pick up the receiver and inhale,
unexpectedly short of breath. But it's only Laurie, suggesting that I drop by the cafe later on today. It concerns
something in Frank's journal, but she refuses to talk about it
over the phone. I hang up and return to the table, feeling
both intrigued and on edge about the possible tidings that
journal might impart. Is it possible that Stanley has the right
idea, after all? Could Frank have been mixed up in this
germ warfare research—even the research which spawned
AIDS—right from the beginning? Or if not from the
beginning, at least from early on? Is it just possible, in fact,
that the preposterous spy story which hit the media
yesterday evening is in some part true, and that Frank has
been some kind of 'consultant' for the CIA?

I order another espresso. Read. Wait. Where the hell is
Stanley? And receive a second call. This time from a Miss
Frannie Richardson, Philip Kaufman's secretary in New
York, calling to inform me that she has received my
message.

"Mr. Kaufman is in Washington D.C. for the week-end,
but we are making every effort to contact him. I will be
passing your message along to him just as soon as we do."

"So you don't have a Washington number for him?"

Oddly enough, she does not. I turn our little arrangement
around, promising to call her back at her office at six
o'clock, on the assumption that she will have a way for me
to contact Mr. Kaufman by that time. After hanging up, I
linger there by the door, speculating on the palpable
agitation in that woman's voice. How much does this
'secretary' of Kaufman's know about this entire affair? Why
wouldn't she have some way of contacting her boss in
Washington, if in fact he is in Washington? And how long is
it ultimately going to take her to track the man down? The
sooner the better, of course. Assuming that the necessary
material has arrived on schedule in Stanley's morning mail.
Right on Cue, Stanley strolls into the restaurant, passing by
me as he makes his way to the back of the room.

"Stanley," I murmur, falling in behind him. He turns,
looks about, turns away. Then turns back again in a classic

double-take. Staring incredulously at me for one long moment in time before a short, bark-like guffaw escapes from his throat.

"Did it come, dammit?" I hiss, prodding him toward our table.

"No, it didn't."

"Shit. . . . Are you sure?"

"Of course, I'm sure," he says, settling into the chair opposite and staring at me with what looks like a combination of poorly stifled amusement and disbelief. "What on earth did you do to yourself, Sarah?"

"Look, Stanley. Things are bad enough as it is. Kaufman is loose somewhere in Washington D.C. and his secretary doesn't even know how to track him down. And now you tell me the envelope hasn't arrived yet? . . . . I knew I never should have mailed the damn thing. No zip code. No real address. Trouble is, Laurie's mind was workng so much faster than mine. I'm not sure how much better, but definitely faster. Do this. Do that. I never had the time to think out whether any of it made sense or not."

"She seems to have had the right idea."

Stanley's right, of course. More than right. Without Laurie's assistance, there is no way I ever would have pulled the whole thing off. I fill Stanley in on my two phone calls. He tells me of another call I received on Thursday night. From Angelica.

"Shit, yes. We were supposed to have dinner together. Did she leave any kind of message?"

"Just that she's at the theater every afternoon. I had to drop by the office this morning," Stanley adds, bringing a news clipping out of his sport coat. "Picked this out of our files while I was there."

It's a 1983 AP news photo of Philip Kaufman, sitting behind some desk and holding a book up to the camera, *The Carrington Story* in black block letters across the cover. He is a slightly balding, barrel-chested man with a dark, bushy beard and intense dark eyes. The caption below the picture reads:

In his four million dollar law suit against Chemix
Pharmaceutical and Fielding Publishing, now being
filed in U.S. District Court, Kaufman claims that top
management at Chemix, after reading a leaked prepub-
lication manuscript of his book, became so alarmed at
its potential for damaging the company's image that
they launched a corporate plot to scuttle the book.

"You know, it's funny, Stanley. But the guy actually looks
like I pictured he would. I feel better already. I mean, about
having to hand the stuff over to him." I reread the caption,
indulging in a little wild speculation as to the kind of sordid
revelations which might have been part and parcel of
Kaufman's text. What horrors could the Carrington family
and Chemix be directly or indirectly responsible for over the
last thirty years to have made a corporate conspiracy of the
scale Kaufman alleges necessary in the first place? Aside
from the more obvious horrors, of course, of napalm, agent
orange, and toxic waste dumps leaking into America's
backyard from coast to coast. . . . The Bay of Pigs? The
military takeover of Allende's Chile? JFK's assasination? Or
his brother's? The Falkland War? Vietnam?

"Also dug something up on the United States Chemical
Corps," Stanley adds.

"No kidding."

"How much do you know about those biological warfare
experiments the Japanese conducted during the Second
World War?"

"On the Chinese? Not a whole lot, actually."

"It wasn't only the Chinese who were dragged into it,
Sarah. Russian and American POWs were part of the
experiments, as well. In total, I think some three or four
hundred soldiers were forced to participate. Every one of
them infected with any number of viruses and bacteria.
Mostly of the lethal variety. Needless to say, none of the
participants survived. After the war, the Russians wanted to
prosecute all the Japanese scientists involved. But the
United States military had other ideas. We made a secret
agreement with the Japanese government: immunity for the

men responsible for these barbarities in exchange for sole access to the data they collected over the four years time. Apparently we wanted to become experts in biological warfare in the worst way."

"In exchange for all the information they gave us, we let all those war criminals off scot free?"

"Some of them now head Japan's largest pharmaceutical firms."

"Jesus. Figures, doesn't it? And where does the Chemical Corps fit into this horror story?"

"That was the arm of the military which engineered the whole deal. More to the point, it was the Chemical Corps which got primary access to all the Japanese biological warfare research."

"I see. And if the Chemical Corps was so interested in germ warfare back in the forties, we can assume they're just as interested today? You suppose they were the driving force behind the Haiti fiasco?"

"A possibility. How was it again that their name came into the June Mail file?"

I take out my spiral notebook and read over the last page of notes. "Something about the Chemical Corps passing data on to Dr. Walters. Jesus, Stanley. This Walters character starts looking more and more diabolical with every new fact we learn."

"And Frank. . . . ?"

I would like to discuss Stanley's accusation and implications further, but he doesn't have the time, having agreed to participate in a public affairs television program to be taped at KQED this afternoon. Would I care to tag along? I have to get back with Laurie, I remind him. And Angelica, as well. On the off chance that she has anything more to say.

I call up Jennifer, filling her in on the latest and persuading her to accompany me down to the Mission district, where both Anglica and Laurie can be found at this hour of the day. Our first stop is the Eureka theater on 16th. Angelica is seated with four or five other members of the company down in the first row of seats, watching a couple of actors walk through a scene on stage. She nods in our direction as if she were expecting us. And after murmuring something to the man beside her, joins us in back.

"So it's true?" she asks, hands set on her hips in an attitude of hostility I have come to expect from the woman. "Our mutual friend is now a famous Russian spy?"

"I think the whole story's a crock of shit, Angelica."

"Well, I don't."

"You . . . ? Why? You know something we don't?"

She looks from Jennifer back to me, taking her time in articulating any kind of response.

"Did Frank ever tell you where we first met?" she finally asks.

"Never in so many words, no. I've always assumed it was at that SoHo party, back in the spring of 80? 81?"

She shakes her head, biting her lower lip. "We met a year earlier. In Brazil."

"Brazil? What in god's name was Frank doing in Brazil?"

"Right," Jennifer intervenes quietly. "Frank did go down to Brazil a few years back."

"But why?"

"He was part of a group of scientists sent there to investigate some kind of strange epidemic that broke out in the area."

"And he was working for the CIA, no?" Angelica confirms for Jennifer.

"Not at all. It was done through the Department of Public Health."

"Of course," I murmur, flashing back on Frank's Time Inc. file.

"Yeah, well you can call it whatever you want. But I saw the offices that Frank and the others were working out of, okay? In downtown Rio. And it wasn't no Department of Public Health, neither."

"So what was it?"

"AID."

"AID? You mean AIDS?"

"AID. Agency for International Development."

"What's that?"

"Where I come from, it's just another name for the CIA. Plain and simple. A front, okay? Everybody knows that. It's no secret, believe me. You Americans can be so dumb sometimes. Don't you know what your country is doing around half the world? You play it so innocent you make me sick." And with a shake of her shoulders which aptly reflects her degree of contempt and disgust, Angelica turns on her heels and walks off.

"Why didn't she tell me any of this earlier?" I demand of Jennifer once we're back out on the street. "Why didn't *you* tell me any of this earlier?"

"About his trip to Brazil? It didn't seem related. Is it related? He's been part of that group of trouble-shooters since 1971. Virologists. Bacteriologists. Geneticists. Any time some new disease turns up somewhere, they're sent to check it out. Even when it happens here at home. Remember the Swine Flu virus? Legionnaire's Disease? They worked on those two cases, as well."

"Where else have they gone? In Latin America, I mean."

"The Dominican Republic once, back in '77. Maybe Guatemala? I know what you're thinking, Sarah. But he was never longer than a week in any one place. They were there to investigate medical problems, nothing more."

"Then why didn't I ever hear about these medical junkets of his before? Ten months of listening to that guy talk shop, and never once did he refer to this work for the Department of Public Health. Now why?"

Laurie catches our eye as soon as we walk into the cafe and beckons us into the back room. She closes the door and sets both of us down in the two available chairs while she paces the floor between us.

"What is it, Laurie?"

She stops moving, stuffing her hands into the pockets of her overalls and looking anxiously from one of us to the other. "Frank's dying," she finally murmurs.

"What are you saying!" Jennifer jumps back out of her chair.

In answer, Laurie digs the journal out of her backpack, thumbs through it to a particular page of Frank's familiar tight script, and sets it on the table between us. We read:

July 9

The night sweats continue. Diarrhea and general
fatigue.

July 22

Swollen lymph nodes in neck and under arms. Chronic
low grade fever. Fatigue continues.

August 13

Antibody test positive. Which proves nothing in itself.
To be expected that I've been exposed to the virus
along with everyone else in the lab.

September 9

Blood blister—left leg. Also on both ears. Fatigue
overwhelming.

September 14

Lesion bioped—positive. Karposi's sarcoma. The
fuckers got me.

I flip over to the following page. But September 14 was
apparently the last entry Frank ever made. "Karposi's
sarcoma? What . . . ?"
  "Skin cancer. Most AIDS victims come down with it at
one point or another."
  "AIDS victims? Frank has AIDS?"
  "But that's impossible!"
  Laurie shakes her head, her face set in a grim frown as
she places the notebook into my hands. "Not impossible.
He could have been infected by somebody in the lab. It
would have been a relatively uncomplicated procedure. A
needle jab in the arm would be all it would take. An infected
needle, of course."
  "You mean on purpose, or what?"
  "What else could that last statement of his mean? Frank,

he . . . well, I just wish. . . . Shit." Laurie and I stand there eyeing each other wordlessly, as Jennifer breaks down in dry, muted sobs. One of Laurie's co-workers stumbles onto the scene.

"Uh, Laurie . . . well, see ya." And he darts back out again.

"I have to get back to work," Laurie finally murmurs, with a light touch to Jennifer's shoulder, and then mine, before starting for the door.

"Wait a minute, Laurie. Doesn't the AIDS virus have to incubate in the body for like years, before it starts taking effect?"

"They could easily have been working with more powerful mutations in their lab. . . . Call me, okay?" And she moves on out.

I turn back to Jennifer, watching helplessly as she stands there in the middle of the room, face buried in her hands and shoulders heaving. I'm not sure which unnerves me more. The horrible news about Frank, or Jennifer's anguished reaction to it. I had no idea she still cared for the man so after all these years. She certainly gave no evidence of such feelings prior to this. Could it come down to the fact of Frank being the father of her only son? Whatever the reason, she is taking the news very, very hard.

"You okay, Jennifer?"

She shakes her head. Slows down. Stops. Wipes off her face with the bottom of her sweater. And absurdly enough, apologizes. As if all this havoc were somehow her fault. Just when I'm beginning to wonder if it isn't all mine. She washes up in the cafe's restroom. Then joins me out front. We hike back through the city without exchanging a word. Each in our own way trying to digest and make some sense out of the latest curve ball thrown our way.

"How can I possibly explain all this to Jaimie?" Jennifer murmurs, as we stand there on the corner of Polk and Clay. A few tears running unimpeded down her cheeks.

"Jennifer, I . . . it's a shitty world. That's all there is to it." And on such a banal note as that, we take our leave until tomorrow night.

"Missy. I wouldn't go in there if I was you." It's the bag lady. The one who sits on the bench across from Amy's apartment 24 hours out of every day. Sitting there now with a styrofoam cup of coffee in one hand and a half eaten donut in the other.

"Why not?" I ask, stopping short and following her gaze up to the bedroom window.

"The same two men who was in there last night making trouble, just come back today. Just walked through your front door, as a matter of fact."

"Thanks," I murmur, whipping around without so much as a backward glance and tearing down Larkin to California. Then ducking into a Gala supermarket around the next corner. Now what? I ask myself, skirting up and down the aisles as if the answer might lie somewhere in the shelves of canned fruit or freezerfuls of poultry and meat. I don't have a dime on me and am finally obliged to 'borrow' a quarter from an elderly lady rolling past me with a cartful of cat food and Sara Lee frozen cakes. She directs me to a public phone in back. I put through a call to KQED, ask for Stanley, and am put on hold.

"London, here."

"Stanley! Thank God! They're back in the apartment! You know, the two guys from last night!"

"Calm down, Sarah. Where are you?"

"Some Gala food store. Corner of California and Polk."

"Be there in ten." And he hangs up. I pace the aisles. Up and down. Back and forth. Wondering how far these guys will go to get their hands on the damn file. My relationship with Stanley must serve as a protective agent of some sort, one would think. . . . Ten minutes are up and I dash into the parking lot. No Stanley. I wait one minute. Then two. And finally catch sight of him turning east onto California in the same old beat-up black sedan.

"Where are we going, Stanley?" I demand, as he veers onto the expressway off Van Ness.

"Does it matter? Out. Away."

"Are they assuming I have the stuff? If none of their own people could come up with the file in Frank's bungalow, why are they under the assumption that I could?"

Stanley doesn't have an answer for anything at the moment. He's not talking. Obviously angry. At me, I should think. For having dragged him into this increasingly more vicious affair. It doesn't help matters when I tell him about Frank. The latest news must obviously force his thought processes through the same gauntlet my own thoughts went through a few moments ago: if they are willing to kill off one of their leading scientists in order to keep this thing under wraps, what next?

As we speed north into wine country, I flip through Frank's journal, surprised to find many more pages of notes than I had originally assumed were here. A scattered and seemingly haphazard array of scribblings and notations, comprising in sum what would appear to have been an internal and ongoing debate he had been carrying on with himself on the subject of what?

Biological warfare research seems to have been the general topic. Perhaps in preparation for an article he was going to write? Or some speech he was planning to present? And where could his interest in all this have stemmed from, if not a growing certainty that the AIDS virus had been spawned by just such biological warfare research?

Early on, he discusses Defense Department allegations concerning Soviet use of mycotoxins or "yellow rain" on mountain tribes in S.E. Asia and Afghanistan. As well as an outbreak of anthrax within the Soviet Union which our Defense Department links up with intensified Soviet biological warfare research. Further back, he thrashes over allegations made by the Chinese and North Koreans, concerning U.S. use of biological weaponry as early as the Korean War. And the claim made by Cuban medical authorities that we have been using that country as our proving ground for biological weaponry since 1970; germ warfare 'experiments' which have allegedly resulted in great harm to Cuba's sugar and tobacco crops from smut and blue mold, in the slaughter of hundreds of thousands of pigs from swine fever, and in the death of any number of Cuban citizens from Dengue II hemorrhagic fever over the last several years.

The most interesting point Frank makes in the notebook—whether it is intended or not—is not made with words, but with pictures. Two pictures. One of the Soviet politburo, and on the opposite page, one of our president and his advisers. Both ruling bodies packed with nothing but older white males in dark suits. And looking very, very much alike.

The Frank of this notebook is not the Frank I knew five years ago.

Some two hours after leaving San Francisco, Stanley swings the car in front of a tiny Bed and Breakfast Inn just outside St. Helena, shuts off the motor, and rests his forehead on the steering wheel.

"You okay, Stanley?"

"Beat."

"Me too. Let's get something into our stomachs and hit the sack."

But first we must go about securing a room for the night. And then I call Kaufman's secretary in New York. Incredibly enough, she has not yet been able to contact her boss. I'm to call her back again at ten o'clock. Before heading downstairs for dinner, we watch a bit of the evening news. The story on 'double agent' Dr. Frank Winslow is heating up, usurping even more space on tonight's telecast than the night before. But a slimy twist has been added onto tonight's report, in the form of alleged statements made by co-workers and friends—none whom are identified—concerning Frank's supposed deterioration into the heavy use of alcohol and drugs.

"I can't believe this!" I rage quietly, snapping off the set. "Isn't it bad enough that they kill him off with the damn virus? And then accuse him of being some kind of Soviet spy? Which by the way Stanley, he most assuredly is not. Now they have to drag him through the muck of these other lies? It won't wash, Stanley. No way. Anyone who is even remotely acquainted with the man will see through all these absurd allegations. Frank is quite simply the most disciplined person I have ever met. He never smoked. Rarely drank. Never overate. Never overslept. Always out of bed by six a.m. for his cup of ginseng and five mile jog around Central Park. No kidding, Stanley. They're not going to get away with this."

"Let's eat."

We wait for a table in their vestibule, sipping silently on complimentary glasses of white wine. By the time they finally seat us, my appetite has snowballed enough to order the evening's special of pesto pasta and vegetable soup. Stanley orders the same, along with a bottle of the house red.

"Forget the damn cat, will you?" Stanley curtly advises me halfway through the meal, as he reaches for the bottle of wine and refills his glass.

"But how can I? God only knows what those gorillas might do to the poor thing just to prove some ugly point. I never should have left her alone like that. Never."

"You're really incredible, Sarah. The entire world's falling apart all around us, and all you can worry about is that lousy cat."

"What would you prefer I worry about, Stanley? AIDS? The Dengue II virus? Yellow rain? What?"

"Keep your voice down."

"Sorry. . . . Why are we acting like this anyway? Why are you so angry with me?"

"I'm not angry with you. I'm just a bit edgy. And beat. Can you understand that?"

"Of course I can. I'm not sure why I had to drag you into this whole mess to begin with."

"A very good question, Ms. Calloway." I look up to find a middle-aged gentleman standing by our table, sporting a shiny dark suit and tie, shiny black shoes, and a hair cut that has FBI written all over it even before he brings out his badge. "Lieutenant Scott Nemmens, here. I need to ask you a few more of those questions, Ms. Calloway. Might I join you?"

"Well actually, we're right in the middle of—"

"I'll only be taking up a minute of your time." And he sits down. Nodding briefly in Stanley's direction before shifting his chair into a position which faces me more directly. I wait for the man to speak, feeling inexplicably calm inside. Even a little relieved, that someone has finally decided to confront me head-on concerning this entire unwieldy affair.

It doesn't hurt any that the man looks about as intimidating as a soggy slice of french toast. Well-disposed light brown eyes set within a sallow, pasty-complected face. The kind of complexion which must stay pent up in fluorescent lit, air-conditioned offices the better part of any day, any week, any year.

"We have reason to believe you have some very important papers in your possession, Ms. Calloway." He pauses.

"What are you talking about?" I finally ask, for lack of a more acrid retort.

He smiles. And rears onto the back legs of his chair while reaching for our bottle of wine. Which he proceeds to empty into a water glass from an adjoining table. He takes a sip. Then begins passing the glass back and forth from one hand to the other. As if it were a baseball. Or better yet, a lump of clay he were molding into shape. His light brown eyes never leaving mine throughout this entire charade.

"It will suit your purposes much better if you cooperate with us, Ms. Calloway. Dr. Winslow has admitted to everything. Including the relevant detail that he has passed certain papers onto you for safekeeping."

"When were you talking with Dr. Winslow?"

"I'm the one asking the questions, Ms. Calloway."

"Look. You guys are raking the poor man over the coals with all those damn lies. Not to mention his son and ex-wife. And he sure as hell isn't any Soviet spy. You people make me sick," I add, in an unintentional echo of Angelica's pronouncement on myself earlier in the day.

"And what were you doing snooping around the doctor's residence in Paradise Valley last Thursday night?"

"Looking for Frank."

Another smile. Another sip of wine. "And did you find him?"

"We didn't find a goddamn thing, if it's any of your business. But whatever thugs hit the place before us sure as hell found something. The place had been turned inside out."

"You're lying, Ms. Calloway. . . . We could make a lot of trouble for you. And your friends," he adds, his eyes flicking sideways in an obvious reference to Stanley sitting there at his back. "I'm sure you can appreciate that. You do not strike me as a stupid woman, Ms. Calloway."

"Flattery will get you nowhere." I can see Stanley scowling over the agent's head, obviously a bit less enamoured with my performance than I am myself. "Look, Lieutenant Nemmens. I don't have these goddamn papers you're talking about. Understand? Talk to the guys who broke into the place before us. They're the ones with the damn papers. Trust me."

Lieutenant Nemmens turns to look at Stanley. Then back at me. Taking a last swallow of wine before setting the glass down on the table with a certain note of finality and standing up. "We have reason to believe that Dr. Winslow will be getting in touch with you in the near future. If such is the case, would you be so kind as to pass a message on to him from us?"

"From the FBI?"

"Close enough. Tell him the deal's back on."

"Back on?"

"That's correct."

"Why should I do you guys a favor? You've been treating the man like shit."

The Lieutenant winces. Not the first time. "It's to Winslow's great advantage to be informed of the situation. Good night, Ms. Calloway. And rest assured that we will be back in touch." With a vague bow, he turns and walks out of the room.

"I don't get it," I whisper to Stanley once the man is out the door. "Was that it? Wasn't the guy terribly easy on me? At the very least, I expected some patriotic spiel on the subject of our national security. At the very least! For that matter, he could just as well have laid some accessory spy charges on me and hauled me off to jail, couldn't he have?"

"Apparently you're more valuable to these people out of their custody, than in. As long as they can keep you on a very short leash."

I take Stanley's left hand in both of mine. Turn it over. Trace the deeper lines of his palm with my finger. His life line. Which runs clear off his hand. Obviously he's meant to live a long life. My own life line is relatively short. "Are you my leash?"

"What the hell is that supposed to mean?" he snaps, withdrawing his hand.

"I'm not sure, Stanley. It's just that. . . . well the way that Lieutenant Nemmens acted back there. The way he looked at you. I mean, why wasn't he more concerned about you being here at the table with me? For all he knows, the whole stupid scene could wind up in your Monday morning column, couldn't it? Even more to the point, how in hell did they know I was up here in the first place? Who could possibly have seen us leaving the city when we did?"

"For Christ's sake, Sarah. Would you just use your head for one damn second! The papers are coming to my address, aren't they? If I'm working for the FBI, as you seem so bent on convincing yourself that I am, then their problems would be over, wouldn't they?"

"I guess so."

"Be up at the bar," he mutters, dropping his napkin onto the table and stalking out of the room. What the hell am I doing alienating the one sure and constant ally I seem to have in this case? I push aside my plate and go join him at the bar.

"Try to understand what I'm going through, Stanley," I say, slipping onto an adjacent stool. "I don't even know how to think anymore. It's like, I'm beginning to lose my grip on reality. No, I mean it, Stanley! All the predictable patterns my thought processes have been flowing into all these years just don't seem to be working anymore. Can't you see?"

"What I see, sweetheart, is a woman digging a hole for herself that's so deep, so wide, I'm not sure she's ever going to be able to climb back out."

"Gee, thanks for the encouragement. Just what I needed to hear, pal."

"You just damn well perjured yourself back there, Sarah. With a representative of the United States government."

"With a what? Since when did you get so self-righteous, Stanley? Of course I just perjured myself. What did you expect me to do? Hand over the papers? Just like that? Look Stanley, you better understand one thing here. I'm committed to helping Frank out on this. Right or wrong, it's what I'm going to do. To the best of my ability, anyway. Besides, that was no perjury. I wasn't under oath or anything, was I? And when it comes down to it, I don't have the papers, do I?" A point which reminds me of the need to contact Kaufman's secretary in New York. I ask Stanley to order me a Manhattan while I head up to the room.

Just as I unlock the door, and before I turn on the light— before I even turn around and see the man sitting there in the chair by the bed—I see the man sitting in the chair by the bed, via an image which flashes across my mind's eye. In the process of translating terror into sound, a large hand is clamped over my mouth and I am yanked back against an invisible hulking presence. My free arm twisted up behind my back.

"No one's going to get hurt, Miss Calloway," says the man sitting in the chair by the bed. His voice that of a cultured British salesman. "We're here as your friends. Do you understand? We want to help you. We want to help Dr. Winslow. But I must insist that you cooperate with us. Or it is going to be very difficult for us all."

I stop struggling. The hulk behind me slackens his grip. I shake loose and turn around to check my adversary out. Expecting an Arnold type, if not Arnold himself, the man before me seems surprisingly thin, and surprisingly young. He nods and smiles at me, as if he had been caught playing some childish prank.

"What is this?" I demand, looking from one man to the other. "Who are you?"

"You're going to have to do better than that, Miss Calloway," says the gentleman in the chair, his finger going up to his lips. "It's going to work against all of us if you bring our presence to the notice of anyone in this hotel."

"So who are you?"

"Let's just say we are people with the same interests at heart as you have. And your friend Dr. Winslow has. Your purposes serve our purposes, and vice versa."

"So who the hell are you?" I try for a third and last time.

In answer, he brings a card out of a vest pocket and places

it on the desk by his side. I hesitate a moment, then walk over and pick it up. And jump—visibly I'm afraid—at the printed words on the card. Soviet Consulate General across the middle in block print. An address on Green street in the right hand corner. And a telephone number on the left.

"What is this, some kind of set up?" I demand, glancing frantically about for hidden cameras. Or Lieutenant Nemmens, lurking in some dark corner of the room. "Your partner comes in one second and asks me to help in the name of the FBI? And then you come in the next and ask me to help out in the name of the KGB? AC-DC. Is that it? You figure, if I won't go one way, I'll go the other?"

"This is no set up, Miss Calloway."

"Like hell it isn't. Since when do Russian agents have British accents, can you tell me that?"

"That is where I learned to speak English, my friend. It can't be helped." The man is actually smiling. All these congenial government agents are baffling the hell out of me. He certainly doesn't look Russian. Neither does his friend. At least not how I assume a Russian should look. No thick neck or heavy jawline to confirm a vague Slavic descent. "Are you ready to listen?" he finally says, motioning me to sit down on the bed as if I were a guest in his room rather than the other way around. I take another look about. Walk into the bathroom. Come back out and sit.

"Your friend Dr. Winslow is in a lot of trouble. We believe we can help him out." He stops, as if he expects me to say something. But I'm determined to keep my mouth shut for as long as I possibly can. He says something in Russian to the character standing by the door. Whereupon the young man settles crosslegged upon the floor. "To set the record straight," he continues in English. "I'm not working for the KGB, as you put it a moment ago. I work with the Soviet Consulate. If you do not believe me, just call over there tomorrow morning. . . . Dr. Winslow made contact with us a month ago and asked for our help. Then he disappeared. Or perhaps he changed his mind. Or had his mind changed for him. We do not know. But what is very clear at this point is that the man is in most serious trouble. Is he not?"

"Why would Frank have ever gone to you for help, for God's sake?"

"This material he—or you—hold on genetic military research. Oh yes, Miss Calloway. He told us everything. Why? Because he fears the material may well fall into the wrong hands."

"And you're the right hands?"

"As I said earlier, Miss Calloway, we have the same interests at heart. He wants that information out in the open. So do we. For the obvious reasons." And he smiles again. This one a little more sinister than the last.

"Look. Even if I could help you, which I can't, I couldn't. You understand? I mean, even if you are who you say you are, which I don't believe for a second, I couldn't help you. I don't have this material you're talking about, number one. And number two. Frank obviously decided to follow another strategy that leaves you out."

"Listen to me, Miss Calloway. Your doctor friend is in very serious trouble. Very serious. With no one to turn to. Whatever plan he—or you—may have up your sleeve for the exposure of these papers, it will not, *can not* work. Do you understand? Your government, your corporate military-industrial complex—this is no laughing matter, Miss Calloway—your military-industrial complex will never allow such a thing to come about."

"In this country we still have something called a free press, Mr . . ." and I look down at the card. "Mr. Tzortizis?"

"We know everything about your free press, Miss Calloway."

"Look," I say, standing up. "This is all really a waste of time. I don't have this material you're speaking of. Really I don't. The whole situation is out of my hands."

He stands. So does his friend, a paperback dropping out of his coat pocket. I could swear it was a book on chess. The young man bobs his head and backs out of the door. My Russian agent hesitates, his hand on the door knob. "I must urge you to reconsider your options, Miss Calloway. To reconsider and to call. Many things hang in the balance with the possible exposure of all this. I am sure you feel the way we do. At least on this most important issue."

"Was it your goons who broke into my apartment last night? Roughed up my friend?"

His eyes narrow slightly. "We don't work in such ways, Miss Calloway."

"Like hell you don't. Look, don't expect me to be *too* naive, okay?"

"You're making a very grave mistake. This attitude of yours is only hurting yourself. Yourself and Dr. Winslow. Good night, Miss Calloway. And remember, I can be reached at that number 24 hours a day. Do you understand?" And with a last nod, he backs away and closes the door.

A few minutes pass, as I stand there in the middle of the room mentally reviewing the scene which has just taken place. Then I walk up to the door, open it, and take a peek out. The hallway is empty. I lock the door and pick up the phone, beginning to dial New York. Then hang up and head downstairs, on the assumption that the wires into our room could already be tapped. Stanley is sitting where I left him, at one end of the bar, chatting with the bartender. I walk right past them and put through my call on the public phone out in the lobby. No answer. I hang up and try again. Still no answer. I check out the time on the clock over the front desk. It's 10:45 P.M. Which translates into 1:45 A.M. back east. Did I blow it? My only option is to try again tomorrow morning, as soon as I get out of bed.

"You're *not* going to believe this, Stanley," I murmur, sliding onto an adjacent stool and smiling up at the bartender. I make a quick survey of the room and stab at the cherry sitting at the bottom of my drink.

"What's up, Sarah?"

"It's kind of private," I allow, giving the bartender another smile. He moves to the other end of the bar.

"Who do you suppose—who could you imagine in your wildest dreams—was waiting for me just now up in the room."

"Frank."

"The KGB."

Stanley sets his glass down very carefully on the marble bar top and turns to look me straight in the eye.

"No kidding, Stanley. Not that they actually admitted to being KGB. But we can assume. . . . What they—or he—the other one never said a word—what he actually said, was that he worked for the Soviet Consulate. In San Francisco. Can you believe that, Stanley! How in hell does everybody know where we are? That's what I would like to know! This is turning into one big fucking party up here. We might as well have printed invitations. And you know what he told me? That Frank had gone to them for help a month or so back. Who can say whether or not the guy was being straight with me. But I must say, he put across a damn convincing argument."

"Which was?"

"In so many words, it stands to reason that the Soviet government would want the AIDS-U.S. military link brought to light, just as much as Frank or anyone else, doesn't it? Obviously for different reasons. But the common ground is there, all the same."

"You're not considering cooperating with these people, are you Sarah?"

"Of course not. . . . Though it had crossed my mind."

"Then cross it right out again. For all you know, this is nothing more than some crazy counter-plot set up by our own intelligence network."

"Don't you think I thought of that, Stanley? Besides, the real problem here is that even if they are who they say they are—and even if they went ahead and broke the scandal in their own press—what good would it do? Who over here would believe them? Our government would no doubt write off the whole preposterous story as nothing more than communist propaganda. And as usual, our press would docilely follow suit. And that would be the end of that. Obviously what we want here, is for our own papers to break the scandal. Not theirs. But the question is—will something that damning ever be allowed into our press? Assuming, of course, that Frank and Kaufman's strategy is to pass those papers on to the press. Which it obviously must be, right?"

We finish our drinks and head up to the room. Stanley makes a quick check of walls, curtains, and furniture, unwilling to go to bed until fully satisfied that the place is clean of bugs. But as soon as his head hits the pillow, he's off and snoring. Sleep doesn't come quite so easily for me tonight. I pass many long and restless hours, waking in and out of dreams which seem to brim over with contradictory images and double negatives, all of them at cross purposes with each other and everything else. The blue iceman over at Chemix fuses in and out of a looking glass image of Philip Kaufman, who is in some vague manner linked up to Lieutenant Nemmens, who has features not unlike that of my Russian visitor of a few hours ago. Who, at closer inspection, bears an eerie resemblance to Frank himself. And then Arnold looms into the picture, puffing on a large Cuban cigar. Or is it Stanley? Blowing ominous black smoke rings into the young Russian's face.

Romping through the middle of this phantasmagoric mirror-play is The Fool herself, manila envelope in hand, drawing inexorably closer to the edge of that cliff, with a herd of reptilian creatures waiting open-jawed in the steamy valley below.

"Stanley!" I hear myself call out, seconds before I realize that I am the one doing the crying. I wake to find myself being rocked in Stanley's arms.

"How long have I been talking in my sleep like that?"

"Just relax, sweetheart," he murmurs, continuing to rock me back and forth in his arms. The primal, reassuring motion gradually dispelling the terror in my throat, the knot in my stomach, and the chill over my heart.

"I need you so much, Stanley," I whisper. Certainly an absurd moment to be admitting to any such emotion or want, God only knows. But then again, no more absurd than the rest of this day has been. Stanley's only response is to hold me tighter and to continue rocking. Sometime before dawn, I finally fall back asleep.

JUNE 27

I awake this morning to the sound of Stanley singing in the shower, a wave of well-being and hope rushing through me. Which is immediately negated by a sense of foreboding, when I recall the seemingly unsolvable quandary which we—or at least I seem to find myself enmeshed in.

"Good morning, Sunshine," Stanley announces upon strolling back into the room.

"Good morning! What put you into such a good mood today?"

He settles onto the edge of the bed, ruffling my new set of bangs. "You know, Sarah. Those things are actually sexy in a certain Mickey Mouse, primary schoolish sort of way. . . . Have a rough night?"

"I guess so. Feel a hell of a lot better today, though. What time is it?"

"Nine fifteen."

"I have to call New York," I say, scrambling out of bed and into my jeans. "Can you believe I still haven't been able to get hold of that guy? The irony of it all! Here, everybody and their brother is trying to get their hands on the damn file, and the one person I can actually give it to is incommunicado. God, what a gorgeous day," I add, moving over to the window as I button up my blouse.

"Certainly is. And we're going to make the most of it."

"What are you talking about? You don't expect us to just . . . ?"

"Why not? It's beautiful country up here. Lots of wineries to visit. Good food and drink to be had."

"Come on, Stanley? After last night?"

"That's precisely the point, sweetheart. What better subterfuge for all these bastards—Russian, American, or otherwise—than for us to simply spend the day enjoying ourselves. We'll confound them all."

"What's gotten into you, Stanley! Yesterday, you were so . . . I love it!"

"Guess I finally woke up to what a great story there could be in all this."

"Ha! You don't say! Well, don't think for one minute that you're going to be stealing it from under me, Mr. London," I say, jabbing him in the stomach. He grabs me and kisses me on the lips. In a way, quite frankly, that he has never kissed me before.

"What *has* gotten into you, Stanley!"

A light tap on the door freezes us both in place.

"Yes?" I ask hollowly.

"Coffee, Ma'am."

"Right," Stanley says, striding over to the door. "I ordered some for us down at the bar last night."

A young lady enters, bearing a trayful of coffee-attendant paraphernalia, including a silver urn, a silver creamer, a silver bowlful of sugar cubes, cups and saucers, and two large glasses of fresh juice.

"I have to call New York," I remind Stanley, following the young woman out of the room.

"So call from up here."

"But what if . . . ?" I shut the door. "What if the phone is tapped?"

"It isn't."

"How can you be sure?"

"Because I used it this morning. Had to cancel an interview, among other things. Trust me woman, it's not tapped."

"How did you become such an expert on these things, Stanley? You're going to have to fill me in on your mysterious past someday. You know that, don't you?"

I put through the call. Miss Richardson answers on the

first ring, sounding greatly relieved upon hearing my voice. She passes on a phone number where I am to contact Philip Kaufman at five o'clock this afternoon. Why must I wait until five, I wonder? But do not ask. As soon as I hang up, I memorize the number, ask Stanley to memorize the number, and then put a match to the piece of scrap paper I had scribbled it on.

"213. That isn't a Washington D.C., area code, Sarah. That's out of L.A."

"Yeah? So apparently this Mr. Kaufman gets around. I tell you right now, I cannot wait to drop the whole kettle of fish into his lap!"

We head downstairs for a walk about town, Stanley stopping off at the front desk to set us up for a second night in this inn.

"Does it make any sense for us to spend another night up here?" I suggest, once we are out the front door.

"What good will it do us being back in San Francisco? The longer we stay up here, the better chance we have of putting them off the trail of that file. The mail won't be getting in tomorrow before eleven o'clock. I'll have us back in the city by ten."

We stroll down the main street of town, up one side and then the other, before returning to our Inn for their Sunday brunch. This afternoon's theme is California-Mex: ranchos huevos and cut-rate champagne. Stanley forgoes the champagne for our own private stock of tequila and lime.

"A little on the early side for my tastes," I say, pushing my glass over to his side of the table and digging into the steamy basket of corn tortillas there between us. Before Stanley gets down more than a bite of breakfast, a waitress approaches to inform him of a phone call at the front desk.

"Wait a minute, Stanley," I murmur, as he pushes away from the table. "Who could possibly know you're up here?"

"Jesus, Sarah. I made a couple of phone calls this morning, if you recall. You just won't give up, will you?" And with a weary shake of his head, he disappears into the dining room beyond.

As two minutes slide into five, and five into ten, I check

out for possible signs of the enemy out here on the patio, while taking intermittent sips on my tequila and lime—surprised at how pleasantly pungent the combination tastes, even at this early hour of the day. Tequila in the afternoon. Could make a provocative title for my next story, I think, helping myself to another sip. It would be the story of a love affair, of course. Between say . . . between a middle aged American housewife and a young Mexican priest. They will run off to Mexico together. Why not? And visit the tiny, impoverished—but beautiful—village where he was born. One week in the life of a passionate but doomed affair.

I take another sip as a core scene materializes: a shady river bank on a beautiful summer's morning. The sun rippling off the water in piercing rings of light. It's the river which runs through his village, of course. The river which he used to swim in as a boy. On impulse, he tears off his clothes and jumps in, the water cool like electric satin on his skin. He beckons her to join him there. But she dare not, knowing full well that her aging body will not stand up to the cruel test of the early morning light. And it is at this precise moment that she is forced to face up to the impossibility of it all. This young man before her, just beginning to wake up to the sensuality at play all around him, at the very time when she herself is on the brink of closing down.

By the time Stanley returns to the table, the combination of tequila and an imagination run amok, have totally submerged me in my theme. The gut sensuality of life seeming to assert itself wherever I turn. In the sultry Roberta Flack number coming through the speakers by the door. In Stanley's blueish-grey smoke rings, rising so languorously toward extinction in the sharp-edged afternoon light. In the sweet-sour smack of the lime juice on my lips. Stanley is very good at picking up the signals. With or without breakfast. And in no time at all, we find ourselves back up in the room, taking full advantage of life's keen and sensual sway.

"The door, Stanley," I call out, stepping out of the shower and into my jeans and sweater once again. He goes to answer it. "Stanley?" I walk into the room to find Fatso and friend standing over by the door, waving ugly looking pistols in my general direction. Stanley is lying unconscious in the middle of the floor.

"Stanley," I murmur, crouching low over his inert form, while ten or more divergent strategies, feasible or otherwise, stampede through my head. Fatso's partner gives me a quick kick to the ribs. No pain. Only a suffocating panic. It takes a good sixty seconds to get back my breath, as the two men stand over me, their Nazi boots only inches from my face.

"Okay, Hotshot. Miss Wonderwoman," sneers Fatso, hauling me up from under the arms and pitching me onto the bed like a sack of potatoes. "The fun is over."

I sit up, pulling my sweater tighter around me.

"Let's have it, Hotshot."

"What are you talking about?"

He belts me across the face with the back of his hand, sending me reeling over the bed. This time there is plenty of pain, the sharp dizzying kind, from my right jaw clear through to the back of my head. I lie there, cowering behind my hands as he readies another blow. "I don't have it," I whisper weakly. Too late, as his hand comes down again, the force of the blow mainly on my knuckles and right ear. He grabs me by the hair and yanks me up to a standing position, his ugly mug only inches from my own.

"Do I got to repeat myself for the lady? The fun is over. No more games. Now where are the fucking papers?"

"Let go of me," I whine, well-nigh incapacitated by the way he's jerking me around. Miraculously enough, he does let go. Shoving me back onto the bed.

"Should we make it easy for the princess?" he says, looking over at his partner and then back at me. "We got your doctor friend, see? And he's nothing but dead meat unless you cough up those papers for us. Clear enough?"

"I don't believe you," I murmur, realizing my mistake as soon as the words are out of my mouth. Flinching under my arms in preparation for the next inevitable blow.

His sneer widens into a thin, repulsive smile that sends a wave of nausea into my throat. "Charlie," he says, holding his free hand out toward his buddy. "Bring it out for the princess."

Charlie draws a small box out of a jacket pocket and passes it on to Fatso.

"A message from your doctor friend," he says, tossing the box onto my lap. "Stop gawking, lady. Open it. See what your friend has to say."

I take off the lid. Inside is something wrapped up in yellow paper towelling, spots of fresh red blood seeping through the layers. Slowly, I unwrap the paper, letting out an involuntary gasp at the sight of a purplish-red human ear lying there, one of my burglarized jade earrings jammed through the lobe.

"It's in my purse," I mutter through gritted teeth. "In the goddamn purse."

Fatso kicks my purse across the room to where Charlie still stands, there by the door.

"Nothing here," Charlie says, burrowing through all the crap.

"In my wallet. A key."

"Got it, Benny." And he tosses the key over to Fatso, who turns it over in his hand and holds it up to the light.

"Greyhound. San Francisco," he reads. "You wouldn't be playing anymore of your fucking games with us. Would you, Hotshot?"

"You got what you came for. You better damn well let go of Frank."

"You hear that, Charlie?" he says, drawing a rope from somewhere inside his coat. "Hotshot is giving the orders now. Come over here, bitch," he snaps, dragging me by the hair onto the straight-back chair by the dresser. He hands the rope over to Charlie, who proceeds to bind me hand and foot to that chair. Fatso does nothing but stand back and watch, an ugly sneer still plastered across his face. Then he walks over to the bed, picks up the bloody ear, and dangles it in front of my nose. "Open up, Princess." I hesitate one moment too long and another blow cuts across my jaw. "Open your fucking mouth." He stuffs the ear inside, followed up by a balled-up dirty rag drawn out of his back pocket. The gag is secured with some electric tape he winds around and around my head.

"Ain't she a pretty sight, though?" he jeers, wagging my

chin back and forth. His hand slithers down to my neck, his thumb pressing gently into my throat. Then not so gently. "Okay bud," he adds, stuffing his gun into his belt and buttoning up his coat. Holding the door open for Charlie, he flips the "Do Not Disturb" sign on to the outer knob, bends over Stanley to check him for any signs of life, then apparently satisfied, follows his partner out of the room.

I listen to their footsteps fade away down the hall. Then make a vain attempt at turning off all my senses. Doing my best to obliterate the throbbing pain in my head, the aching numbness in my hands and legs, and above all, the taste and feel of that bloody, fleshy ear pushed against the roof of my mouth. After interminable wriggling and writhing, I am able to work my legs free enough to lurch my way across the room to where Stanley lies. There is a dried trail of blood leading out of a gash over his right ear to a small puddle there on the rug. I start giving him short, ineffectual kicks in the stomach. One minute, two, and he begins to stir, moaning softly in a pitiful replay of his predicament just two days before.

"Jesus," he mumbles. Or I think he mumbles. I try to make some kind of sound myself from around the crap in my mouth. But nothing comes out. His eyelids flutter. Then stop. I kick some more. At long last his eyes really open, as his right hand goes to the back of his head. "Sarah?" He struggles to his knees, then falls backwards. And turning over onto his stomach, he manages to bring himself back up to his knees once again. "Good God, what happened?" He sways to his feet and begins to fumble away at one or two of the many knots locking me down to the chair. Swearing steadily as he goes, and taking what seems like an ungodly amount of time to get anywhere at all.

At long last my hands are free. I yank the tape off my head and spit all the shit out of my mouth. Then help him with the rest of the knots, all without saying a word. I'm too nauseous to dare open my mouth. When I have finally shed the last of the rope, I rush straight to the bathroom and throw up brunch.

I return to the bedroom to find Stanley back down on his knees, looking like he just might black out again. I help him into the bed and call downstairs for a hot water bottle, some tea, and a bottle of aspirin. Then, stuff the ear into the box and toss it into the dresser, and scrub the blood stain on the carpet into a dull brown blur. When the waitress arrives with the order, I inform her of our change in plans. We will no longer be taking the room for a second night.

By his third cup of tea, Stanley seems to be partially revived. At least to the point where a wry smile appears on his face.

"What could you possibly be finding amusing in all this?" I demand, holding warmed washcloth up to his temple.

"Nothing really. It's just that . . ."

"What?"

"Well, I'm certainly glad we came all the way up here to avoid any unnecessary confrontations."

"You find that funny? It's damn spooky, if you ask me. It's beginning to look like wherever we go, we can count on my muckers being close behind."

"Who were those last pair of freaks connected up to?"

"God only knows. They sure as hell didn't tell me. They were vicious bastards, that's for damn sure."

"So how the hell did you get them off your back?"

"I gave them the key."

"What key?"

"When Laurie and I came into the Greyhound station Friday afternoon, I rented a foot locker. Got myself a key. Guess I was figuring a red herring might come in handy one of these days."

"I'm impressed, Sarah," Stanley says, looking like he means it. "Would never have thought you had it in you to be so devious and sly."

"Me neither. I'm learning, I guess. I learned something else today, Stanley. When the chips are down, I turn into a lily-livered coward. No, I mean it. Just glad you weren't around to witness my pitiful performance. Those characters scared the shit out of me. How do people ever manage to stand up under pain and torture like that? One mean belt across the kisser and I was ready to throw in the towel. Well, until I remembered the key. You haven't seen the worse of it, Stanley,'' I add, going over to the drawer and bringing specimen A out of the drawer, dropping it by his side of the spread.

"What the hell. . . " Stanley murmurs, gingerly handling the box. "My God . . . who the hell's is it?"

"They want me to believe it's Frank's."

"Christ almighty."

"But I don't think it is, Stanley. No blood blisters, see? In his notebook, Frank talked about blood blisters on both of his ears." We continue to stare down at the dismembered ear for a moment or two longer in mute, repugnant fascination, before I drop it back into its box and back into its drawer.

"Then who the hell does it belong to?" Stanley asks.

"Who knows. Fucking awful to even contemplate, right? That they might have lopped off some poor sucker's ear just to make their point? What now?" I ask, after an extended pause. "I mean, we obviously can't stay around here tonight. Once those low-lifes get a peek at that locker I'm in big trouble. The real question here is, how the hell am I ever going to manage passing the stuff on to Kaufman with all these gorillas breathing down our necks?"

"There might be a way out of this, Sarah. If you're willing to enlist a little outside help."

"What kind of outside help?"

"George Faccio's."

"How the hell can he help us out?"

"Friends."

"Yeah? What kind of friends?"

He waits a moment or two before answering. "Gorillas in their own right. Look at it this way, Sarah. It will take one to beat one."

"But who are these people, Stanley?"

"People who can be trusted. And who have had plenty of experience with this kind of thing."

"You're not talking about bringing the mob into this thing, are you Stanley? Jesus, as if we didn't have enough different parties messed up in this fucking shooting match, as it is."

"Do you have any better suggestions?"

Needless to say, I don't. So I go along with Stanley's scheme, on the condition that Faccio is told no more than is absolutely necessary.

"That was it?" I ask Stanley, after his one or two minute conversation on the phone.

"That's it."

"So what now?"

"We're to meet them at a steak house in San Rafael. Three o'clock. They'll take it from there."

2:45 and we're settled into a corner table of Freddie's Steak House somewhere east of San Rafael, downing another pot of tea. I'm concerned about Stanley's chances of recognizing our 'friends', when and if they should ever turn up. How to distinguish one set of gorillas from another? But my worries are groundless. It is Sid, George's more than portly younger brother who strolls through the door, approaches the bar to ask for some change, and strolls back out again. We follow suit, and are promptly ushered into the back seat of a silver-plated Rolls Royce. A distant cousin to the number I smashed into on the expressway just a week or so ago.

No introductions are made. It's strictly business here, as our driver, a bearded gentleman who himself looks vaguely familiar, guns the motor and takes us on a strangely exhilarating joyride through the foothills of Marin. Maybe it's the incredible beauty of the countryside we're passing through. Or maybe it's the relief which comes from abdicating responsibility for oneself and one's mission, if only for a circumscribed amount of time But there's a certain unreal, almost antic quality to the next few hours, as Stanley and I hold hands in the plush back seat of this handsome vehicle while our hard-nosed consorts, who damn well seem to know what they're doing, take over the entire show.

We wind up in a split-level colonial set high on a bluff overlooking the city of Tiburon and the San Francisco Bay. The view from up here is prime time. The entire set up is prime time. Panoramic picture windows and fireplaces in every other room. Redwood beams, skylights, and hand woven carpets enhancing every ceiling and floor. Northern California at its most extravagant, sumptuous, and lush.

"Who the hell owns this place?" I whisper to Stanley, as we wander into their large, supermodern kitchen, our chaperons close behind. Stanley shrugs off my question, as if he doesn't know the answer, then heads straight for a bottle of scotch over the sink, as if he does. Sid steps into the den and switches on the set. Football. The beard checks out the cupboards and refrigerator, and heads back out to the car.

"Scotch, Sid?" Stanley offers, bringing out a bucket of ice and setting up an impromptu bar on the kitchen table.

"Nah." Which is the first peep I've heard out of that guy since we got into the car.

"How about you, sweetheart?"

"What is this? Some kind of party we're having here, or what?"

"Might as well relax and enjoy ourselves. It's going to be a long night."

"Is Sid the only protection we're going to have, Stanley? Did that other fellow leave for good?"

"He'll be back. *Relax*, Sarah," he adds, passing me a Manhattan I never ordered. "These guys are pros."

So were the others, I think leerily, moving upstairs to make my call. I trace down a pink princess in the master bedroom and settle on the bed for a moment or two, sipping my drink and running through the possible permutations on my conversation with Kaufman before dialing L.A.

He sounds like he looks. Intense, clipped, and to the point. And at the moment, none too happy that I yielded the precious envelope into the hands of the United States Post Office. And less happy still, when I tell him I mailed it to a certain friend, whom I choose to leave nameless, and whom Mr. Kaufman is clearly indisposed to trust.

Our dialogue is riddled with pauses—the weighty, censorious kind—and by the time we hang up, I find I have developed a distinct dislike for the man. Put off by his abrupt and arrogant disposition. Or more to the point, by his utter lack of appreciation for the blood and sweat I have donated in the interest of resolving this affair.

"Quite unsatisfactory," I tell Stanley, joining him at the kitchen table downstairs. "Even forgot to ask what he plans on doing with the stuff once I hand it over. I have the right to know that much, don't I?"

"So ask him tomorrow. It's all set?"

I close the door between the kitchen and the den, and return to the table. "He's meeting us in the coffee shop on the ground floor of your building. Eleven o'clock. We decided it would be too risky meeting in your apartment, on the chance your place is being cased."

Stanley scoops up our glasses, dumps out the watered down ice, and freshens up our drinks.

"Funny, isn't it?" I say, once he hands me the fresh drink. "To think I'll be going back to New York in a few days time."

"What's your hurry?"

"For one thing, I'm broke. The sooner I get home, the sooner I can finish up that moronic health spa article I was working on and get some money in the bank. The Ten Spots To Lose Ten Pounds within Ten Miles of Manhattan. Can't believe the crap I agree to write."

"Why *do* you agree to write that stuff, Sarah?"

"Because I need to eat, that's why. We can't all be as lucky as you, Stanley. You pick your stories. I get them picked for me. Well, in a manner of speaking, anyway. I mean, I know the kind of junk they'll print, and that's what I give them. So be it."

"You sound like you've given up. At thirty-five."

"I haven't given up. The important part of every day is devoted to my fiction. From the moment I get out of bed until lunch. That's hardly giving up, is it?"

"If you put it that way, you could just as well be writing out here, as back in New York."

"But I have a rent-controlled apartment back in New York. Which I'll probably be chained to until death do us part. I'm serious, Stanley! I was priced out of the housing market years ago. Unless I want to go back to working full time in some stinking office, which God knows I do not."

"Parts of San Francisco are considerably less expensive than Manhattan."

"Like where? Sixth and Market?"

"Like the Mission district, for one."

"Yeah . . . ? I don't know."

"I thought you liked that neighborhood."

"I do. With the sun up and the cops cruising, it's a groovy place. But after dark, I have a feeling most single women crawl into their holes and watch *Miami Vice.* . . . What are you smiling at?"

"Just thinking."

"About what?"

"About the first time I ever saw you."

"At Verdi's?"

"Sitting at that table with your book and basket of calamari. Looking so perfectly content in your own company, I hated to butt in. But I couldn't resist."

"Thank God. I shudder to think I might never have met you, Stanley. I mean it! . . . You want to know what I first liked about you? From the very start? The way you listen. Not many men around who can listen the way you do, Stanley. I mean, like you're really interested in what the other person is saying. And of course it goes without saying, a great listener makes a great lover."

"Is that so?" Stanley murmurs, a hand creeping up my arm.

"Absolutely. I've found that to be true down the line. Either a person can tune into other people. Or he can't. . . . You can."

The beard makes a most untimely entrance at this point in the conversation, depositing a bag of groceries in the sink. After sharing a few words with Stanley in Italian, he takes a six pack into the den where he joins Sid in front of the set.

"Jerry says you can cook dinner anytime," Stanley informs me, when I go over to take a peek at the goodies the man brought us.

"He did, did he? What is this? 1952? The women cook and the men watch football?"

"1985, doll. Catch up."

"Look at these suckers," I murmur, bringing out five individually cellophane wrapped, two inch thick rib-eye steaks. "I didn't know people actually ate these things anymore. Classic white American male grub," I add, momentarily forgetting these guys are Italian as I haul out a couple of boxes of Kraft cheese style macaroni, a can of baked beans, a loaf of WonderBread white, a bottle of Heinz, and another six pack of beer.

"Shall I tell them dinner at eight?" Stanley suggests, making a move to join the other two men in the other room.

"Get back here, Stanley! I've never cooked up one of these damn things in my entire life. I mean it!"

"It's not terribly complicated, Sarah. You stick them under the broiler and watch them burn."

"And that, no doubt, is precisely what I'll do. And not one of these babies under three bucks."

Stanley broils up the steaks. I boil the macaroni and heat up the beans. When the meal is ready, Sid and his buddy take their plates back into the den to watch the kick-off of another game. Stanley and I move into their palatial living room with our steaks. But try as I may, I'm unable to get down a single bite. Something in the texture of this medium rare rib-eye which revives in graphic detail the taste and texture of that bloody dismembered ear as it pressed against the roof of my mouth. But dismembered ears aside, I'm quite content to lounge on this cushy sofa, taking in a prodigious sunset as it settles into the Bay. Asking myself what it must be like, coming home to a spread like this every night. Fixing oneself a cocktail, turning on the incredible sound system they have installed in here, and mellowing out. But of course, the guy who owns this place probably never gets home before nine or ten o'clock, watches Johnny Carson, and falls into bed. Which is one of the many kinks in how our system works. The people with the luxurious set-ups, never have the time to enjoy them. The people with all the time in the world, live in dumps. Or nowhere at all.

"Are you going to tell me who owns this place, Stanley? Or is that against house rules?"

"A cousin of George's. . . . He and his companion are in Hawaii for a couple of weeks."

"Companion? Must be some companion. Have you checked out the closets upstairs? Never seen anything like it. Except maybe in the movies. Racks upon racks of all these clothes. Mink coats. Silk gowns. And shoes! Must be at least two hundred pair of high heels up there. Not to mention drawers full of cashmere sweaters and the kind of lingerie I thought was reserved for *Hustler* magazine."

"I see you made yourself right at home."

"Yeah, well. . . . How well do you know these people, anyway? And where did you learn to speak such good Italian?"

"Lived in Italy for a couple of years."

"No kidding? I suppose that's where you met your ex-wife?"

"Nope. Met her right where I met you."

"Yeah?" Ick. "Are you starting to see her again, Stanley?"

"What gave you that idea?"

"You saw her Friday night, didn't you?"

"That was strictly business, Sarah."

"I see," I say, making it perfectly clear that I don't see at all.

"Listen, Sarah. . . . I have a child."

"A what?"

"A little girl. A four year old little girl."

". . . So why didn't you tell me this before?"

"She was born mentally disabled. Very. We were finally obliged to put her into an institution."

"I'm very sorry, Stanley. That must hurt a lot. . . . Do you visit her often?"

"Not often enough."

"Was that what . . . ?" And I stop.

"What's that, Sarah?"

"Nothing."

"Come on. Out with it."

"Was that what broke up your marriage?"

He doesn't answer immediately. Pursing his lips and bouncing the fingertips of both hands off of each other at a nervous rate. "Thousands of marriages survive something like that. Ours didn't. . . . I blamed it all on her, you see. An unforgivable thing for me to have done. But sometimes we do the unforgivable, don't we?"

"But why on earth . . . ?"

"She was very much against having the child in the first place. I suppose she was too much of a child herself. . . . I went from there to convincing myself she had purposely brought on the whole mess. Accused her of sabotaging the pregnancy. If not consciously, then unconsciously. Of drinking too much. Smoking too much. Went so far as to accuse her of attempting an abortion behind my back. It was a very ugly time, Sarah. I'd like to say I wasn't myself back then. But that would be too easy, wouldn't it. . . . She visits Amy every afternoon. Hasn't missed a day in the last three years. Not a single day," he repeats, as if to himself. His voice a disturbing mixture of anguish and awe.

I stand up. Walk over to where he sits. Reach out to touch his hand, thinking, here is a man. A man I love. That is all.

Much later that night, in bed, I mull over the word lovemaking. Rolling the syllables over and over on my tongue. Thinking what a really beautiful word that is. A word that I have never truly appreciated before.

JUNE 28

The four of us share a coffee cake the Beard picked up at a neighborhood Adeline's, and head straight into the city, arriving at Stanley's apartment complex right on schedule at ten a.m. On first impressions, the building looks clean. As does the lobby, the coffee shop, and the bar. Stanley remains out in the lobby to await the arrival of the postman. Our two escorts join me in the coffee shop, settling at one end of the counter while I head for a table in back.

10:15. I make a mental review of information I want to milk out of Kaufman when the time comes. Frank's involvement, to what extent? The AIDS vaccine, why the hold up on the trials? The fate of the June Mail file, where to from here?

10:30. The way I see it, I should be crawling the walls by now. Considering that the last three frenetic weeks in time have—in their way—led up to this very moment. But not unlike my reaction to Lieutenant Nemmens a few evenings ago, I am infected with an inexplicable and stoic calm. The die is cast, as they say. I have done my best. The rest can only be left to fate.

10:45 and he walks through the door, his dark eyes darting quickly about the room before he takes a seat at the other end of the counter from my friends.

"Good morning, Mr. Kaufman," I say, sliding onto an adjoining stool.

He gives me a long hard look. The waitress approaches. He orders two coffees, three fingers strumming nervously on the formica counter top.

"So?" he murmurs, eyes set straight ahead.

"Mail hasn't come in yet. By eleven o'clock."

His only response is to strum more fiercely, his eyes roving to the ceiling overhead. The waitress appears with our coffee, pushing a creamer and sugar bowl our way before returning to her cigarettes in back.

"Why am I giving these papers to you, Mr. Kaufman?"

"It was Dr. Winslow's request, was it not?"

"Yes, but why? What do you plan on doing with them once I hand them over?"

"I'm not sure that's any of your business, is it?"

"You goddamn better believe it's my business."

He turns to study me again, those sharp black eyes probing under the surface. Then turns back to his coffee, dumping three heaping teaspoons of sugar into his cup.

"Shall I make myself a little plainer for you, Mr. Kaufman? I don't plan on giving you the file until a few muddy issues have been cleared up."

I can feel him bristling at my side. A man not given to taking orders. Especially from dames. Well fella, live and learn.

"Jerry Sanderson has agreed to spotlight it in his column."

"How soon?"

"Tomorrow morning."

"My god. . . . So you're flying back east today?"

"Twelve o'clock flight."

"And he's going to lay it all on the line? Tell where the information came from? Who's responsible? The whole bit?"

"He's promised us a complete exposé. From there, we hope to get it into Congressional committee. Get a full-fledged hearing focused on the whole issue."

"On AIDS and biological warfare research? Great . . . Mr. Kaufman, how deeply is—was—Frank involved in all this? Particularly in the monkey viral research down in Haiti?"

"He wasn't."

"So why did you make contact with him down in Paradise?"

"Chemix was involved in Haiti. Frank was involved in Chemix. He has also been working with ARPA for the last ten years. Suspected he might be able to give me some answers."

"ARPA?"

"Acronymn for Advanced Research Projects Agency. A group of elite civilian scientists doing research and development projects for the Defense Department."

"For the Defense Department? So how does the Department of Public Health fit into all this?"

"ARPA funding is channelled through Public Health."

"I see. So no one has to know these scientists are dirtying their hands in nasty war games. Is that how it works?"

"More or less."

"But the scientists themselves are perfectly aware of who they work for?"

"More or less."

"Meaning?"

"Meaning, they can turn a blind eye to the obvious if they wish to. Many of them do. But ARPA projects are blatantly military in nature. And the results of ARPA research is automatically classified. Never published. That in itself is a dead give-away for these people."

"And this group of trouble shooters Frank was a part of,"

I say, beginning to see the light. "They were checking out possible accidental epidemics which may have resulted from some of this ARPA biological research?

"A reasonable assumption." He looks down at his watch.

"Was Frank ever directly involved with the CIA?"

"All a smoke screen."

"For the AIDS-genetic engineering link?"

"For that. For ARPA. For project AGILE. For the JASON group. For AIMS. For all the biological warfare research going on all over the goddamn place."

"What *are* all these groups? AGILE? JASON? AIMS?"

"More of the same. Counterinsurgency research programs. All going under the official heading of U.S. Military Options in the Third World and dedicated to soft-war research."

"*Soft*-war?"

"The so-called limited warfare technologies. Biological and chemical weaponry. The kind that can be used covertly. No soldiers needed. No body bags. That's the ticket, these days. How to wage subtle little wars. The kind the American public can turn a convenient blind eye to. Bombs have become too noisy for our purposes, you see. Bad press."

"Biological-chemical weaponry to be used in the Third World?" I repeat. He nods. "Counterinsurgency meaning counter-revolutionary? Meaning counter-Cuba?"

"Meaning counter-Nicaragua," he picks up where I left off. "Counter-Angola. Counter-guerillas in El Salvador. Counter guerillas in the Philippines. Counter guerillas in Guatemala." And his arm waves on down the counter to indicate a non-ending series of examples at hand. "Counter any damn system that might threaten our corporate hegemony abroad."

"How do you find all this stuff out, anyway?"

"Look," he says curtly in answer. "I have a plane to catch. When did you say your friend's mail usually arrives?"

"Any time now. . . . One last question, Mr. Kaufman.

Why was Chemix delaying trials of Frank's AIDS vaccine?"

Another pause. Another look. "For starters, the general opinion is that his vaccine wasn't ready for human trials. The protein coat still too mutable. Too unpredictable. And then there was pressure on his team to convert from an oral vaccine into an aerosol."

"Aerosol?"

"Defense Department policy."

"But we're talking about Chemix Pharmaceutical."

"Very difficult to say where one starts and the other leaves off."

"So why aerosol?"

"It should be fairly obvious, I should think."

"So more people can be vaccinated in a shorter amount of time?"

"No. So *our* people can be protected without being aware they are being vaccinated prior to any possible military release of the virus."

"But why ever. . . . ?"

My question falls on deaf ears. Kaufman's attention is set on Stanley who has just stepped up to my side.

Until this very moment, a good part of me doubted I'd ever be seeing this envelope again. But here it is before my eyes, Stanley's Fox Plaza address scribbled in my jagged handwriting across the front jacket, evoking the trauma of chase three days ago. I hold on to it a moment longer, and then pass it on to Kaufman's waiting hands.

"Need a ride to the airport?" I suggest, nodding in the direction of Sid and his partner at the other end of the counter.

He shakes his head, eyes on the envelope as he slits it open with one finger and draws out the ream of papers. "That's all taken care of," he murmurs, rifling quickly through the pages before shoving it all back inside.

"Well, best of luck, Mr. Kaufman. Getting all that into the open. And getting that book of yours out someday too. Judging from our conversation today, it must be a real sizzler."

"I think so," he says, smiling for the first time since our

little interview began. And with a last tap of the envelope to the counter top, he nods and walks out of the shop.

"So that's it?" Stanley asks, his gaze following Kaufman on through the outer lobby.

"That's it. You know who's picking up the story, Stanley? Jerry Sanderson!"

"Sanderson?"

"Didn't sound right to me either. I mean, that guy's gotten so wishy-washy the last couple of years. I find it hard to believe he'd be willing to break a story like this. But then again, if it's going to break anyway, why not get first shot. . . . Kaufman's talking about committee hearings and the whole bit. . . . So what feels wrong here?" I add, slapping the counter top.

"It's over, sweetheart. That's what feels wrong. It's all over."

JUNE 29

My eyes pop open at dawn. The cat on my chest. Stanley by my side. And the same nagging questions disturbing my peace of mind this morning, as were disturbing it last night. Why was Amy's apartment left untouched? What were my two thugs doing up here on Saturday afternoon, if not tearing the place apart again in quest of the missing file? And where are those two men now? Why haven't I heard a peep out of anyone—neither the FBI, nor the KGB, nor Fatso—since passing the papers on to Kaufman yesterday morning? The total absence of crisis or confrontation is unsettling to the extreme.

I can't keep still a moment longer. Slithering quietly out of bed and into my clothes, I move out of the bedroom, step over our chaperons sacked out on the living room floor, and head out the door. I ask myself where I can possibly pick up a paper this early in the day. At Verdi's, of course. I head over, ordering a double espresso and taking my coffee and the morning edition to our table in back. A moment to catch my breath, and I turn quickly to the Panorama page, where Sanderson's column can always be found. His heading today reads—*AIDS Research Controversy.* I read on:

Some medical researchers suspect that the federal government is discouraging tests which might identify a mutated SV40 monkey virus or a Marburg monkey virus as the primal cause of AIDS, fearing that discovery of such a link-up would unnecessarily curtail ongoing and valuable medical research. U.S. officials have discounted any researchers' suggestions of a connection between AIDS and one or another mutated monkey virus, saying that all government tests have proved negative.

While these government officials claim scientists are sounding needless alarms, the researchers themselves are charging that their work toward establishing such a link is being impeded by the Department of Public Health, which controls material necessary for monkey virus tests. The Department "is concerned that genetic engineering research, which makes extensive use of monkey viruses, would be harmfully restricted if one particular laboratory mutated virus or another were to be related to AIDS," says Dr. Jonathan Friedman of Yale University.

Internal memos of the Center for Disease Control in Atlanta indicate that doctors there believe sufficient testing on a possible AIDS-mutated monkey virus connection has been done. "From the outset," states one memo, "wideranging observation of specimens from AIDS patients have been carried out which would have identified the SV40 or the Marburg monkey virus should either of them have been present." The memos

reveal that tests did show some positive reactions.
But Public Health officials dismissed these results
as "false positives."

One Public Health consultant, Dr. Francis Conway, said he would like to see further testing of
the two viruses. "I don't think either virus could
cause AIDS by itself," Conway says, "but many
people feel there are co-factors helping the AIDS
virus along." Conway added, "I have a feeling
the government is not at all interested in this type
of research."

That's it? I ask myself incredulously, finishing up the
piece. No mention of Haiti? No mention of biological
warfare research? No mention of Frank? Or Chemix? Or
ARPA? No commitment to any side. To any source. To any
point of view? "That's it?" I murmur out loud.

"That's it."

"Arnold! What in God's name . . . ?" I glance around
for others.

"Came to say goodbye," he says, taking a seat.

"Good bye?"

"I'm off the case."

"My case?"

"Right. I'm going to miss you, Ma'am. 24 hours a day.
Three weeks. Feel like I kind of know you. Feel like I
should at least say good bye. And set you straight."

"About what?"

"You passed those papers into the wrong hands, lady.
Nothing's coming out. Not now or ever."

"What are you talking about? Kaufman—?"

"Made a deal. Handed the file over to Chemix. Chemix
is cutting the reins on his book."

"Why should I believe. . . . How do you know all
this?"

"Let's just say that I do. It's the way the system works,
Ma'am. The sooner you learn that, the better off you'll be,"
he adds, shoving back his chair and standing up.

"Wait a minute, Arnold. Don't leave yet. I have so many
ques—"

"Gotta split," he says, looking over his shoulder. "It's been real." And with a tap to his forehead and a smile, he walks back out of the cafe.

I sit there a minute or two, waiting for the walls to crumble. Then grab up the paper and race homeward, to confront Stanley with the horrible news.

"Do you believe it!" I seethe, joining him at Amy's breakfast room table. "Do you believe it! That double-crossing fat ass! All this risk and trouble, and for what? A fucking zero. A fucking blank slate!"

Stanley sits there, nodding slowly, taking it all in.

"Couldn't you write the whole thing up yourself, Stanley? Put the story into a couple of your columns?"

"No smoking gun. I'd lose all credibility trying something like that."

"So what do I do?" I wail. "Chalk it up to experience? The whole damn thing?"

"Write it up yourself, Sarah."

"What are you talking about? I don't have any smoking gun either. Who the hell would ever print *my* story?"

"Turn it into fiction. Then the only smoking gun you'll need is yourself. Tell everyone exactly what you've been living through these last few weeks. It will make a great story, Sarah. Whether people choose to believe you or not."

"Not such a bad idea," I murmur, hopping back up and pacing the floor. "Not such a bad idea at all."